"Keeshah!" I called.

The great cat leapt gracefully over the high wall to my right. He kept his distance, padding back and forth along the wall, watching me and growling.

"I have brought you water, Keeshah. Come and drink."

He stopped pacing and came a few steps nearer, stretching out his head to sniff in my direction, then sidled off.

Markasset?

I felt a pulsing from somewhere inside me, familiar, compelling. A warm touch directly to my mind —friendly, yet wary. I understood then that the special bond between cat and Rider was a telepathic link.

No longer Markasset but same friend. Keeshah's friend.

He rose to his feet. A single bound and he was looming over me. His mouth opened, and my breath dried in my throat. The razor-sharp teeth closed gently on my shoulder.

THE GANDALARA CYCLE

I

THE STEEL OF RAITHSKAR

RANDALL GARRETT & VICKI ANN HEYDRON

BANTAM BOOKS
TORONTO · NEW YORK · LONDON · SYDNEY

THE STEEL OF RAITHSKAR
A Bantam Book / May 1981

ISBN 0-553-14607-6

Published simultaneously in the United States and Canada

Bantam Books are published by Bantam Books, Inc. Its trademark, consisting of the words "Bantam Books" and the por-
trayal of a bantam, is Registered in U.S. Patent and Trademark
Office and in other countries. Marca Registrada. Bantam
Books, Inc., 666 Fifth Avenue, New York, New York 10103.

PRINTED IN THE UNITED STATES OF AMERICA

0 9 8 7 6 5 4 3 2

*This book is dedicated,
gratefully and with love,
to our brother Greer.*

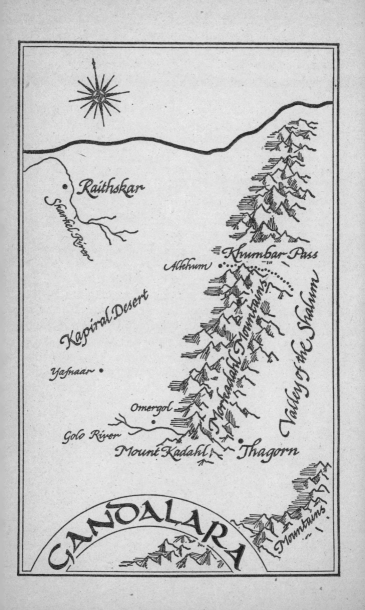

PRELIMINARY PROCEEDINGS:

INPUT SESSION ONE

—*You understand what you must do. You have undertaken and completed your training for this task. You know that what you are about to do is of the utmost necessity for the further continuance of the well-being, and perhaps the existence, of our descendants. Are you in agreement with that concept?*

—*I am, Recorder.*

—*Good. What goes into the Record must be of the highest quality. No truth can be absolute, but the truth of the Record must be as close to absolute as it is possible for us to make it. Do you understand and believe that?*

—*I understand and believe it, Recorder.*

—*Then you know that every detail, down to the slightest, should go into the Record. Every impression, no matter how fleeting; every nuance of thought and emotion; every memory that can be made available must be brought forth.*

For all that the work will be purely mental, and not physical, you will find it the hardest labor you have ever undertaken in your life. Do you willingly undertake this labor?

—*I do willingly undertake it, Recorder.*

—*Are you ready, then, to begin this Recording?*

—*I am ready, Recorder.*

—*Then make your mind one with mine, as I have made mine one with the All-Mind . . .*

1

WE BEGIN!

1

Heat, pain, and blinding light, burning through my skin and my eyelids. And the taste of bitter salt in my mouth.

The sensations filled me, rooted me in consciousness while that part of my mind which *could* think floated away and returned. Among the jumble of wandering thoughts, one came clearly:

The fireball killed me. This is what Hell feels like.

But it had no real meaning and it ebbed away into a blankness which seemed eternal.

At last I became aware of directional sensation. The incredible heat surrounded me, but under my fingers as I moved them weakly, pressing against my left cheek, scattered in my eyes and mouth, there was a grittiness that was somehow familiar. Rationality was returning. It was sand.

I was lying on the ground somewhere, on gritty, salty sand.

I lifted my head and tried to spit out the sand, but my mouth was too dry and all I could do was push the sand out with my tongue. With one hand I brushed grit from my eyes and opened them.

I groaned, and lurched up into a sitting position. I sat there with my hands covering my eyes and wept away the savage sting of salt.

When I could open my eyes again, I did so very cautiously, shading them with my hands. At first I thought that I had been blinded in a reverse way, that instead of blackness I was destined always to see only a brilliant white glare. Slowly the light grew tolerable, and the whiteness resolved itself into understandable divisions.

Above me a thin cloud layer diffused the sun's light, but had no discernible dimming effect on it. Light and heat beat down on a fierce white desert, which amplified and reflected them. I had never believed that *anything* could be that hot.

As I turned my head to look around, the pain in my body focused sharply. A lump on my head, above and behind my right ear, was throbbing mightily. And my neck was so stiff that I was forced to wonder how long I had been lying here, slowly frying on the floor of this desert.

3

What I saw around me was a broad vista of nothing. Or almost nothing. In the flat, nearly featureless desert, two things stood out.

One was nearby. A few yards to my right lay a man, perfectly still, with his face turned away from me. The bright yellow and green of his clothes was oddly comforting, a single spot of color in the gray-white desert.

The other was distant. Toward every horizon but one, the desert flowed unevenly. Here and there were short bushes, spreading almost flat just above the ground. In the sand, crawling around me, were small, pale ants. Yet all this life was a part of the vast, deadly desert, blending smoothly into the endless panorama of nothingness.

Except in one direction.

The land rose slowly to touch the white cloud layer of the sky, and in the far distance a strip of blue, parallel to the horizon, marked their meeting. I had no way of knowing what that line of blue meant, but it was far more attractive than the grayness which surrounded me. It was the only way out of the desert, and I knew I had to move in that direction.

That desperate need carried me clumsily to my feet, and I was instantly grateful that I had managed to stand. My clothes had been crumpled and pressed against my body, but the movement jarred them loose, and, as they fell away from my skin, the heat became almost bearable.

A weight dragged on my right shoulder. I looked at my clothes, touched my chest, and discovered a folded strip of sturdy tan fabric supporting that weight. A baldric—and a sword?

The sword was too heavy for my trembling hands to hold it up for examination, but behind it was hanging a small pouch. At the thought that it might contain food, I was suddenly very hungry. But when I opened it, I found only five large golden coins.

Perhaps the other man had some food . . .

The other man!

I staggered over to him and fell to my knees. I hadn't the faintest notion who he was, but if he were still alive . . .

He wasn't. The stiffness of the corpse as I rolled him over told me he had been dead for long. And the blood-caked shreds of his tunic made it obvious that he had not died of thirst. He was an ugly sight.

The dry heat had desiccated what could never have been a handsome face. The supraorbital ridges were prominent beneath a high brow. The nose had a pushed-in look, like

4

that of a gorilla, so that the nostrils showed. The chin was massive and squarish.

The dead mouth was open. Cracked and shrunken lips had shriveled back from large, even teeth; the canines were unusually long. Ants were crawling in and out of the open mouth.

I looked away quickly.

But I searched the body thoroughly, hoping to find a bottle of water or some food. All I could come up with was a sword I took to be like the one I was wearing, and another pouch. This one was filled with smaller coins of different sizes, and, without thinking, I poured them out of his pouch and into mine. Some of the coins spilled over my shaking hand. I didn't pick them out of the sand; it was just too much trouble to try.

I stood up then, and looked around again. There was still nothing that promised change except the tantalizing blue ridge at the edge of the visible world. I started to walk toward it, but something drew me back to the dead man. His sword.

Clumsily I pulled the baldric off the body and tried to lift it over my head—but I hadn't the strength to lift the sword. So I set off toward the horizon, holding the baldric and dragging the heavy sword behind me. I didn't know why, but I knew I didn't want to leave the sword out in the desert.

For an endless time I stumbled across the desert floor. My feet slipped in the sand; I tripped over low bushes I was too tired to avoid; sometimes my legs just let me fall. Tiny, sharp-edged rocks, concealed by the sand, cut my hands and face. Each time I fell, the salty sand ground into my raw wounds, until my skin was on fire.

I kept moving. The only *real* thing in the world was the faint line of blue, always ahead of me but never any nearer. I knew I had to keep walking to reach it, so walk I did. One foot in front of the other, struggling back to my feet when I fell, I forced my way across the desert.

I realized dimly that I must be moving north. The sharp glare in the sky which must be the sun above the cloud layer was behind me and moving toward my left. But it didn't matter. Nothing mattered.

I stopped once with a feeling of surprise. Why couldn't I move? I traced the problem to my left arm—something was pulling at it. I looked down and saw that I still held the loop of the baldric in my hand. Somehow the sword had become too heavy to move. Why was I dragging it, anyway?

5

I had no answer. I let go the baldric and almost fell. I started walking again, with a feeling of satisfaction that I had solved an immense problem.

I was suddenly convinced that I was being followed. I whirled around, the violence of the turn making me stagger, and looked for the follower. Nothing. As far as I could see, the desert was empty except for me. But the sensation persisted: I was not alone.

Now my steady, straight-ahead plodding became a zigzag course. I walked a few yards, then jumped around to try to catch whoever or whatever was trailing me. There was never anything: no movement, no sound. So I turned back and walked on—not quite in the same direction I had been going.

So, for a time, I forgot about the blue line. My attention was behind me, and almost as if it were a game, I walked and turned, walked and turned.

My strength failed. My legs suddenly quit, and I slammed heavily into the salt-thick ground. I simply lay there. I knew I could not stand up again.

Could I move at all? Yes. I could crawl.

The shock of this last fall had knocked some sense back into me. Forget the whatever-it-is that's following; *blue* means salvation. I sighted the line of blue and aimed for it again, began to drag myself through the sand.

I heard a rumbling noise behind me. I was too weak to turn around, so I rolled over on my back and dug my elbows into the sand to lift my head. I wasn't afraid; rather, I was glad to find the answer to the mystery.

A few yards away from me stood the biggest damned cat I had ever seen.

No wonder I hadn't been able to spot him. He was covered with a grayish pale tan fur that blended almost perfectly with the drab surroundings. The low coughing sound came from his throat as he paced restlessly back and forth.

He began to walk a spiral, moving slowly around me and coming gradually closer.

I was sure that the cat's shoulders would have brushed my chin if I were standing. He—I had never thought of him as "it" after I saw him, and as he prowled around me, his maleness was obvious—was built like a tiger, with a powerful chest and a long, agile body. When he growled I could see well-developed canines in his mouth. The image of a sabertooth came to me, but these teeth were nothing like the exaggerated knives of that animal.

I watched the cat watching me. He came in closer, sniffing.

6

I became aware of *his* odor: vaguely muskish, not un-pleasant, and somehow familiar.

My neck was getting tired, following the cat's circling. Suddenly he stopped and looked directly at me.

I couldn't defend myself against a kitten, I thought at him. *You might as well come eat me. It's better than dying of thirst.*

The cat didn't move.

Come ahead, I urged. *You're welcome.*

As though he had heard my thoughts, the cat let out a roar that literally shook the ground, and bounded eagerly toward me.

I knew that I had invited him. I was even willing to let him eat me, in a tentative sort of way. But the sight of that great cat closing in for the kill drained away my remaining strength. I collapsed back into the sand and my mind slipped away from me.

2

Water!

It was dripping on my lips, and I licked at it weakly. More drops fell. I licked again.

"Not too much at first," said a voice. "When a man has been too long without water, it is a strong shock to his system to give him too much."

The voice was that of a man, but he spoke with an odd, faintly guttural accent that I couldn't place. I was fully awake now. But I didn't open my eyes. I was perfectly content to lie there licking the water as it dripped on my lips.

"More, Respected Father?" The voice of either a woman or a young boy. The accent was the same.

Drip. Lick. Drip. Lick. Nothing in my life had ever tasted quite that good. It seemed that the water even *smelled* good. Drip. Lick.

I was flat on my back, resting on something noticeably cooler than the desert floor. The air around me and the delicious water were cool and fresh. Suddenly the dripping seemed too slow. I wanted a *drink* of water. I opened my mouth.

"See." The man's voice. "He responds. A little more now, Lamothet. Not too much."

When my mouth felt moist enough to talk, I said: "Has Keeshah water?"

"The sha'um will take it only from you, Rider."

I knew what I had said, and I understood what had been said to me. But it had no meaning. I blinked and sat up. What the hell were we talking about? My mind seemed fuzzy, as if it were slightly out of focus.

The room I was in was cool because it was protected from the desert heat by thick walls made of huge translucent blocks. Sunlight penetrated the walls and suffused the room with a soft light, which was a welcome change from the painful glare I had first seen.

More of the large, regular blocks stood free around the room as furniture. On some of these, and hanging on the walls, were finely woven cloths, richly embroidered. One served as a pad for the man-sized block on which I had awakened.

There were three other people in the room with me. A young boy—Lamothet, I presumed—was holding a small, delicate cup, adorned with tiny geometric designs. There was a strong-looking man who could only be "Respected Father", and another man not quite as young as Lamothet. The older man wore authority with the same ease that he wore his long, clean, white tunic.

My voice sounded as strange as theirs when I spoke.

"Where am I?" I asked. "How did I get here?"

"You are in the Refreshment House of Yafnaar, and are most welcome, Rider," said the elder. He put gentle hands on my shoulders and pressed me back. "As for how you got here, why, you came on the back of your sha'um, of course." He unstoppered a small-mouthed jar that matched the cup's design, took the cup from the boy, and filled it. He lifted my shoulders and helped me drink.

"You must rest a while longer."

I lay back and looked closely at the man's face, and realized with a start that he could be related to the corpse I had left out in the desert. He was by no means as ugly, but he had the same high forehead, jutting brows, and pug nose, all a little less pronounced. Even the canines. They weren't the pointed fangs of a movie vampire, but wide, strong teeth, more like short tusks than fangs. The other two had that same look—a family resemblance?

I decided not to mention the corpse. If these were his

8

family, they might think I had killed him. And it troubled me in an unknown way that I had left his sword out on the desert.

I closed my eyes to a wave of weakness, and again an unfamiliar word came naturally to my lips. "Keeshah?"

"You may tend your sha'um when you are more rested. He is strong—stronger than you. Relax."

My sha'um. Funny word. *Shah-oom*. With a glottal stop.

I remembered.

The big cat looming over me, not attacking but nuzzling in an urgent way. Trying to get his huge head under my unmoving bulk. I understood at last, and put my arms around his neck. He surged upward, lifting me to my knees, then lay down on the sand in front of me. I fell across his back, managed to turn my body to straddle him, and again locked my arms around his neck. Then he carried me across the desert in long, loping strides. The last thing I could remember before waking here was the regular, comforting motion of the strong body beneath me.

Yes, Keeshah was stronger than I could ever hope to be. He was a sha'um.

Sha'um. Great cat. Or, literally: cat great. This language put the adjective after the noun, as the Romance languages did.

What? I started from my half-doze. *What the hell is going on in my head?* It suddenly became very important for me to find out who I was.

I tried to sit up and ask my new friends, but I couldn't. That last cup of water must have been drugged. I gave in and relaxed again. *I think I'm better,* I told myself with crazy logic. *At least I know now that I don't know who I am.*

I dozed off, still puzzling over a language I understood perfectly, and at the same time knew damned well I had never heard before.

I dreamed a dream.

"The Mediterranean is beautiful on a moonlit night, is it not?" said a voice at my elbow. A woman's voice, huskier than contralto, a voice that suited the evening. Her Italian sounded Milanese.

I turned to look at her, sure before I saw her of what I would see. I had just been thinking of her, remembering the happy laugh I had heard across the dining room, wishing that during this cruise I might meet her on deck and share just

9

such a lovely night with her. If I have learned anything in my long life, it is that wishes occasionally come true.

She was tall, five feet seven or so—she would have said 170 centimeters—with the blonde hair and the svelte figure of the Lombard. Her gracefully and delectably low-cut gown had the unmistakable, expensive look of Alderuccio of Rome.

"It is made even more beautiful by your presence, Contessa," I said. A man of sixty can afford to be gallant, especially if it's the truth.

Her lovely laugh rang out. "I am not the Contessa, signore."

"You must be, my dear. At dinner this evening, the gentleman next to me—Colonello Gucci—distinctly said to me, 'Dottore, you see that most beautiful woman sitting a few places down from the end, at the Captain's table? That is the Contessa di Falco.' Since you were the most beautiful woman at that table—indeed, on the ship—I concluded he meant you."

"No." She shook her head and made the silver-set dangles at her ears wink in the moonlight. "That is my sister, who was sitting next to me. I am Antonia Alderuccio."

I gestured at the dress. "You are Alderuccio of Rome?"

"Wrong again, signore. That is my uncle." She moved closer to the railing, and the breeze brought the light scent of her perfume past me. "I am sorry, signore, that no one pointed out to me such a distinguished man as yourself. You are Dottore . . . ?"

"Ricardo Carillo, at your service, signorina."

She turned to face me. The surprise on her face was a fine compliment. "You are Spanish? You speak Italian perfectly!"

"Thank you, but I am Spanish only by ancestry. I am an American."

"Naturalized, then?"

"No, native born. My ancestors were living in California before the English ever heard of the place."

"How wonderful! I have seen the cinema films of the early Californians." She drew up the skirt of her gown, assumed the en garde, and attacked me with an invisible rapier in her right hand. "Zorro! So! Zzzt-zzzt-zzzt!"

She stopped. I looked at her in astonishment, then laughed as I had not laughed in years. She dropped her pose and laughed with me.

I was grateful to her. She was young enough to be my granddaughter, yet with her exuberance, she had not so much

10

flaunted her own youth as reminded me of mine. We were closer now; friends.

When we could speak again, she said: "But that still does not explain how you speak Italian so well."

"The truth is dull, I'm afraid. I have the honor to be a Professor of Romance Languages, University of California at Santa Barbara."

"But I think of *professores* always as intense and stoop-shouldered, wearing glasses and not quite looking at one." She looked at me critically. "You look more like a military man."

Her zaniness was infectious. I snapped to attention and saluted crisply.

"Master Sergeant Ricardo Carillo, United States Marine Corps, Retired; at your service, *signorina*." I relaxed and added, "Actually, I only made corporal in the regulars; the six stripes came from reserve time."

"I know the reputation of the Marines of the United States—they are the finest fighting force in the world. How brave you must be!" Was she laughing at me? A little, perhaps, but not entirely. I had indeed impressed her; knowing that I could impressed me.

"Not brave, *signorina*. Cautious. The Corps has a saying: 'There are old Marines, and there are bold Marines, but there are no old, bold Marines.' It's funnier in English, I'm afraid."

"But it makes sense in any language," she said seriously. "Why are you sailing the Mediterranean on a cruise ship, Ricardo?" The sound of my first name was very special in her voice. It was a gentle intimacy between us.

"I'm taking a sabbatical leave, Antonia. I've been to Europe before—often, in fact. But always on business. Linguistics research, conferences, and other such mundane activities which didn't allow me to appreciate the countries I saw. This time it's just for fun: a pleasure trip."

I told her only what she needed to know of the truth. Could I tell her that my health was bad, that diabetes and kidney infection and just plain old age had caught up with me? I don't think the knowledge would have driven Antonia away, but I was afraid that it would drive her closer, which, under these circumstances, would have been even more repellent to me. Besides, the deck of a cruise ship, surrounded by the shimmering, restive Mediterranean, was no place to speak of death.

"Oh, look, Ricardo. Look!" She had been watching the sky with that thoughtful look that is so appealing in young

11

women, but now she pointed upward, completely alert. "That star! It is getting brighter and brighter."

I did look. There was a pinpoint of light in the sky, unmoving, which was indeed growing brighter second by second.

"Is that what the astronomers call a nova?" she asked. There was excitement in her voice.

I watched the light closely; it changed color. It was orange, then yellow, finally white. And still it grew brighter.

"I'm afraid that's not in my line, Antonia," I told her. "But I'd say it has to be at least a supernova."

I tried to keep the fear from my voice. But now it was a small ball of fire, visibly growing, which did not seem to move. I thought I knew what it was.

A meteor, I thought. It's coming straight at us.

A falling star, a boloid, a great hunk of rock or iron—it wasn't my field, as I'd told Antonia, but I knew enough to be frightened. It was a huge mass of space debris, coming in from the sky at a velocity measurable only in miles per second. To say "thirty-six thousand miles an hour" doesn't mean anything unless you think about it, and we had no time to think.

But I had time to feel. I had come to terms, more or less, with my own death long ago. I had half expected to die before I got home; only the manner of it was an incredible surprise. But I felt a totally irrational guilt, as though this disaster were my fault, and because of me, everyone on the ship would die, too.

And Antonia. I was angry on her behalf. So young . . . Too young . . .

I didn't tell her what I knew. I didn't even try to give an alarm, because I knew there was no time. We simply stood together and watched it grow in eerie silence—it was moving far faster than the speed of sound. From the time she had first seen it until it struck could not have been more than ten or twelve seconds.

Brighter and brighter . . . larger . . . closer . . .

It became a great ball of unbearable light . . .

I woke up screaming.

3

I opened my eyes. The soft light around me, diffused through the frosty walls, told me that day had come again. I sat up slowly, surprised to find that I was feeling quite well.

The young man was seated on a nearby white block, padded, as mine was, with colorful tapestry. He stood up with the silent grace cultivated by those who tend the sick, and smiled at me tentatively.

"You had a bad night last night," he said. "Are you better this morning?"

"Much better," I assured him. "I'm sorry if I worried you. I had a—a dream." As I said it, I knew it hadn't been *precisely* a dream.

"You screamed," he said. There was a look of consternation on his face, as though he wanted to ask me why, but hesitated. He compromised. "Were you sent a portent of disaster?"

"No. A . . . memory of a past one." I smiled at him; I didn't want more questions right now. "Don't disturb yourself, please. It was nothing."

The worry fell away from his face. "Good. I am Keddan of the Fa'aldu. I think you will have more water, then we will bring you a porridge. These things must not be done too swiftly, or you will be sick at your stomach and waste much water."

I watched him as he unstoppered the decorated pitcher and poured water into two of the fragile cups. He moved with studied care and spilled not a single drop. He was wearing the same kind of long white tunic as the "Respected Father" had worn, and I wondered briefly if the white robes were a uniform of some kind. I put the thought aside as Keddan brought the two cups over to me.

He offered both of them, unmistakably inviting me to choose one for myself. I understood the gesture; he was assuring me that *this* drink was not drugged. And it wasn't until he dismissed it in this way that I realized the suspicion had been in my mind. Gratefully, I took one of the cups and drank thirstily—though I was careful not to spill any.

13

The water was cool and had a pleasant flavor which I didn't recognize at first. I realized as I finished the cup that it was brackish. There was salt in the water—enough, at least, to taste it.

The well must contain a trace of salt, I decided; that would hardly be surprising out here in the desert.

"I will go now to prepare your breakfast," Keddan said, when he had placed pitcher and cups in a narrow recess cut from one of the blocks that formed an inside wall. "Is there any other service you desire?"

"No, thank you, Keddan. May I sit here and rest a little?"

"That would be good, Rider. When you are ready to water your sha'um, you have but to ask." He pushed aside a tapestry which concealed a doorway and was gone.

I was glad to be alone. I had a lot to think about. And I was infinitely glad to be *able* to think again. The day before had been a jumble of confusion and exhaustion; an incoherent desperation had driven me across the desert. Yesterday I had only wanted to survive.

Today I wanted answers. *What the hell has happened to me? Where am I? Oh, I know*, I told myself impatiently, *in the Refreshment House of Yafnaar, among the Fa'aldu. And where does that get me?*

Today, at least, I had a rational mind. I had defined the problem and could approach it logically. The first step: assemble all the facts I had—the facts, that is, as I understood them.

FACT ONE: My name was Ricardo Emilio Carillo, lately of California. *All right, face the toughest one first. Do you mean "lately" or simply "late"?* Yesterday I had considered with utter detachment the possibility that I had died and arrived in Hell. Certainly I had believed, when the fireball was coming toward me, that I was about to die.

I had never thought much about the character of Hell—or, for that matter, of Heaven. But I had always assumed, I realized as I thought about it now, that I would *feel* very different. Whatever the place was like—either one—I should not feel as . . . well, as *alive*.

And right now, with my head still dully throbbing, the hardness of the block beneath me intangible even through the thin padding, the pleasant salty taste of the water lingering in my mouth, I felt very much alive.

I made up my mind, then, to set aside the question of my death in another life. In *this* life, in *this* world, I was alive; and the world around me was absolutely real.

14

It occurred to me that my decision followed classic lines of thought: the nature of reality *à la* Bishop George Berkeley, and the Cartesian *cogito ergo sum*. Whatever it was based on, having made the decision made me feel much better. And it led me to examine the next fact.

FACT TWO: This place did not exist on the Earth as I knew it. It had similarities to Death Valley in California, the great salt flats of Utah, and the desert areas around the Dead Sea. But I had been to all three places; I knew for a certainty that this desert was different. Nor could it be the Sahara or the Gobi, which I *hadn't* seen; I knew they had nothing like the salty quality of this place.

Could I be on an entirely different planet? Only, I decided, if it weren't in Earth's planetary system. Even *I* knew that there were no planets except Earth in the Solar System with breathable atmosphere.

I didn't have enough information to settle this question at the moment. I set it aside.

FACT THREE: I had studied languages all my life, specializing in the Romance languages, but along the way acquiring a nodding friendship with most of the languages of my world. I had never even heard of this language. Where, when, and how did I acquire such an automatic command of Gandaresh?

There! It happened again! A word I need pops out of nowhere—a word I know, and yet I don't.

Gandaresh: people-talk.

The word was there in my mind as though it had always been there. With it was another one: *Gandalara.* People-place. I had one of the answers I had been searching for. Where was I? Why, in Gandalara, of course.

But where, damn it, is Gandalara?

No answer.

So I had a memory I hadn't had before, but it was limited to things of this world, the Gandalaran world. It would be no help in solving the puzzle of my presence here. *But,* I thought with relief, *it's going to be a hell of a lot of help in getting along here!*

FACT FOUR: I had a very painful bump on the right side of my head, just above and behind the ear. What was *that* contributing to my state of mind?

It didn't matter, I decided. I had done all the logical thinking I could or wanted to do. I'd relax a while and simply accept things as they came.

I got up from the padded stone and stretched experimentally. I could feel an annoying sting here and there on my hide—and winced at the memory of my trek across the desert. Looking back, it was almost as though I had *bounced* across it: up on my feet, flat on my face, up on my feet, slam to the ground . . .

All in all, it was remarkable that I felt so good. Abrasions all over my body, of course, and the palms of my hands felt very tender. I was a little stiff, but the stretching helped that. It could have been worse. Very much worse. By comparison to the condition I might have been in, I felt terrific.

I walked a few steps around the room, intending to look at everything, but I was first drawn to the wall of the house. Its translucent stone intrigued me; it was like no building material I had ever seen before. It had a random crystalline quality: it was generally more translucent than alabaster, but in some places it was as transparent as glass, in others as opaque as fine white marble. The closest familiar comparison I could make was to rock crystal—quartz.

The engineering problem seemed enormous. It took precision and skill and *lots* of power to mine and shape that hard mineral, and the impression these people had given me had no suggestion of that kind of power. How on Earth—*try to think like a native: how in Gandalara?*—could they mine and handle blocks about the size and shape of a case of beer?

Faen. Beer. *Thank you, memory.* It was nice to know that fermentation was practiced here. Oh, a beer—how I wanted an ice cold beer!

I withdrew from that line of thought as fast I could. I had to concentrate on learning about *this* world, not waste time in longing for the one I had lost.

Still fascinated by the stone, I ran my dry palms over the wall. It was smoother than I had suspected. In fact, it seemed too smooth to be a natural mineral. Could it be some kind of cast glass? No; the crystalline structure was quite apparent. As I stared thoughtfully into the block which was at my eye level, I began to see something familiar in it. Distorted as they were, the crystals seemed cubic and they reminded me of *something* . . .

It came to me. To confirm it, I wet one forefinger with my tongue, rubbed it on the wall, and tasted it.

Son of a bitch! I thought. *The place is made of rock salt.*

Now here was knowledge I could use. It meant, of course, that rock salt was readily available to the Fa'aldu, but besides that: One, it hadn't rained here since this house was built; and Two, rain must have been unknown here for a long time *be-*

16

fore they built it. Surely nobody would go to the trouble to build a house like this if he expected it to be washed away at any moment. Building materials have to suit the environment. Adobe works fine, for instance, in the arid Southwest United States, but try building a 'dobe *hacienda* on the coast of Maine.

I moved over to the draped doorway through which Keddan had gone. The heavy curtain seemed to have been woven of several different thicknesses of yarn. Some were merely thin threads, as smooth as tanned leather, but others were three times as thick, some of them fuzzy and bristly, like fat twine.

They were all different tones of the same medium blue, except for a wide strand so much lighter than the rest that it stood out from the blue background. It formed no pattern that I could see this close to it, so I stepped back a pace—

—and caught my breath.

The overall effect of the thing was a sheet of water—cascading from ceiling to floor.

An indoor waterfall in the middle of the desert! It was incredibly beautiful—even cooling.

I wondered, suddenly, if one of the people I had met had crafted that amazing tapestry.

As I looked around the room for more wonders, I caught sight of a polished bronze plaque set shoulder-high in the outer wall. I was seeing it from a shallow angle which should have made visible anything etched on its surface, and I could see nothing there. Curious, I walked over to stand directly in front of it.

For a moment, I thought I was looking through transparent metal—a window of some kind. Through it I saw, looking in, another member of that same family of heavy-browed, pug-nosed people. Embarrassed by the confrontation, I opened my mouth to speak—I don't know what, a greeting, an apology—but I never said anything.

The man "outside" moved when I moved.

I was looking at my own reflection in a Gandalaran mirror—except that the face I saw in it was *not* my face. At least, it was not the face of Ricardo Carillo.

I stared into the eyes of a face I had never seen before, and they began to look terribly frightened. I looked away and examined the rest of the face instead. I was wearing it, after all; I should get to know it.

The supraorbital ridges were quite pronounced, making a semicircle of bone that hooded the eyes. The eyebrows were

17

faint and sparse, composed of fine dark-blond hairs that followed the bony ridges across the top of the nose, around, and down to the corners of the eyes.

Above the supraorbital ridges, the brow was high, and short dark-blond hair swept down from the scalp in a sharp widow's peak. I reached up with my left hand and touched it. It was short all over, like a crew cut, but it lay nearly flat against the skull. It was fine and soft, almost like fur.

I followed the line between the eyes down to the nose, and as I watched it, it wrinkled with distaste. Pug. Not as flat as that of the corpse in the desert, but most definitely a pug nose, and I have never been fond of them. They offend me for some reason—maybe because I don't care to be looking up people's nostrils.

I looked down to the mouth. Firm and large, perhaps a little too thin-lipped, but a very pleasant mouth—a mouth I could live with.

I smiled at the mirror image, just a little. Only the great canines showed. I smiled wider.

Look at those beautiful teeth!

Strong and white, even those tusks were gorgeous. I made faces into the mirror, trying to see all the way inside my mouth. Not a single cavity that I could see. I grabbed my upper teeth with the fingers of both hands and shook them until my head wobbled. They didn't budge. They were rock-solid in this new mouth of mine.

No more dentures and their problems: Would my teeth click at the faculty meeting? Let's see—no, I'd better not have a cob of corn. Trying surreptitiously to get a seed out from under my lower plate. No more of that now.

My own teeth again. *Hot damn!*

I liked the chin, too. It was wide and strong and well-formed. So far, it was the most familiar part of the face; I fancied it was much like the Carillo chin.

The ears were a bit on the small side; they lay almost flat against the side of my head. Not bad ears at all.

The skin was dark, like a heavy tan on an Amerindian. Much darker than the skin of Ricardo Carillo. That was all right, too—I hadn't had a decent tan in years.

Now I could look into the eyes of my new face, and I was pleased to find that, aside from their frame, they were very much like the eyes I had always known. Darker brown, perhaps, and clearer around the iris.

I stepped back to take a look at the face as a whole. Not bad, actually, once one got used to it.

18

I accepted the incredible truth: what I saw in the mirror was *my* face.

I was *behind* it, looking out. I controlled it. It blinked or smiled when I told it to. It *belonged* to me—and yet it didn't. I reminded myself that the English "face" and the French *façade* are cognates. Yes, I told myself, it *is* my face.

Now: *Who am I?*

A few minutes before, I could have answered without hesitation: Ricardo Emilio Carillo. But that was before I saw myself. Coupled with the odd, unearned memory that popped up now and then, my new appearance changed everything.

As I groped for understanding, it occurred to me that sometimes amnesia acted this way. A concussion destroyed a man's memories, and he had to start life over again. Years later a second blow on the head restored his memories of the early life and wiped away the years immediately past.

It wasn't a true model for my situation, of course. But it helped me think things through. For me it was as though the "second blow" had called up only vague memories of that early time. I was still consciously Ricardo Carillo, but I was also someone else—someone whose memories were not quite available to me.

I wondered with a flash of panic if they would ever be entirely mine. I had to live in *his* world; without knowing who he was, without understanding this Gandalaran as well as I did Ricardo (which, after all, was little to ask—do we ever really know ourselves?), I would never make this world *my* world.

The amnesia model fell apart when I considered the physical change which had taken place. At that point in my thinking, I looked down at my new body. A man is more than his face.

I undid the drawstring and dropped the loose blue trousers I was wearing. Were these the same ones I had worn across the désert? I couldn't tell. Then I removed a loosely-woven undergarment that was very much like boxer shorts with a drawstring.

I stood back far enough from the mirror to see my whole body, and I was very pleased with what I saw.

My neck was short, thick, and muscular, like that of a wrestler. My shoulders and chest were broad and well-muscled. They tapered slightly to a waistline fuller than the one I remembered, but flat and harder even than mine had been in my youth.

My genitals seemed quite adequate and appropriate for my

19

size and weight. I would have to see how they stood up to the ultimate test if the opportunity arose.

My legs were muscle-corded, and ended in feet which looked quite ordinary. The toes were a little longer, I thought, but when I flexed them, they worked fine. What more can you ask of toes?

I looked at my hands then, wondering how it was that I had not noticed the difference before now. Ricardo Carillo's hands were not in any sense delicate, but these made them look weak. The fingers were long and fine, full of strength. The hands themselves were large, though not massively so. With the corded wrists that held them, they were appropriate to the long, thickly muscled arms.

The dark-blond hair of my head grew downy-fine along my forearms and over the backs of my hands, more coarsely on my chest, on the back of my neck, and around my genitals.

I turned and posed in front of the mirror, getting acquainted with my body as I had with my face.

As Ricardo Carillo, I had been tall and reasonably strong; my muscles had remained firm until only a few years ago. The height of this Gandalaran I couldn't judge until I compared it to others, but he was unquestionably strong. "Rider," they had called me. I could well see that clinging to the back of that cat for any length of time would develop every muscle you could find.

Whoever it was who shared this body with me, he had taken very good care of it, considering the short time he'd had to develop it . . .

It hit me then, with more of a shock than looking in the mirror. This was the body of a *young* man.

I'm young again!

I had been ready to die. In the only way I could reckon it, less than two days ago I had come to terms with the fact that I would be dead within a year. To face such a truth, to let it penetrate down to the core of your being, demands incredible effort and indescribable pain. No matter how much life you've had, you want more. There are things undone, words unsaid, potentials unexplored. You know you could have done more with your life, and you beg fate, or whatever god you believe in, to give you more time. You know in your heart that another entire lifetime would not be sufficient, yet you pray for just a few more years. You've been goofing off, you think; please, just an extra year or two to finish all those abandoned projects!

20

But you know it can't be done. Your time has come, and there's no changing it.

So then you look back and count what you *have* done. And, all in all, the balance is really in your favor.

I looked back and realized that I had spent most of my adult life doing exactly what I wanted to do; exposing younger minds to the variety and the history of the world that I had discovered through languages. Some of my students had taken the time to tell me how much I had changed them. Their viewpoints had broadened, their lives had felt richer. They were aware of themselves as individual units in the composite of civilization. And those words of thanks were precious trophies.

There had been personal relationships, friendships I remembered warmly. Coming back from the war to find "my girl" married to someone else had been a blessing in disguise. I was left free to study all over the world, and to make friends wherever I went. Many of them were women, and some were very special. We shared our lives for a time. It was always—at least for me—very satisfying, and it ended naturally and without bitterness. Yes, I could say to my credit that I had never made a friend, man or woman, who was not still my friend.

So I had accepted, at last, that my life had been full, and well worth living. I had contributed what I could to the lives of other people; hopefully, through them and their memory of me, to the human race as a whole. An extended pleasure trip, to see the places I'd always traveled *between*—that was what I had wanted to do with what remained of my life.

I had made that adjustment. Painfully. Finally. I had been prepared to die.

And now I am alive in another world, young in another world, with another lifetime of experiences—new experiences—ahead of me.

I stood motionless for some time, taking it in. Letting the silent raging joy wash away the musty taste of death. And giving thanks in an incoherent, inexpressible way. I knew that I might never know why or how this had happened. But, *Oh, God!* was I glad!

A grumbling roar that I remembered well sounded from outside and brought me back into focus. I dressed again quickly; Keddan would be back soon with my breakfast. And then . . .

I would have to go out and face that monster cat.

21

4

The door curtain was swept aside, and the older of the two men came in, followed by Keddan, who was carrying a bowl. I glanced quickly from it to the recess where the stoppered pitcher stood. Yes, it was the same pattern. These people appreciated fine craftsmanship, if they did not, in fact, create these lovely things themselves.

They stopped a few paces from where I stood and Keddan, still in the background, said in formal tones: "Rider, I present the Respected Elder Balgokh."

Help! I thought. *What am I supposed to do? What are the customs?* No answer was forthcoming, so I followed my instincts; I bowed slightly and spoke, relieved to find that the words, at least, were there.

"Greeting, Respected One."

"Greeting, Rider." He did not return my bow, but he showed no offense. In fact he smiled, and waved Keddan forward. "We bring you breakfast. You seem to have recovered well. How do you feel?"

"Remarkably well, all things considered," I said. I accepted the good-smelling bowl of food from Keddan and smiled at him. "Thank you."

A quick smile lit Keddan's face, then he left the room. I looked at the imposing figure of Balgokh in his floor-length white robe. He was older than I had first thought, but that did not affect the attitude of accustomed authority which emanated from him. He was a little taller than I, his hair darker and sparser, his hands thinner. He moved them in a gesture of invitation.

"Sit, Rider, and eat," Balgokh said.

I sat down and took up the eating implement which was partially imbedded in the contents of the bowl. It was ceramic, shaped very much like a spoon, except there were two slots in the end, which formed three fork-like tines. It matched the other pieces of the serving set, and said something about basic values in Gandalara: graceful utility.

The bowl contained what appeared to be finely chopped vegetables and chunks of meat. I scooped a small bite into my mouth, braced for anything. It was pleasantly warm, and tasted something like oatmeal with bits of lamb—a distant relative of haggis.

"This is delicious," I said, meaning it. Balgokh bowed slightly, accepting the compliment.

"We offer the best fare we can to those who pass through out compound. Please, eat. We will talk when you have finished."

As I ate—I was intensely hungry, and had to try not to wolf down the food—I considered what they had called me: "Rider." It was a title, not a name.

The bowl of food was quickly gone and, surprisingly, I was quite satisfied. When I finished, Keddan came back in to take away the bowl and fork-spoon. Had he been watching through the curtained doorway?

When he had gone, Balgokh reached into his flowing robe and took out a small pouch and handed it to me. "Your money, Rider. Your sword will be returned when you are ready to leave."

I accepted the purse with new misgivings. Hesitantly, I asked, "Do I owe you for your hospitality?"

Oops.

The tall man stiffened, and his voice lost the note of familiarity that had been present earlier. "We sell water to the caravans," he said with deadly formality, "for that is the living of the Fa'aldu. But we demand nothing of the distressed, and we *never* accept coin."

Hurriedly I stood up and bowed with what I hoped was formal grace. "I ask your pardon, Respected One."

Boy, do I need more information about this culture—for that matter, about the person I'm supposed to be. But how the hell can I ask questions about things which are absolutely obvious to other people? A man wandering around California asking questions like "What are grapes?" or "Who is the president of the United States?" is going to be suspect as a mental case. If I don't want to head straight for the local equivalent of a twitch bin, I'd better think about everything I say before I say it. Unless . . .

I decided to tell part of the truth.

I touched the side of my head gently. "This blow on my head has left me confused, Respected One. My memory is addled."

To say the least.

He thawed instantly, and looked so concerned that I felt a twinge of guilt. "I have heard of such cases," he said. "I saw one, myself, many years ago, when I was an apprentice. An unfortunate man. He was a caravan driver, who had been kicked in the head by one of the vleks. He did not know his name or where he came from."

"What happened to him?" I asked, glad to hear Balgokh's voice lose its frostiness.

"He died." Then, at what must have been a look of utter shock on my face, he added quickly, "But he was in much worse shape than you. It was a miracle that he lived the three days he spent with us."

I laughed a little. "I'm not going to die." The words held infinite meaning for me. "But I admit I can't remember my own name."

He grinned broadly. I was interested to see that, old as Balgokh was, he, too, still had all his own teeth. I was getting used to the large canines; Balgokh's smiling face was not what I could yet call handsome, but I was beginning to like it. Especially when Balgokh said:

"I am delighted to be of help to you in that respect. Four days ago, the caravan of Gharlas stopped by, trading food and cloth for water. You were with them as a mercenary guard—at least, so Gharlas said." His grin faded, and a look passed across his face which I couldn't read. It might have been dislike, or wry humor. "He confided to me—not at my request, I assure you—that he intended to bypass Thaggorn in order to save that portion of his freight which would go as duty to the Sharith."

Sharith. Catfolk. There was something about the carefully neutral tone in which Balgokh spoke that word that worried me.

"You said 'so Gharlas said'?" I prompted him.

"Yes." He began to walk around the room. There was too much dignity in the slow movement to call it pacing. It dawned on me that he was embarrassed, and I recalled Keddan's reluctance to ask personal questions.

It must be a code of privacy, I decided. *Or self-preservation. The Fa'aldu don't get involved with their clientele. But I'm a mystery he couldn't resist thinking about. Could he be afraid of offending me with his opinions?*

"Respected Elder," I said, and he stopped. He turned to look at me. "Do you know my name?"

"Your name was given to me as Lakad."

Nice phrasing, I thought. The name meant nothing at all to me. "But who am I, really?"

Balgokh sighed, and seemed to make a decision. "My first

24

thought," he said, "when you returned as a Rider, was to believe that you had been a Sharith agent, planted on the caravan. But after we had cared for you, and I considered carefully, I wondered why your sha'um hadn't taken you directly to Thagorn, given the time you must have been exposed on the desert.

"If you were not Sharith, as I had begun to suspect, your identity was obvious. I know of only one Rider in this part of Gandalara who does not reside in Thagorn. He and his sha'um live in Raithskar. When you named this one Keeshah, the proof was complete." He paused for emphasis.

"You are Markasset, son of Thanasset."

"Thank you, Respected One," was all I said. I had to push the words through a chilling rush of associations too tangled and jumbled for me to read them yet. "My mind is still clouded, but at least I know my name. You have been a great help."

Markasset. Yes, it was my name. It *felt* like my name. But it wasn't. Not quite. Not completely. I still felt like Ricardo Carillo, too.

Thanasset. My father. As I thought of his name, I could see his face quite clearly. I would recognize him when I met him. But how would I feel about him? There was no emotion connected with the memory. A picture only—a face much like mine, but older and etched with lines. A good face, but only that. Like a photograph.

But instead of solving everything, my new knowledge only led to more questions. If I had been with a caravan, how did I wind up alone in the desert with a dead man? Why was I traveling under an alias? What happened to the rest of the caravan? The old man was looking at me speculatively. I assumed he was thinking those same questions. But I was wrong.

"I am not a Recorder, Rider Markasset," he said gently, "but it has been said of me that the All-Mind has touched me with the power to read men. And I tell you now that you have changed greatly since you came through here four days ago. Has some Ancestor given you wisdom?"

"Changed?" I asked, avoiding his last question because it made no sense to me at all. "How have I changed, Respected One?"

"As I said, I did not speak to you. But I observed you, and heard what you said to others—in the caravan and here in the compound. Let me say only that now you are . . . less

25

prideful. Less arrogant. And yet, you seem much more sure of yourself."

If I'm more sure of myself now, I thought, *I must have been really confused four days ago.*

"If I was disrespectful to the Fa'aldu, I am shamed, Respected One," I said. And meant it. The Fa'aldu and their water meant survival in the desert, Markasset's memory told me. Only a fool would offend these desert-dwellers.

Balgokh came a little closer to me, and looked intently into my face. "There is honesty there," he said, then nodded sharply. "Yes, I believe an Ancestor has touched you with wisdom." He bowed gracefully. "You are most fortunate, Rider Markasset."

"Thank you, Respected Elder Balgokh." What else could I say?

From outside I heard again the low roar of the huge cat, and I glanced toward the outer door. When I looked back, Balgokh was staring at me.

"I only hope," he said, "that you are not too changed for your sha'um. If you have been too radically altered by your contact with the All-Mind, your mount will not recognize or obey you. If that is so, we are all in danger."

"Danger? What danger threatens the Fa'aldu?"

Balgokh almost laughed as he gestured to the door—obviously beyond the door to the animal we had heard. "Perhaps you do not consider the rage of a sha'um dangerous? At the moment he is only restless and unsettled, waiting for you to come to him again. So far, he has done nothing, but he prowls incessantly. Our women and children are staying behind bolted doors. If you do not take command soon . . . If you *cannot* take command . . ."

I know, now, about the sha'um. A Rider and his sha'um are together from the time the boy is twelve and the sha'um is a year-cub. And it's strictly a one-to-one relationship; one man, one cat. If Markasset had died in the desert, Keeshah would have returned to the wild, grieving. But Keeshah had accepted that confused, exhausted wretch in the desert as his master and had brought him here for help.

If he doesn't recognize Markasset in me, I thought, *he'll blame the Fa'aldu for changing me—or, rather, for causing Markasset to disappear. And he'll avenge "me."* Probably starting with me.

As though I were seeing it again, I remembered the way the corpse had looked in the desert. I had noticed, then, only that his clothes were torn. As I looked back now, they seemed to have been shredded by some giant animal's claws. Keeshah?

Damn! I wish I could understand this whole thing. I have Markasset's memory, I can remember—not dependably, either, damn it again—what he knows. But I don't remember being Markasset. And if I have no real sense of the identity of his master, how can I expect Keeshah to have any? To recognize me now that I know I'm strange?

"I will take care of Keeshah," I said. "If I am too changed, my own death will be enough for him."

I was more scared when I said that than I had ever been in my life. But, what the hell; you only live once.

In the back of my mind an impish voice said, *"Oh, yeah?"* and I answered, *Yeah! I'm not fool enough to try to parlay miracles.*

"May it not be so," Balgokh said. There was sincerity in his voice. "We have a haunch of glith for him, and plenty of water. *Keddan!*"

Keddan brought in a hunk of raw meat that seemed to be the rump and one hind leg of a sheep-sized animal, and a tanned skin that might have been the hide of the same animal. The skin was tightly sewn where the legs should have been, and thick twine tied the neck. It was stretched taut with the weight of the water inside it.

I slung the haunch of meat over one bare shoulder and tucked the skin under my other arm. I looked a wordless, hopeful farewell at Balgokh and Keddan, and went out into the blistering heat of the compound.

Keeshah wasn't there.

Far from being disappointed, I was relieved to have a moment to get my bearings. The Fa'aldu compound was a large rectangle marked at either end by a man-high wall of rock salt blocks. There were openings in the walls to permit the passing of caravans, but these were covered now with thickly-woven cloths tied through holes carefully drilled near the edges of the top and bottom blocks. They were not designed, obviously, as defensive barriers. But they were a symbol that entrance to the Refreshment House of Yafnaar required the consent of Balgokh, as eldest of his family. And they were sufficient, once a caravan had entered, to keep the contrary and exceptionally stupid vleks from wandering out into the desert.

The sides of the rectangle were formed by seemingly identical rows of buildings, individual units sharing one side wall with its neighbor, each one opening onto the compound

27

through a small square-cornered doorway. Markasset knew that the doors I faced across the compound led only to cubicles lined with sleeping blocks which were padded with the plainest possible pallets.

The room I had left, however, was only the beginning of the larger compound which was the living area of the Fa'aldu. From somewhere in its private interior, the Fa'aldu brought the water. I searched Markasset's memory as closely as I could; he had no idea how the Fa'aldu drew water from the wasteland of the desert. He did know about wells, it seemed, and was certain that they were not used here. It was a generations-old secret among the Fa'aldu clans.

Wondering about it was pointless—and it was putting off the inevitable.

I walked out to the watering troughs in the center of the large yard. There were three of them, the larger two almost exactly twice and three times the length of the smallest. They were made of large, semi-cylindrical tiles laid with the rounded side down and supported by short walls of brick-shaped salt blocks. The smallest trough contained only one tile, flanged at both ends and fitted with half-discs of tile. It was a darkish brown in color, and glazed to be watertight.

The longer troughs were made of two and three of these tiles, the edge of one fitted exactly within the flanged lip of the next, the extreme edges sealed as this one was.

I set the meat down on the edge of the trough, and untied the knot at the neck of the waterskin, carefully holding the opening closed until I had the skin in position over the trough. Then I let some of the water run out, feeling my arm indent the lower surface of the skin. I re-tied the opening, set the skin on the ground, and took a deep breath.

"Keeshah!" I called.

As though he had been waiting for that summons; the sha'um came easily, gracefully, over the high wall to my right. As he had done out on the desert, he kept his distance, padding back and forth along the wall, watching me and making growling noises in his throat.

"I have brought you water, Keeshah. Come and drink."

He stopped pacing and came a few steps nearer, stretching out his head to sniff in my direction. Then, with a roar, he shook his head and sidled off.

Does the water smell bad, Keeshah? I thought. *Or is it me? Scratch that—it's a silly question.*

It had never occurred to me that the cat might accept me simply because I *looked* like the Markasset he knew. Even in the world of Ricardo Carillo, domestic cats were sensitive to personality changes and moods in the humans they chose to live with. No, Keeshah knew I was different. He had proved it already by hanging back for so long while I made my way across the desert. And if he had been confused then, when I wasn't sure who I was, he must be even more skittish now that I had a strong conviction of an identity which was alien to him.

I watched the huge cat pacing, and fear gave way to admiration. I had never seen such a powerful animal. His muzzle was a broader wedge than that of a tiger, the mouth cut deeper into it and, I thought, lined with even more teeth. Ridges of muscle flowed from the powerful jaw along his smooth throat to help form the wide shield of pectorals that rippled across his chest as he paced about.

His legs were thick, his paws easily the size of my head; their claws, retracted now, must be proportionately large. His long body looked lean, but I remembered how it had felt beneath me: wide, supportive, secure.

Markasset?

At first I didn't know what it was. A pulsing from somewhere inside me, familiar, compelling. A warm touch directly to my mind—friendly, yet wary.

Of course: Keeshah.

Markasset? came the thought again. It wasn't really the name, simply an identifying thought and a sense of question. Uncertainty.

I understood many things then. The special bond between a Rider and a sha'um was a telepathic link. The huge cats could not verbalize or think in exactly the same way that a man can, but they were intelligent in a feline way, and they had a low-powered type of telepathy. They could communicate with men.

That is, *one* sha'um chose to link with *one* man. And the basis for that link was mutual loyalty, a friendship which went deeper than human friendships. When Markasset turned twelve, he had gone to live for a season in the Valley of the Sha'um. The cats had accepted him as their own; a huge gray female had allowed Markasset to take with him his "brother," her only cub—Keeshah.

Markasset had passed the judgment of the sha'um. That gave me a deeper impression of him than anything I had yet learned about him. Now I had to face that same judgment, and there could be no deception in this mind-to-mind relationship.

29

The question came again: *Markasset?* With a growl of impatience.

I walked toward the sha'um, and as I moved, he grew still. Only the tip of his great tail moved, barely twitching.

I was still afraid. Not of death under the teeth and claws of a huge, dangerous cat. But of failing to win Keeshah's trust. In Markasset's body—*as Markasset*— I had shared the special, wonderful friendship of the sha'um. I was desperately afraid . . . that I might lose Keeshah.

I stopped directly in front of the sha'um and looked up into his face. Even his eyes were gray, flecked with silver, and as unreadable as any cat's. He made no move, though he was tensed to leap in any direction.

No longer Markasset, I spoke to him in a way that was automatic, a way I didn't understand. *Not the Markasset who brought you from the Valley.*

The big head moved then, up and down my body, sniffing.

Same smell. Different. Who?

I answered the most honest way I could. *Myself.*

Not Markasset? Keeshah relaxed a little, sat in the classic cat pose. His tail curled around his feet, and its tip still twitched restively. He tilted his head and wrinkled his mouth and regarded me with a perfect look of puzzlement.

Suddenly I laughed: a loud, raucous sound that filled the courtyard as Keeshah's roar had done. The cat laid back its ears and fled in startled confusion. He stopped a few feet away, turned in an incredibly small circle, and crouched to the ground, watching me.

"I don't blame you for being mixed up, Keeshah," I said aloud, conscious that I could choose to speak at the same time I was projecting to him mentally. I walked toward him slowly and muscles rippled along his side as he crouched even lower. The claws on his hind feet were out, digging into the sand for better traction.

Who? he asked again.

Myself, Keeshah. Someone who is neither Markasset nor Ricardo Carillo. Someone who is both. Myself. I have had a hard time accepting it; I know the change puzzles you.

But I am certain of this, Keeshah. I knelt in the sand and looked levelly into the cat's solemn gray eyes. *I need you as Markasset did. More. Already you have helped me. And I think you—and only you—understand how strange I feel. How alone.*

Not Markasset, Keeshah. Markasset is gone. Please let me take his place.

30

For a moment, the cat gazed at me steadily. Then his head darted forward in a light nudge to my midsection. I fell over and rolled several feet, once more tasting salty sand.

Not Markasset, he said as he rose to his feet. A single bound and he was looming over me. His mouth opened, and my breath dried in my throat. The razor-sharp teeth closed gently on my shoulder. *But same friend. Keeshah's friend.*

He released me, and rubbed his great soft-furred head against my chest; his whiskers tickled my abdomen. I laughed and grabbed the huge head with both arms, burying my face in the fur on his wide forehead.

Keeshah lifted me from the ground as he had done out in the desert. I released him and we walked without touching toward the water trough. I dipped my hand in the water and held it to his muzzle.

While among men, a sha'um always eats or drinks first from the hand of his Rider.

5

The caravan trail led north across the salt wastes, toward the base of the Great Wall, where Raithskar lay. The Respected Elder had offered me simple directions, as well as a pouch of dried meat and a small leather canteen of water, assuring me that it was but three days' trip for a sha'um. I soon found that directions were unnecessary; once Keeshah knew where we were going, he knew the way. I lay my head upon the wide back and dozed as he moved with long, seemingly effortless strides across the desolate land. He did not gallop headlong, as I fuzzily remembered him doing in his urgency to bring me to the Refreshment House, but fell into an easy lope which ate up distance without tiring him. An easy, rhythmic, soothing motion—I drifted in and out of sleep as the distance passed.

At first I had been hesitant about riding the sha'um. Especially was I hesitant about mounting him. I remembered the scorn I had felt as a kid, watching a cowboy comedy and laughing as the greenhorn tried to swing into the saddle from the horse's right. There was no one watching, as by custom I would not ride my sha'um within the walls of the Refreshment House. But Keeshah was there, and I most certainly didn't want to make a fool of myself in front of *him*.

There was no saddle to give me a clue. The sha'um is the only animal in Gandalara big enough for a man to ride, and the great cats would not have put up with a saddle. Even the cargo-carrying vlek, with hardly enough mind to get mad, threw a fit every time a pack-harness was tightened around its low-slung belly. It could carry only as much weight as that of a ten-year-old child, but it was untrustworthy as a child's pet. So there was no such thing in Gandalara as a riding saddle.

But I need not have worried. My body behaved in an almost automatic fashion. Keeshah lay upon the ground, and I sat astride his back, seating myself near the base of his spine. Then I lay forward, drew my knees up against his sides, and reached up with my hands to grasp his huge shoulders. My knees were just below his rib cage, my feet tucked up just forward of his thighs. I could direct him with slight pressure from my hands or my knees—but, as I have said, Keeshah needed no directing.

We traveled for some hours across the desert, the only sound in that vastness the *pad-pad-pad* of Keeshah's thickly calloused paws against the hard-baked bed beneath us. Occasionally I would hear the cry of a bird, and look up to see a flash of wings, or a distant, almost stationary soaring form. But there seemed to be nothing larger than the sand-ants alive on the desert floor except for Keeshah and me.

I had accepted the leather canteen of water from Balgokh with formal thanks and unspoken skepticism. Keeshah would need no water in that time—he could go for several days without it. But the canteen contained, at a guess, somewhat less than a pint of water, four or five hundred milliliters. Hardly enough for a man for three days in the desert. I felt it wouldn't be politic to ask for more; I decided I would have to make it last.

I soon found that it would be plenty. In the first place, I didn't feel thirsty very often—not nearly as often as I should have in this heat. In the second place . . .

I was a water saver.

We had been on the road for some hours when I noticed a pressure in my lower abdomen which indicated a need that should be taken care of. *Stop,* I directed Keeshah, and when he did, I sat up and swung my right leg over his back, sliding down to the ground. I walked a few paces from the smoothly worn area that was the road and urinated.

32

I passed very little liquid. As it touched the dry, hot desert floor, the dark urine crystallized rapidly, leaving a little heap of yellow crystals. I stared at them for so long that Keeshah walked over and nosed my back, anxious to get going again.

Wait, I told him. *Just a little while.* Absently I rubbed his jaw and moved my hand up to his ear to scratch lightly. He agreed with some impatience, and lay down by the side of the road.

You find truth in the oddest places, I was thinking to myself. The concentration of organic and inorganic salts in that urine solution must have been *high. Very* high! Like the kangaroo rat of the American southwest, my kidneys were designed to save every possible drop of water.

With a concentration like that, a human being would have died of kidney stones or other renal failure long since. And here was the truth I had found in a simple, natural act.

I am not Homo sapiens. *Whatever I am, wherever Gandalara is, I am not a man as I knew men.*

Keeshah growled, and obediently, almost in a daze, I mounted him and we set off again. For a long time I simply clung tightly to his back—as though he were my own humanity and I wanted to hold it as long as possible. I pressed my face into his fur and closed my eyes and tried not to think. But by the time I detected Keeshah's complaining thought—I was pinching his shoulders, and he could sense my distress and was worried—I had accepted it.

I was not human.

I apologized to Keeshah and rode more lightly, turning things over in my mind. The whole situation made less and less sense. And this last twist was cruel. The problem wasn't so much that I knew I wasn't human, but that I was so damned *nearly* human. I had already speculated that Gandalara might be, fantastically, on some world that orbited Alpha Centauri or Procyon. If that were true, I wouldn't really expect to be human—but it was far less likely that I would *look* human.

Parallel evolution was a little too much to swallow. Look at the wide and wild variety of life that had evolved on Earth during two or three thousand million years. The notion that a water-oxygen world much like Earth would necessarily evolve a dominant, human-shaped, intelligent species was nonsense on the face of it. The Earthly dolphin has a brain as fully evolved as the human.

I don't think I'd have gotten as much pleasure out of waking as, say, a highly intelligent, good-natured spider, I specu-

33

lated. *But after the first shock, it might have been philosophically easier to accept. And I'd have known, positively, that I wasn't on Earth.*

I think.

Information, damn it! I need more data before I can place myself in the "grand scheme of things."

For the rest of that day, I tried to keep my mind a blank. I failed, of course. The questions kept circling and spinning, seemingly in rhythm with Keeshah's powerful movement under me.

The cloud layer diffused the diminishing rays of sunlight as night approached, so that the light dimmed only gradually. When the sun finally set, the world was plunged into darkness with startling suddenness. I called Keeshah to a halt, slid wearily off his back, and was asleep almost before I touched the ground.

It was full light when I woke again, and I realized that I was not fully recovered from the desert ordeal yet. I ate a light meal and drank sparingly of the water, still surprised by the tiny amount which satisfied me. Then I mounted Keeshah and we were on our way again. I rested my head on his furred back and dozed as he carried me.

Keeshah angled toward the left, and I raised my head from his back to see what had caused the slight change in direction. The caravan trail had turned, and Keeshah was following it. If we had continued straight ahead, we would have had to cross an area of the desert that had a strangely smooth and shiny look about it.

I caught a picture from Keeshah: anyone stepping onto that shiny area would break through the crust and sink. It was a bog of some kind. Though I had known, intellectually, there was more to Gandalara than the dry waste of the desert, the sight of anything wet surprised the hell out of me.

I sat up a little and looked around, glad to have a new puzzle to distract me. In the distance I could see things growing in the marsh. Farther ahead, thicker now as we approached it, was the line of blue that had drawn me through the desert. I knew now that it was the Great Wall, at the foot of which lay Markasset's home city of Raithskar.

The city has to get its water from somewhere, I decided. *This bog is the end of the line for whatever source feeds the city.*

It had to be a river which flowed down from the mountains, through or beside the city, and picked up more and more salt as it ran south into the desert. Here the intense heat

34

caused such rapid evaporation that the water simply disappeared. Some of it might soak into the ground, but I'd bet money that the hot, dry air sucked up most of it.

At the final edge, the brine concentration was so great that nothing could live in it except some stubborn algae and bacteria. Farther upriver, less hardy plants could live with water that was merely brackish. But this bog contained a saturated salt solution, into which no more salt could dissolve. It was thick, stagnant water covered by a mush of salt crystals which formed a thin, shiny crust.

Keeshah was right; it would not be a good place to walk over.

By noon, the marshy area was dotted with clumps of reeds and an occasional sickly-looking tree. Keeshah slowed, stopped.

Too hot. Rest.

I was willing. Riding a sha'um is less work than being one, but it was no picnic.

I ate a bit of food from the pouch and leaned up against Keeshah's heaving side.

"I don't wonder you're pooped," I told him, and he turned his head to look at me. I poured a little of the precious water into my hand and offered it. He lapped it up carefully, the big raspy tongue flipping it *under* itself and into his mouth. Then, deliberately, he licked across the palm of my hand, lightly enough that he didn't quite scrape off hide.

For a while we sat in companionable silence, staring at the Great Wall. I glanced at Keeshah, and smiled. He looked for all the world like a sphinx in informal dress. I leaned up against his shoulder and scratched under his chin absently as I surveyed the wall.

It looked like a range of mountains stretching to the horizon on the east and west. There didn't seem to be any high peaks or deep valleys, though; the top edge was a little uneven but, all things considered, remarkably smooth. I'd never heard of any such long, *high* wall as that, anywhere on Earth. China's Great Wall might be as long or longer, but it was certainly not so incredibly high.

Keeshah's eyes were closing, and finally he shoved me aside so he could stretch out. I lay down against his back and fell asleep in the shadow of his body.

I woke to a nearly inaudible whining noise and a very definite nudge. As I started to complain, Keeshah's urgent thought reached me.

Silence. Danger. Hide.

35

I woke up fast.

We crept quietly away from the road and lay flat behind a shallow rise. It was dotted with scraggly bushes that wouldn't have hidden a jackrabbit in the daytime—but it was the best cover available.

It was already night—the sun must have set some time ago. In the east there was a white glow that was the moon shining beyond the thin overcast. It spread an eerie silver radiance over the bleak landscape.

Soon I could hear what had alerted Keeshah. Carrying over the flatland came the sounds of a group of men moving toward us. The low murmurs of men's voices. The muffled pacing of many feet. An occasional sharper voice calling commands. An organized group of men, coming at a fast march from the north.

It was several minutes before I could see their shadowy figures moving along the caravan trail in the veiled moonlight. Their voices became clear before their bodies resolved from the shadowy silver of the night.

"Might as well be chasing a wild thaka!" grumbled a deep voice. "I say the stone's somewhere in the city."

"Aw, you been singing that fleabitten tune for hours, Devok. It don't matter *what* you think. Orders is orders. Anyway, Klareth's group is still searching the city."

A third voice added, "Yeah, Devok, and if the fleabitten thing *did* get shipped out with the caravan, we'd best catch it now. If they get to Chizan or Dyskornis with it, we'll *never* get it back."

I could see them clearly now: a dozen men, each leading a pack-vlek.

"What we ought to have done is arrest the fleabitten old man and persuade him to tell us all about it."

"Arrest a City Supervisor with no evidence? You're crazy, Devok. Shut up and march. We want to make it to Yafnaar before sundown tomorrow."

They marched in silence for a while, drawing nearer. Then I heard a new voice.

"What *I* can't figure is why anybody'd try to steal the Ra'ira. It'd ruin its value to cut it up, and if you leave it like it is, anybody in Gandalara would know what it was and whose it was."

"Not if it was kept hid for a while." That sounded like the first voice which had replied to Devok.

"How's that? What good would that do?"

An exaggerated sigh. "One of these days, Mord, you ought

36

to go to a Recorder and pick up a little education. That's how *we* got the fleabitten jewel."

"Awww. That thing has been in Raithskar for hundreds of hundreds of years."

Another voice. "Not that long. Several tens of hundreds, maybe. But he's right, I've heard the story myself. Tell him, Ganneth."

"Serkajon himself stole it from Kä," Ganneth supplied. "Brought it to Raithskar and set up the Council."

"Didn't know that!" said a voice down the line.

"Dummy!" came another voice, disgusted. "Whatcha think Commemoration Day is all about?"

The words brought a flash of memory. Parades and celebration, the statue of a man riding a sha'um carried through the city, and his image miniaturized and multiplied in banners displayed everywhere. In one large building, encased in glass so that it might be viewed and appreciated by the public during that annual celebration, a pale blue stone about the size of a glass doorknob. Its surface was unfaceted, but the blue color darkened as one looked deeply into it, and hinted at an imperceptible crystalline structure.

The Ra'ira.

"Him?" another voice bantered. "Give him free faen and he'd drink to his mother-in-law!"

Laughter, then Devok's voice again, challenging. "So what? Kä's been long deserted; nobody even knows where it is, anymore. And that was a long time ago. Way I hear it, we never even got a complaint from Kä when Serkajon ran off with it. But you can bet we'll raise a holler if some other city has heisted it from us! Raithskar ain't deserted by a long ways.

"Naw, no other city'd have the nerve to swipe the Ra'ira; I still say it's inside Raithskar!"

"Not again!"

"Knock it off, will you Devok?"

"Yeah, ain't it bad enough we gotta march—"

The straggly column was abreast of us. I hadn't noticed that there was a slight breeze . . . until it changed direction. The vleks caught Keeshah's scent, and all hell broke loose.

I've never heard any sound that can compare with the harsh bawling of a frightened vlek. The pack animals screamed and stamped, straining against their leads and doing their best to trample anybody who got in their way.

Two or three of the vleks seemed to be carrying live cargo of some sort. A horrendous, terrified clacking rose from the

37

woven-reed cages and drove the vleks into an even higher frenzy.

Beside me, Keeshah was tense as coiled wire. I tried to see what was in his mind, but it was seething and unreadable. Anger and contempt for the vleks mingled with predatory desire, frustration and a flash of . . . guilt? If a sha'um could swear, the silver night around us would have been tinged with blue.

It's all right, I tried to reassure him. *How could you have known the wind would shift?* No response. He moved his hind legs, getting ready to lunge into the melee. Eagerly.

No, Keeshah! I ordered sharply. *They don't know we're here. Keep still; they may yet pass us by.*

He didn't move. But he didn't relax.

For that matter, neither did I. My hand was on the hilt of my sword.

They were beginning to make sense of the chaos. I could hear Gandalaran voices above the vleks braying.

"Settle down, you fleabitten . . ."

"Hey! Ganneth tripped! Get him out from under . . ."

The wind shifted again, and the frenzied animals calmed almost instantly. There was a moment of stunned silence, broken by the now familiar voice of Devok.

"Didn't I tell you we shoulda never left—"

"WILL YOU SHUT UP!" roared a voice I hadn't heard before. "Now, anybody know what set 'em off?"

"I dunno," someone answered. I knew they must be peering into the shadows on either side of the trail—I pressed my face into the hard ground, willing myself to disappear.

"There's nothin' out there," someone said disgustedly.

"Almost anything will spook these fleabitten animals. We should just be glad it's over and nobody's hurt."

"Whaddya mean, nobody. My foot . . ."

"Didn't hurt you none .. ."

"AWRIGHT!"

When a muttering quiet had set in: "Your jabbering probably set 'em on edge. It sure as Gandalara was makin' me nervous.

"Let's get moving again. And this time do less talkin' and faster walkin'. We've wasted enough time, and you'll need your breath before dawn. Let's go."

They moved away in silence. Only when the sound of their feet on the hard-worn trail had faded completely did I dare to breathe again. I let what I judged to be another twenty minutes go by before I remounted a restless Keeshah and we were on our way.

From what I'd heard, it sounded as though the cops were out in force tonight. I didn't know what instinct had driven Keeshah to conceal us from them—a natural wariness of the unidentified, probably—but I was glad he had done so. In my travels, I have learned that even a respectable university professor is wise to steer clear of the police if he doesn't know what all the laws are.

6

Raithskar was itself a jewel.

It sprawled uphill, following the slope that had risen gradually from the salt bogs. Now the slope steepened swiftly to merge at last into the majesty of the Great Wall, some miles beyond the city.

We had stopped several yards distant from the huge main gate, over Keeshah's anxious protests. I needed time to get reacquainted with this city.

Through the gates I could see a portion of the wide boulevard which led into the city, and I could *hear* the marketplace that filled the boulevard. Voices haggling over prices. The squealing of children forced to tag along on a shopping trip. The clinking of coins.

I could smell it, too—the tang of blood from the butcheries, sweet fruits, sharp spices, perfumes I could not quite identify.

Raithskar seemed familiar to me in many ways. The smells, the sounds, the look of the place made me feel I had been here before—yet I did not recognize it in the sense of *knowing* it. And it called up Earthly memories. The clustered roofs climbing the slope in a riot of color made me think of San Francisco before skyscrapers spoiled the natural line that was so beautiful when viewed from the bay. Some of the roofs had small interlaced tiles like the one which had formed Yafnaar's watering trough. They were dark brown in color, but otherwise much like the Spanish-style roofing that had been a feature of Santa Barbara.

Raithskar gleamed and glittered in the early morning light.

In different ways, it made both Ricardo and Markasset homesick.

I found my gaze drawn to the Great Wall, four or five miles away. It stretched clear to the sky and disappeared in the clouds. How tall was it, I wondered? A mile? Two miles? Maybe three? There was no way to know for sure, but I'd have said at least two.

And directly behind Raithskar was a sight I had never expected to see. From out of the mists at the top of the great escarpment, water cascaded down the almost sheer face of the cliff. At its base was a rainbow-crowned lake which foamed continuously as the tons of water thundered into it. The lake narrowed to a river, which rushed down the slope and through the city.

This had to be the source that wound up miles later as a treacherous salt bog. The Skarkel Falls—the name surfaced from my memory.

The base of the falls was shrouded in mist—the water, falling from such a height, virtually pulverized the lake, sending up an endless spray of water vapor.

I could see then why Raithskar glittered so in the sunlight. Even this far from the falls, there was *moisture* in the air, cooling off the fearsome heat of the desert. Invisible droplets coated the roofs of the city, causing them to shine as though they were polished.

After the hot, dry journey, the coolness of the city called out to me.

Keeshah and I had traveled through the night. From his back I had watched the dimly-lit countryside change around us. The vegetation in the swamp had grown denser, the mucky ground gradually solidifying to support short grasses and bushes. I saw trees more frequently, and they seemed taller and healthier—although I had seen larger manzanita bushes in California. Just as the land began to look all overgrown, with fields of grass and shadowy clumps of growth that might almost have been wooded areas, the moon set.

The blackness was complete; it was as though I had been suddenly blinded. The cloud layer had diffused and distributed what little moonlight remained, so that I hadn't noticed the gradual dimming.

Frightened in the abrupt blackness, I ordered Keeshah to stop. He did, but he protested.

Soon there, he said.

Can you see through this darkness?

40

No. Follow road smell. He was panting heavily; he had been running for hours without a break.

We'll wait till dawn, I told him.

I slid off his back, and when I moved away from him he was completely invisible. But we were still together. He was a large warm presence in my mind, and I was no longer frightened of the dark.

Rest, Keeshah.

He agreed—not with reluctance, but with some puzzlement. I heard him moving around in the bushes, settling to the ground. I lay on my back in the tart-smelling grass and looked up into the darkness.

As though the sky had been waiting for me, the clouds broke apart and I was looking at the stars.

But not *my* stars.

I had spent enough romantic moonlit nights gazing into the sky to know that for sure. There wasn't a single constellation up there that I recognized. And there was one bright configuration that I knew I had *never* seen. Then the clouds swept together and left me again in darkness.

I'd had enough of questions today. So the stars were different—I listed that among things to think about and sort out later. It was another datum, only that.

I was emotionally drained, tired past the point of sleeping, afraid that if I slept, I would dream of unfinished puzzles, mazes with no end and no beginning, paths that led only into other paths. So I listened to the night.

Riding with my head on Keeshah's body, the soft sound of his paws striking the ground had blocked out all other aural input. I had noticed the landscape changing visually; now I became aware of the different sound of it.

The desert had been so quiet. The cry of a bird had been an intrusion out there. Now I could hear the flutter of wings all around me, and the soft rustling of small animals moving through the grass and bushes. Skittering sounds made me think of squirrels and their nervous, rush-and-stop zigzags.

What did these night creatures look like? Would I ever see them clearly in the daytime? I could well understand that even here, where the desert was fading, the cooler night was more inviting than the day. And I wondered then whether the vast savage desert, so desolate in the heat of day, had its own sort of night life.

As I lay there listening in a sort of sleep-daze, it occurred to me that I believed dawn was imminent because on Earth it would be so. I'd had no evidence so far that I *was* still on Earth. It might be hours before dawn.

I was too relaxed to move right then. But eventually I summoned the energy to sit up, to tell Keeshah it was time to get started. I looked for and found him nestled into some scratchy-looking bushes . . .

Looked? Bushes?

It was gray and dim, but the dawn had already begun. A few minutes later, the red glow of the rising sun spread through the thin clouds in the east, flushing the sky. I stood up and stretched, and watched while Keeshah yawned and *stre-e-e-etched*. I ate a little food, and we shared what was left of the water. Then I mounted and we were on our way again.

The land began to change quickly, the open area giving way to cultivated fields. There were waist-high, grass-like plants that had to be some kind of grain. Evenly spaced humps of vines or low bushes—what they produced I could only guess.

Smaller tracks crossed the caravan road, and as the morning brightened we passed Gandalarans on the road. Some carried wood-handled, bronze-headed tools toward the fields. Others were leading laden vleks in to the market.

I sat up on Keeshah's back and moved forward to ride just behind his shoulders, asking him to slow to a walk. The people who passed us greeted me politely and edged carefully past Keeshah with looks of mingled fear and curiosity on their faces. Those who led vleks simply stood still until we had passed, holding tightly to the looped halters so that the beasts would not stamp around and spill their cargo.

And so we had come at Raithskar at last, and I had paused a moment to absorb my first impressions of the place which was to be my home now.

I yielded to Keeshah's impatience and urged him on; he ran eagerly toward the gate, then stopped.

Well? I asked him. *I thought you were in a hurry?*

He twisted his neck to look back at me.

City, he explained. *Get off.*

Oh, sure. Sorry.

It was logical. Balgokh had said that Markasset was the only Rider not connected with the Sharith. Therefore I was the only man in Raithskar who could ride instead of walk. Common courtesy demanded that I shouldn't flaunt it. I dismounted and walked into the city beside Keeshah with my

42

hand resting lightly behind his left ear. That, too, was at Kee-shah's direction—a ritual gesture to assure the people in the china shop that the bull was under control.

The bustling marketplace reminded me strongly of the older sections of Fez and Marrakesh. The streets here were wider and much cleaner, but the noise and the confusion were the same. There was color everywhere, as though the town itself was rejecting the uniform paleness of the desert. Most of the shoppers wore long- or short-sleeved tunics of lengths which varied from very short for the children to ground-sweeping for some of the women.

Here and there a man was dressed, like me, for the desert: loose trousers tied at waist and ankles, long-sleeved tunic slit to the waist for leg freedom, soft leather boots calf-high under the trouser legs, a piece of cloth tied so that its loose edge hung down the back. More commonly, however, and almost as a rule for the vendors seated in the shade of the selling stalls, the men wore only the loose, comfortable trousers.

No one made any attempt to blend colors or find compatible combinations, and all the colors were bright. A green tunic was belted round with red; yellow trousers screamed against a rich purple tunic; a worn blue tunic was patched neatly at the shoulder with lurid orange.

I blinked at the vivid display, but soon found that the unplanned, fluid melange of colors cheered me. Unmistakably, I had left the desert behind me.

The only *pattern* of color to be seen was in the fabric awnings under which the merchants sat. Each one was a square of canvas supported and stretched by a framework of wooden poles. In places there were several of the same pattern grouped together. Markasset's memory told me that the weave of the fabric identified the merchant, much like a Scottish tartan identified a clan.

Merchandise was arranged in the same neat, hollow squares under each awning. They were spaced so that a customer could walk all the way around them. The merchant or his man sat in the center of the square, calling out the value of his goods and hawking business like a carny talker. A customer could touch, look at and, within reason, test any merchandise as long as he remained standing or kneeling. When he'd found something he wanted, he literally "settled down" to dicker, seating himself beside his choice. Then the merchant turned to him and they began to haggle over price.

The bright, busy stalls lined the boulevard three deep on each side of the wide, hard-surfaced street. The thronging pedestrians were polite and cautious, avoiding collisions with studied care, laughing and smiling. As Keeshah and I threaded our way through them, I felt my spirits lifting. The touch of light mist on my face, the gay color all around me, people who were happy and ordinary, though they might not be human—and an unforced feeling of having come home.

We moved out of the busiest area of the marketplace, where the out-of-town merchants conducted business under their temporary shelters, and into the city's own trade district. Neat, stone-walled buildings crowded together and narrowed the street slightly, offering for sale those things which the townsfolk would regularly need. From the aromas here, as richly confused as the colors of the bazaar, I guessed we were in the food-selling district.

Keeshah and I stopped at the same time. We were outside a meat shop which was a cross between a delicatessen and a butcher shop, and featured both cooked and fresh meat. The roast had stopped me; the raw had stopped Keeshah.

Eat? The quasi-question hung in his mind, and it echoed through mine.

"Markasset!"

I turned toward the high-pitched, slightly breathless voice. A woman was hurrying toward me.

Though there were not consistent or obvious style differences between what I had seen men and women wearing as I walked through the marketplace, the sexual dimorphism in this race was more pronounced, and I had been having no trouble differentiating the sexes. Nor did I now. There was no doubt in my mind that this was a woman. Or that she knew me.

I tried to keep my expression pleasant but noncommittal. I had a faint memory of having met her before, but no name would come to mind. She rushed up to me, smiling eagerly, golden, fur-like hair, no longer than mine, coated with mist and winking in the sun. Her canine teeth were as well-developed as mine. Somehow, they looked even better on her.

"What are you doing back in town?" she asked a little breathlessly. I could hear concern in her voice. "You told me you'd taken a job with Gharlas the merchant!"

I opened my mouth to say something—damned if I knew what. Luckily I didn't get a chance.

"Darling," she rushed on, "once you were gone, you should have *stayed* gone! Worfit is furious because you left town still owing him money, and he probably already knows you're

44

back. Why didn't you leave Keeshah outside the city, so fewer people would recognize you?"

"Well, I—"

"Did you hear that the Ra'ira has been *stolen?* And Zaddorn has been asking me questions about you." She stopped for breath, looked around almost furtively, stepped closer and lowered her voice. Like most of the women I had seen, she was small and delicately boned; I had to bend my head to her to catch her words.

"I told him that what's between you and me is none of his business, but he says that the Chief of Peace and Security has the right to ask anyone questions in a case like this. What with Worfit and Zaddorn both looking for you—darling, coming home right now was *terrible* timing!"

I was trying to put together what I had learned from her with what I had overheard from the police squad on the road the night before. I didn't much like what I came up with.

"Do you mean," I asked, "that somebody thinks *I* stole the—uh—Ra'ira?"

"Oh, you know Zaddorn—he's always been jealous of you. He thinks if he could discredit you, I would turn to him. It hasn't even been officially announced that the Ra'ira is gone, but there are rumors everywhere. I don't know if he really thinks you did it, or is just trying to make *me* think you did. I don't. I know you'd never do such a thing, especially when it was in your father's care."

"Thanks," I said, but I couldn't help wondering about the "especially" qualification. What sort of man *was* Markasset?

"You'd better get home fast," she was saying. She was looking around again as though she expected to be caught at any moment. "Before Zaddorn hears you're back. Your father can give you protection."

"Keeshah needs food," I told her. As Keeshah had been telling *me* during the entire conversation. "I'll get a side of glith for him, then I'll go straight home." The look she gave me was unreadable. "I promise," I added.

"You can't take Keeshah in a meat shop! And you can't leave him out here!"

"I know," I covered rapidly. "I was going to ask you to go in and get it for me, if you would."

I had another reason for asking; I hadn't the least idea of how much glith meat was worth, nor how much the coins in my purse were worth. I handed her the pouch. She looked impatient, but she glanced over at Keeshah and finally agreed.

45

"Oh, all right. If it will get you off the streets sooner. You want a whole side? Wait here and I'll have the meatmonger bring it. I'll be right back." She went into the meat shop.

I stood quietly, scratching Keeshah's ear and trying to digest this new, gratuitous information. There was plenty of it, and I *didn't* like it.

ONE: Markasset apparently was engaged to marry this talkative wench—but we (Markasset and Ricardo) couldn't remember her name.

TWO: A certain Zaddorn, who seemed to be the equivalent of the Chief of Police, was also (?) in love with her and was jealous of Markasset. And maybe not above using his position to ace out a rival.

THREE: Worfit—now *that* name rang a loud bell. A money-lender of the shadier kind, unhandsome, powerful, dangerous. Little Caesar with fat teeth. Markasset owed him a rather large sum of money—I didn't know exactly how much, but I had an impression that it was a gambling debt, and not his first.

FOUR: If Zaddorn had been telling the girl the truth, Markasset might really be suspected as a jewel thief.

None of this spoke well for Markasset. I had the feeling that he—*I*—had not been the most reputable of young men-about-town.

Keeshah rubbed his cheek against my chest, reminding me that I had stopped rubbing behind his ear.

I had to laugh at this huge, dangerous cat that wanted to be petted like a kitten.

I guess if you *liked Markasset, Keeshah,* I told him, *he can't be as bad as all that.*

7

I was distracted suddenly from my own problems. Two monsters were walking down the street.

Part of my mind told me that they were only a couple of working vineh. Nothing remarkable. Nothing to worry about. But I couldn't help feeling like the lead idiot in a Friday night Creature Feature—who hadn't had a chance yet to read the script.

At first, I thought they were blond gorillas. They were taller and wider than I, but on closer inspection I could see that their legs were longer and their arms shorter than those of *Gorilla gorilla*, and they held themselves more naturally erect.

Their faces were definitely apelike. The head sloped back steeply from the supraorbital ridge, leaving little room for prefrontal lobes. The lower jaw was massive and muscular, and the great canines made my own look ridiculously small. Their faces and bodies were covered with short, curly fleece, as though they had grown pubic hair all over. It was a light tan in color, not much darker than Keeshah's fur. But where Keeshah carried his pale bulk with grace, these lumbering brutes were even uglier for their pallor.

To add to their grotesqueness, they were wearing gray-brown shorts and were wielding push-brooms. And as I watched, a third one followed them from the crowd; he was pushing a wheelbarrow-like cart.

No one else was in the least disturbed by their presence or their appearance. Shoppers stepped out of their way automatically as they passed. Apparently they were a normal sight on the streets of Raithskar, a simple street-cleaning detail, sweeping up sand and leaves, and leftovers from passing vleks.

Then one of the broom-pushers caught the cart-pusher in the side with the end of the broom handle. It was purely accidental, a miscalculated backstroke. But Cart-pusher roared, spun the cart out of his way and cuffed Broom-pusher on the side of the head from behind. Broom-pusher swung around, his broom cutting a wide arc and knocking the wind out of Cart-pusher.

The Gandalaran pedestrians were paying attention now, scattering away from the fight. The two vineh were literally at each other's throats, grappling and snarling and trying with single-minded determination to kill each other. The second broom-pusher turned and looked, crouched and eager to join the brawl. I had the feeling that the only thing that stopped him was having to decide which side to join.

A man in a yellow tunic, whom I had seen near the vineh but hadn't really noticed, pushed against the outward tide of people and ran toward the fray, shouting with authority. "Break it up!" he ordered the struggling vineh, who paid him no attention. The third ugly took a step toward the other two, but stopped in confusion when the man yelled, "Gooloo, you stay out of this!"

He was carrying a thick baton nearly as long as his arm. He thrust it between the two fighters, but they ignored it.

47

"Stop it, you fleabitten filth-heads! Stop, I say!" They pulled out of their clinch for a second, and, with a quick flick of his wrist, the man gave each one of the pair a painful smack on the nose.

Both vineh roared their indignation, forgot their quarrel, and turned on the man, who backpedaled quickly. "Back! Back! Stay back!" he ordered. But the note of authority in his voice had been replaced by one of terror. He was the one who was backing, trying to hold the brutes off by jabbing with his baton like an inept fencer.

His heel caught in an irregularity in the hard clay surface of the street and he went down, flat on his back. The two vineh who had been fighting were close now, and the third was converging on them. This decision, obviously, was easier to make. It was going to be a slaughter.

I had to do something. Without my even thinking about it, my bronze sword was suddenly in my hand, and I was sprinting toward the fallen man, who was still poking upward with his baton to ward off the beasts. One of them grabbed, jerked, and took it away from him. I tried to put on more speed.

But before I could reach them, the attack stopped as quickly as it had begun.

The vineh who had grabbed the baton dropped it, looked stupidly around, and went back to pick up his broom. The other went back to the cart. He was limping slightly, and both of them were bleeding slowly from gashes and bites. I marveled at the toughness of their hides. They picked up their equipment and continued along the street as though nothing at all had happened. The third, who had been halfway to the scene of the fight, recovered his own broom and joined them.

The man picked himself up and grabbed his baton. He ran a few steps after the vineh, but stopped when he saw me. I could see him relaxing, the anger and terror going out of him.

"Thanks," he said. "I'm glad you were here. But I don't think they'll make any more trouble."

Someone in the crowd called out: "You ought to have better control over your vineh than that, Foreman; someone might have been hurt!"

The foreman smiled and nodded, but I, standing next to him, heard him mutter, "Fleabite you, townsman."

"You hurt?" I asked, sheathing my sword.

"No. I'll be all right." He smiled at me. "Thanks again."

48

He moved off, following his charges, who were once again calmly sweeping the street.

I turned to go back to the shop, and found Keeshah beside me. Together we walked to where the girl was waiting anxiously. Beside her stood the meatmonger, holding a wrapped bundle half the size of a goat.

"Markasset, what is the *matter* with you? Are you crazy?" She glanced at the meatmonger and refrained from reminding me that news of the fight—and my almost-participation—was sure to reach Zaddorn. "Why didn't you stay out of it?"

I was shocked. "And let a man get killed?"

"Don't be silly. Whoever heard of a vineh killing anyone? He would have been all right. He *was* all right, wasn't he? You didn't do any good by going out there, brandishing your sword, and making a spectacle of yourself."

"I don't know," the meatmonger spoke up for me. "I never saw *two* of 'em gang up on a man before. It could have been nasty."

She gave him a look that might have quick-frozen the meat he held, so hurriedly did he hand it to me. "Here's your side of glith, townsman—er—Rider." Then he disappeared back into the shop.

I laid the bundle across Keeshah's shoulders.

Eat?

When we get home.

The girl handed back my pouch, but came close to whisper to me. "Markasset, why are you carrying around so much money? Do you realize that you have *five* twenty-dozak pieces in here?" I did now. "Why, you might be robbed!"

"With Keeshah around? A thief wouldn't get very far," I said. There was a short silence which was, for me at least, very awkward. Did she expect an explanation for the money? If so, I couldn't help her. "Well," I said at last, "if I hurry, I can get home before Zaddorn gets the word I'm back." I hesitated, then asked, "Are you coming?"

"Oh, no," she said. "I can't come with you now, darling. Mother gave me definite instructions. 'Get your shopping done and come right back,' she said. 'I need that cloth right away.' " The girl sighed.

She looked up at me, and for a moment there was a look on her face that spoke more than all her words. Beneath the chattering, the nagging, the impatience, she was really frightened for me. She cared.

"I'll come by your house later, darling. And if I see Zaddorn I'll try to send him in the wrong direction. Just hurry now and—take care of yourself." And she was gone.

I remembered her name now. Illia.

Keeshah knew the way home, and I followed him through streets which narrowed and twisted as we approached the residential district. The homes reminded me of the Spanish Colonial style—mostly stone and sun-baked clay, plastered over and finished with pastel-pigmented whitewash.

Thanasset's house was larger than most, a sprawling two-story building. On the side facing the street, there were windows only in the upper story, and the front wall continued away from the house to enclose a large yard area. There were two massive parquet doors: one directly into the house; the other one, through which Keeshah and I passed, into the patio garden. It was carefully arranged and tended, patterns of green broken up with colorful and fragrant flowers. A cool and pleasant place.

A broad pathway, inlaid with large flat stones, led through the garden and split. Half of it led to the back of the house on my left. Keeshah and I followed the other half, which took us to the end of the large enclosure. Here there were small storage buildings and a large stone structure that was Keeshah's home. Double doors made of heavy wood stood open, braced against the outer walls on either side of the archway. Inside was a big square room with a roof twice as tall as a man.

Against the rear wall, a broad ledge had been built of stone and laid over with grasses and leaves. In one corner, there was a wide pit filled with sand; in the opposite corner, a stone trough had been built against the wall and lined, as at Yafnaar, with tile. The walls had been built with a pattern of openings in lieu of windows; it was well ventilated, but it had the cool semi-gloom of a cave.

Keeshah, glad to be home at last, went directly to a thick round post, in the center of the room, that I had taken to be a roof support. But Keeshah put first one front paw, then another against it and stretched upward, then back, clawing it joyfully with claws as long as my fingers. It was the trunk of a tree larger than any I had yet seen—and it had been hauled in and placed there as a scratching post for Keeshah.

I unwrapped the meat, and Keeshah, his homecoming ritual complete, attacked it hungrily. I brought water for him from a cistern beside one of the storage buildings, moving automatically and not stopping to wonder how I knew where things were.

Soon I was walking up the stone pathway to the rear of the house. There were lots of windows back here on both floors, letting plenty of light into the interior. They were made of lozenge-shaped panes only as large as my hand, joined together with thin strips of wood. Even the three doors had wood-latticed windows in them.

I came to the central door and stopped, frozen. What was I doing?

Up to this point, I had been merely following a logical line. It had seemed the most natural thing in the world to come here to "my" home, where "I" had always lived. I had begun to accept this world, to feel almost comfortable in it. But all familiarity vanished now in a wave of alienness.

I was Ricardo Emilio Carillo, elderly American gentleman, walking around in what some might regard as a stolen body. I had been about to walk, without invitation or by-your-leave, into the house of a stranger, a man whom I had never seen before. This wasn't *my* home at all. It was the home of a near-human, *not*-human being, a native of an alien world who spoke a language I had never heard before. The mores, laws, customs, and civilization of this world were unknown to me. *I* was the stranger here.

What the hell had I been thinking of?

I wanted desperately to turn and run—but there was no place to run to. Only danger waited beyond the walls which surrounded me. A man named Worfit who might slit my throat for welching on a debt. One Zaddorn who might throw me into prison, or worse, because of some sacred bauble I knew nothing about—or because of his jealousy over a woman. And the woman herself, a promised marriage to a girl who, though she seemed sincere enough, was hardly a rock of strength.

No, I didn't want to stay here, but where else could I go? What could I do? How could I live? Illia seemed to think I had a lot of money with me, but how long would that last, especially when I couldn't tell if I was being cheated? I had strong doubts about the existence of unemployment offices, welfare checks, and food stamps in this world. How could I support myself and Keeshah?

For I knew that I could not leave the great cat behind me if I fled. And the thought increased my despair. I would be instantly recognized anywhere with Keeshah in tow. And that would lead all the dangerous people directly to me.

I had to stay here. I was safe here—for the moment. But I just *couldn't* walk into this house and face a man who was supposed to be my father. What would I say to him? How would I act? He was sure to see through me, to realize that, although I looked just like Markasset, I was *not* the person who had grown up in his house.

In that moment, torn by fear, unable to make any decision, paralyzed by the whole situation, I came as close to total panic as I ever have in my life.

Then the door opened, and the man who had opened it said: "Don't just stand there, son. Come on in."

8

For a moment I just stared at him stupidly. The only clear thought in my mind was a question: how had he known I was out here?

This was the man whose face had flashed through my memory when Balgokh had first told me who I was. It was a strong face, the brows a little more prominent than mine and a faint white scar running from forehead to cheek beside his left eye. The hair on his head had thinned and darkened with age, and fine lines rayed out from his eye-corners and along his mouth.

The tone of his invitation had been neither welcoming nor rude. His voice had held only exasperation. I had a sudden intuition that some of those lines had been put there by Markasset—that Thanasset disapproved of his son in some ways, but still loved him. Very much. I was beginning to like Markasset less and less.

"I don't know why you're back so soon," the old man continued, in a somewhat lowered voice. "I suppose you'll tell me when you feel like it. But have the courtesy to keep your tongue civil until we're alone. There is a guest in the house."

He turned on his heel and walked before me into the house. He was taller than I, with wide shoulders and a brisk stride. He was wearing a sleeveless green tunic that reached to his thighs and his body, though thinning, was still muscular and strong.

We had gone only a few steps when Thanasset turned and looked at me coldly. I stopped hastily, just in time to keep myself from colliding with him. *Have I already goofed?* I asked myself, and the answer was quick in coming.

"As long as you are a son of this house, Markasset, you will not bear arms under its roof!"

"Oh, of course," I said in confusion, and pulled the baldric off over my head. I dislodged the scarf tied around my head, which fluttered to the floor. I bent and retrieved it and stood there with the scarf in one hand and the baldric in the other, feeling utterly foolish.

Finally, Thanasset took the baldric from me and walked back to the door to hang it from a rack mounted on the wall. I took the moment to look around the room, and I was impressed.

Everything about the room bespoke wealth. Not ostentation, but quality. The floor and the walls were finished with fine parquetry in a light, richly grained wood. The floor, highly polished, was a regular pattern of small diamonds, but the walls were random mosaics. Each piece of wood had been cut and matched by hand by some brilliant craftsman.

The room in which we stood was like a wide hallway that led straight through the house. Across from me were the doors I had passed in the street before reaching the garden entrance. Directly to my left was a short, narrow hallway leading to a small door and to a flight of stairs; the outer door at the rear of the house which I had passed opened at the foot of the stairs. On my right were two doorways and, against the front wall of the house, a second staircase.

The walls were decorated with sketches and small tapestries, most of which depicted animals. There was one, quite good, of a sha'um—not Keeshah; its markings were different. On the right wall, between the doors, the mosaic pattern seemed to be less random than elsewhere, but it was not until Thanasset passed me again and led me toward the front of the house that I could see what it was.

Standing opposite that wall, the pattern plainly was the outline of a sha'um. Darker woods had been used here to emphasize a line or to suggest a fur marking. Nothing had been placed on the wall to cover that exquisite mosaic portrait, but mounted above it was a sword—not bronze, like the one I had been wearing, but a gleaming gray-white metal. Steel.

I had time for only a brief glance, then we were walking through an open double-doorway on our left. This room held a comfortable array of armchairs and small tables of different shapes. Their surfaces, too, were parquetry, some of the fitted wood pieces mere slivers. Wood, I thought, must be very precious here; every smallest fragment seemed to find use.

In here, the stone of the walls had been left unfinished. A ledge that served as a bench ran the length of the room along the outside wall, beneath two tall, latticed windows that admitted both daylight and the beauty of the garden. And my earlier question was answered: the windows looked out on the pathway where it entered the garden. Thanasset, sitting in this room with his guest, had seen me as I passed by. When I hadn't come in after a natural interval, he had gone to the back door to find me standing there uncertainly.

Thanasset's guest was a man a little older than my father, a small man with laughter around his eyes. The smile he gave me in greeting wreathed his face in wrinkles.

"Chief Supervisor Ferrathyn," said Thanasset, "I present my son, Markasset."

Chief Supervisor? The old man made no move toward me, so I bowed as I had done to Balgokh and said what seemed right. "Our house is honored by your visit."

Thanasset flashed me a strange look, then turned away to fetch a stoppered glass pitcher with a dark liquid in it.

"Come, come, my boy—you needn't be so formal," said the Chief Supervisor. "Sit down, please, and tell us—what news? What rumors reached you in the marketplace?"

Thanasset refilled Ferrathyn's glass, then his own. Then he brought a third from the stone-and-glass shelves that formed one wall of the room, filled it and handed it to me.

I sat down and took a sip, then a deep draught. This, I realized, must be faen. Good it was, too, but not like beer as I knew it. For one thing, it wasn't carbonated. It reminded me of Japanese *sake* lightly mixed with Mount Vernon rye whiskey—but it was cool and tasted much better than such a mixture would have tasted.

Besides liking the stuff, I was stalling for time, trying to think. Was I or wasn't I supposed to know about the theft of the Ra'ira? Illia said that Zaddorn suspected me. Did my father and Ferrathyn know of his suspicions? And what did *they* think?

A frightening realization swept over me, almost causing me to choke on the faen. I don't know myself whether I—Markasset—was guilty or not!

I set my glass down on the small square table beside my chair. "The marketplace is churning with rumors," I told them. "It is said that the Ra'ira is missing, and that the Peace and Security Department is looking all over for it."

Ferrathyn looked at Thanasset. "I knew we could not keep it quiet for very long, old friend. We'll have to make an official announcement soon." He looked back at me. "Is that all? No mention of how it was stolen, or by whom?"

I hesitated, then said, "No. Not that I know of, sir." That was technically true. Illia had said that everyone seemed to know of the theft, but Zaddorn had spoken to her privately when he mentioned his suspicion of me.

I thought to myself, *If it's all that secret, and I've been out of the city . . .* I took a chance. "May I be told what happened?" I asked them. They glanced at each other, and Ferrathyn nodded.

"Please do tell him, Thanasset. Perhaps, after he has heard everything, he may be able to help us."

"Very well," Thanasset sighed, and took a long drink from his glass. Then he spoke directly to me. Ferrathyn, obviously, had heard the story before.

"It happened on the night you left—Kryfer before last." *Kryfer. Day Two,* Markasset's memory said. "As you know, I had Guardian Duty that night, beginning at midnight. I went to the Council Hall, relieved Ferrathyn, and formally took custody of the Ra'ira."

I *didn't* know. I tried to dig a memory of that day or night out of Markasset's storehouse, but with no success. Thanasset might have been reading *Little Red Riding Hood* for all the personal connection I felt to what he was saying.

"Ferrathyn left me in charge," Thanasset continued, "and I locked the Security Room. I was there alone with the stone.

"About an hour into the watch, the door opened, and two men came in."

He looked at me, waiting for me to bring up the discrepancy I had already noticed.

"Through a locked door?" I asked.

Ferrathyn sighed, but said nothing.

Thanasset stood up and began to pace the room, making little noise on the green carpet that almost covered the floor. "That's the whole trouble," he said. "I distinctly remember locking that door. But they came in as though it had never been locked." He threw open his arms in a very human gesture of hopelessness. "I can't explain it."

"Can't it be unlocked from the outside?" I asked, and instantly wondered if I should already know the answer.

"No," Ferrathyn supplied. "That is part of the whole security program. It is unlocked *by the Supervisor on duty* when the next man arrives. The shift changes every third-of-a-day, and the new man re-locks the door."

"As I did!" Thanasset almost shouted. "For fifteen years, I have *never* failed to lock that door. And yet they came in!"

"Go on with your story, old friend," the Chief Supervisor said in a kindly manner. "We will worry about the locked door later."

Thanasset came back to his seat, and refilled our glasses. "Well—as I said, two men came in. They were armed with truncheons, not swords, and both of them were wearing hoods with eyeholes. I couldn't identify them if I saw them again, except that one of them had the little finger of his left hand missing.

"Neither of them said a word. One came at me, and the other went to the desk where the jewel was resting on its pedestal." His hands clenched and trembled with recalled frustration. "I fought them, of course. I would have given my life to protect the Ra'ira. But even that small dignity was denied me. I was knocked senseless. I lay unconscious on the floor of the Security Room until Supervisor Noddaran came to relieve me at the end of my shift. He found the door ajar, the Ra'ira gone, and me . . . asleep." He took a deep breath and lifted his glass again. "That's all. That's exactly what happened."

"Are you well now, Father?" I asked. He looked strong enough, but I knew what it was like to wake up from a clobbering like that. And his body was older than mine.

Thanasset looked at me so long that I lowered my gaze in embarrassment. "Yes," he said then. "Yes, Markasset, I'm fine now." A short, awkward pause. "Thank you for asking, son."

I tried to bring the conversation back to the point. I remembered a scrap of the discussion I'd heard among the cops on the trail south the night before. I decided it was worth quoting. "Why would anyone steal the Ra'ira?" I asked them. "Its value would be destroyed if it were cut up, and, if left intact, it would be recognized anywhere for what it is."

"Prestige, for one thing," Ferrathyn answered, and sipped from his glass. "Are you aware of its history?"

"Only vaguely," I said, and blessed the talkative flatfeet who had passed me that night. "I know it came from Kä originally."

Ferrathyn shook his head. "Not originally. Many tens of hundreds—perhaps a hundred of hundred—years ago, it was found here at Raithskar, in our own precious metal mines. At that time, the Kings of Gandalara at Kä held sway over the whole of the land between the Walls of the World. The jewel was sent as tribute to either King Beykoth or King Veytoth—the Record is unclear on that point—and remained there for tens of hundreds of years, until the fall of the Kings and the sacking of Kä."

"When Serkajon brought it back," I contributed.

"Yes," Thanasset put in. "Our esteemed ancestor returned it to its rightful home, and for tens of hundreds of years it has been the symbol of the power and authority of the Council of Supervisors of Raithskar."

Our ancestor, I thought. *Markasset comes from good stock. Or does he? After all, to the Kings of Gandalara, Serkajon must have been a thief.* I turned away from that line of thought, only to realize that what Ferrathyn was saying brought me back to it.

"The descendants of the Kings went to Eddarta when they escaped from the sacking, and they rule that city yet. They have long claimed that the Ra'ira is rightfully theirs—with some justice on their side. The Lords of Eddarta claim that since the stone was freely given to the ancient kings, it is theirs by family right."

"Our reply," Thanasset added, "is that the gem was given to the Kings of *Gandalara.* Since there are no such kings anymore, the rights of the stone revert to us." He chuckled—a deep, warm sound. "Besides, we are—or *were*—in possession of it."

Nine points of the law, I thought. Aloud, I said, "Then you think that the Lords of Eddarta are behind this robbery?"

"It's one possibility," Ferrathyn said. "Possession of the Ra'ira would certainly increase the prestige of the Lords of Eddarta—except, of course, in Raithskar." His face acquired a troubled look. "They might well try to re-create the kingdom and rule from Eddarta rather than lost Kä. Some of the cities near them, already dependent on their rich harvests and busy marketplace, might even support them in their claim."

"But many others would not," Thanasset said in a quiet voice. "There would be such fighting as has not been seen since the First King united the Walled World. There would be no safety for caravans—no trade—very little water sharing."

"It would disrupt *everything.*" Ferrathyn was leaning forward in his chair, as though he were trying to impress me with the importance of what he said. "We can't allow it to happen; we *must* get the Ra'ira back!"

I was duly impressed. Even a little frightened by the man's

57

intensity. And puzzled. The men on the trail had treated the whole affair like an ordinary jewel theft—a very special jewel, to be sure, but a simple robbery. It was their job to find the thieves. And their pride was at stake; that someone had stolen *their city's* treasure was galling.

But I had heard nothing in those rough voices to compare with the passion concealed in the quiet tones of these two men. The Ra'ira had a significance for them that went beyond anything the townsfolk had ever thought of. Listening to them, I felt as though Archduke Ferdinand had just been assassinated.

"Are you sure Eddarta is behind the theft?" I asked.

Ferrathyn relaxed back in his chair as Thanasset refilled his glass. He took a hefty drink before answering. "As a matter of fact, we're not certain of anything. When the robbery was first discovered, we tried to keep it quiet for two reasons. First, we saw no need to excite the townsfolk. And second . . . well . . ."

"We thought that someone local must have taken it," Thanasset finished. "The manner and method of its keeping are not widely known. Whoever planned the theft needed accurate information. So we asked Zaddorn to search the city."

"House by house?" I asked, astonished. "Respectfully, that's no way to keep it quiet!"

They laughed, and I was glad to feel the tension in the room ebb away.

"Nothing so obvious," Ferrathyn said. "Zaddorn and his men have contacts—sources of information—that know about everything that goes on in Raithskar."

So even this world has an underworld, I thought to myself, and a name attached itself to the thought. *Worfit. And Markasset? How closely was he involved with them?*

"I hate to ask the same question twice," I said, "but again: why? Why would anyone *in* Raithskar want to steal the Ra'ira?"

"Ransom," said Thanasset shortly, then shrugged. "At least, that was Zaddorn's theory. What other reason would there be? It's the only practical way to make money from the theft."

"*Was* his theory?" I asked. "What changed his mind?"

"A quarter-moon passed with no message from the thieves, and all of Zaddorn's digging brought up exactly nothing," Ferrathyn said. "Either it's the most tightly-held secret in Raithskar's long history, or the rogueworld really does know nothing about it."

"And so he blames Eddarta now," I said, and refrained from mentioning the posse I had seen.

"Yes," Farrathyn agreed. "It was actually my idea that sparked the new theory. When he could learn nothing, Zaddorn came to us—" he gestured to include Thanasset "—in desperation for any clue. He seized on my suggestion of city rivalry and, with his usual sharp understanding, quickly determined that if the Ra'ira left Raithskar, it must have traveled with the caravan of Gharlas."

"Which is where you come in, son."

Here it was at last. I held out my glass for a refill, surprised that my hand wasn't shaking.

"That girl, Illia, delivered the note you left for me. When Gharlas was suspected, I confided in Ferrathyn that you had signed on with his caravan. Naturally, seeing you back home so soon, Ferrathyn and I wondered . . ."

You wondered? I thought at him. *You should be on this side of things!*

"Did you see or hear anything, Markasset," Ferrathyn asked me, "that might suggest to you that our thieves rode with your caravan?"

How the hell could I answer them? Yet answer them I must, and I had only seconds to decide what to say. The truth? *"Sorry, folks, I'm a stranger here myself."* I had a strong hunch I'd get a lengthy tour of the local equivalent of the madhouse. Would they believe me if I told them I was Ricardo Emilio Carillo, and that, in some fashion I did not understand, I had been loaned the use of Markasset's faultless body and faulty memories? I thought not.

But I couldn't lie, either. Not from any compunction over lying to "my" father—though I did feel a reluctance—but from the sheer impracticality of it. A good lie has to be based on a sound knowledge of the truth, or it won't fit in, even for a moment.

Even a censored version of the truth wouldn't work. If I said, "I don't remember," I'd sound like a *Capo Mafioso* testifying to a Congressional committee.

But I had to talk, and *talk fast!*

"I'm sorry, sir, but I can't help you there. I don't recall any suspicious or peculiar behavior on the part of anyone in the caravan."

I waited for more questions, but Ferrathyn only nodded. "Good enough. But—" I had taken a mouthful of faen in my relief; it turned bitter and I had to struggle to swallow it. "—then why did you return early to Raithskar?"

I looked at him directly and brought out my most sincere voices. "Sir, with all due respect, that is a personal matter. I assure you it had nothing whatever to do with the Ra'ira."

Was I lying? Or telling the truth? I didn't know. No wave of guilt surged up from Markasset's memory, but I couldn't count on that to mean he wasn't involved in some way.

The Chief Supervisor gazed at me for a long two seconds. He looked kindly, puzzled, and just a little sad. "I see," he said, and sighed. "Well, we'll know for certain before too long. Yesterday Zaddorn sent out a special squad with only food and water. They can travel half again as fast as a heavy-laden caravan—but even so, we cannot expect them back for more than a moon yet. We shall just have to be patient."

A moon, I thought to myself. *It will be much longer than that. The caravan had a nine-day head start. That means Zaddorn's squad won't catch up with them for . . . um . . . eighteen days, and then it will take them at least that long again to get back . . .*

My chain of reasoning was cut off sharply by the realization that I didn't know just how long a time period a "moon" was in Gandalara. On my Earth, it was twenty-nine and a half days, but if I were on some planet circling Deneb or Fomalhaut, its moon could have an entirely different period.

"If it can be found," Thanasset said, "we can trust Zaddorn to find it eventually. He's tough and he's smart."

Ferrathyn nodded. "He is that. And he hates to give up." Suddenly he chuckled. "He may yet find the Ra'ira here in the city." The chuckle became a laugh and the old face crinkled up with merriment. "Oh," he gasped. "I can see it now. The squad reports back, exhausted, dejected, drained by the heat of the desert, and its leader reports sadly to Zaddorn: 'Sir, we have found no trace of the Ra'ira.'"

"And Zaddorn," added Thanasset, laughing with his friend, "looks up from his desk with that absent expression he has when his mind's on something else, and says: 'Oh, that! We found that thirty days ago!' He'd certainly have twelve very unhappy men on his hands!"

"And it would be my fault," Ferrathyn said, "since it was my idea that sent them after the caravan!" He chuckled again, shaking his head. "And I can't say I'd be sorry for it, either. Zaddorn is a fine man, but his independent ways have given me headaches enough in the past." He drained his glass and stood up. "Well, I must be going. I'll see you in the morning, Thanasset?" It was only half a question.

"Of course," Thanasset replied, standing up and walking with Ferrathyn to the door of the room. "I'll have to see to Tailor's Street first thing; it hasn't been resurfaced in eight moons, and the ruts are getting bad. I received a note on it yesterday. And *then* I'll try to get to the threescore other matters waiting for me. This whole business has thoroughly disrupted my routine."

"I know," Ferrathyn said feelingly. "You should see my desk." He turned to me and smiled. "It's been a pleasure to meet you at last, young Markasset."

I stood up and bowed as I had earlier. "You honor me, Chief Supervisor."

Both men left the room then, and I collapsed back into my chair. I could hear the soft whisper of their sandals as they crossed the polished wood floor toward the door which opened into the street. And I could hear their voices.

"A well-spoken lad," Ferrathyn said softly. "He is a credit to you, old friend."

"Thank you," Thanasset said, and I heard the heavy door swish open. "Until tomorrow, then."

"Yes. Good fortune until then."

Thanasset came back into the room and silently refilled his glass, then mine. But he didn't drink his. He just sat there, across from me, and stared moodily at the surface of the faen, tipping the glass slightly and watching the shifting liquid. The tip of his tongue worried his right tusk in about the same spirit as I might drum my fingers on the table. He was thinking. He was worried.

And so was I—and for the first time since I had awakened on the desert, not just about myself. I liked this man. Whether that was a carryover from Markasset I couldn't tell, but the fact remained that I felt a strong liking for him. I remembered what that cop on the trail had said: something about arresting "that fleabitten old man" and persuading him to tell them all about it. They had meant Thanasset, of course—the Ra'ira had been stolen from him. Did they think . . .

"Father, are you in trouble?" I asked softly.

He looked up at me with the same expression I had seen on his face when he introduced me to Ferrathyn. He seemed about to say something, then apparently decided against it. At last he said, "I don't know, son. Maybe. I'm not suspected of the theft, of course, but—I may be open to a charge of criminal negligence."

61

"The door," I said, and he nodded. "*Did* you leave that door unlocked?"

"*No!*" He slammed the flat of his palm on the top of the table beside his chair. Ferrathyn's glass, which had been left there, jumped clear off the table. Even with the thick green rug covering the parquet floor, it would have shattered when it landed. With a reflex speed I didn't know I had, I leaned out of my chair and caught it in midair. Thanasset barely noticed. "I locked that door when Ferrathyn left!" he said. "My honor on it!"

I took the glass and set it on the shelf where the pitcher stood. "I believe you, Father. The question is, how *did* the robbers get in? It definitely can't be unlocked from the outside?"

"Absolutely not."

I thought for a minute. If that room was *always* occupied by a Supervisor, it was unlikely that visitors, even the son of one of the Supervisors, would be admitted. It seemed like a safe bet that Markasset didn't know any more about the room itself than Ricardo did, and I could ask questions freely.

"What would happen if the Supervisor on duty suddenly became ill or dropped dead? How would the others get the door open?"

Thanasset's eyebrows tried to crawl up over his jutting supraorbital ridges. "That would never happen. A man that ill would never be allowed to take the duty!"

"Not if anybody knew he was ill—of course not," I agreed. "But if something happened unexpectedly? Suppose . . . his heart just stopped?" There was no way to say "coronary thrombosis" in Gandaresh.

His face cleared of its puzzled look. "Oh, I see! You're proposing a purely hypothetical case: that for some reason a man's inner awareness failed to tell him of the possibility of an oncoming malfunction."

Inner awareness? I wondered.

"I've never heard of such a case. But, assuming such a thing *could* happen, I suppose we'd just have to take an axe to the door."

I managed to keep my face straight, but inside I was gawping at him like an idiot. The Guardian shift was a third of a day—eight hours—and Thanasset had *never heard* of a case where a man hadn't *known* of a fatal malfunction *at least eight hours before his death.*

No doctors, I thought, stunned. *No lab tests, no outside opinions. Just "inner awareness." I must have it, too. Perhaps I would have the rare privilege of twice knowing beforehand that I'm about to die!*

But, I reminded myself, that only works for interior failings. My "inner awareness" is giving me no messages about whether or not I'll be executed for the theft of the Ra'ira!

"How does the lock work?" I asked, to cover my surprise and confusion.

Thanasset shrugged. "It is not a thing generally known outside the Council, but I see no harm in telling you now that there is nothing to protect. The building is very old, and the lock on that door has never been changed. But it lacks nothing because of its antiquity—it's the strongest door and most secure lock I've ever seen. The door is a pace wide and half a hand thick, solid wood, reinforced and nailed with rakor."

Rakor. Markasset's memory came through. The word meant "most precious metal"—but the English equivalent was "steel." Evidently iron mines were far from common in Gandalara.

"There is a set of five steel brackets," he continued, "two on the door itself, two on the wall on the opening side, on the left, and one on the wall on the hinge side, on the right. A heavy wooden bolt slides in the brackets. When the door is unlocked, the bolt is pushed clear of the door, to the left. To lock it, you slide it to the right until it rests in the bracket on the hinge side. There's a hole in the bolt that matches a hole in the bracket, and there's a steel pin as thick as your thumb that goes in there. The bolt won't slide until that pin is removed."

"And you put the pin in?"

"I did. I remember it distinctly."

I believed him. And not just because I liked him. It didn't make sense to think he had left that door unlocked on purpose and expected to get away with it. He was not a stupid man, nor an irresponsible one. That the Ra'ira had been stolen from *his* care troubled him deeply, and his anxiety for the stone's return was compounded by his bewilderment over this business about the lock.

Somehow, that door had been unlocked by the robbers themselves. But how? I had no better answers than Thanasset did. I'd read plenty of locked-room mysteries, but this was the first *un*locked-room mystery I'd come across.

"I'd like to take a look at that room," I said.

"As I said before, there's no harm now. Yes, we'll go there

63

tomorrow. I have this day off, and I need the rest." He eyed me, and smiled wryly. "And *you* need a bath. You're all over salt and dust." We both stood up. "Bathe and change your clothes. Lunch will be ready by the time you're through."

A bath and some food! Suddenly nothing was more important.

9

I remembered where "my" room was. I rushed up the stairs that led upward from the street entrance. They were made of wood, but the stepping surfaces had been covered with rough-surfaced tiles—for safety, I presumed, and to protect the precious wood. A hallway led off to my right when I reached the top of the stairs, and the second door on the left side was my room.

Another of the tall, latticed windows in the far wall overlooked the neighboring garden. A cloth hanging was mounted above the window, and would cover it if it were allowed to drape naturally. But now its folds were gathered and drawn to the side of the window, held there by a long wooden peg mortared into the stone of the wall.

Beneath the window was a man-sized woven pad much like the ones I had seen in the Refreshment House. This one seemed larger and thicker, and it lay upon the floor of the room. A light, soft blanket was neatly folded beside the pad. This was to be my bed, and it looked comfortable enough.

I turned to one of the side walls, which was covered completely with narrow bronze-hinged wooden doors. When I pulled at the two handles in the middle of the wall, the doors folded apart, exposing room-length shelves spaced about two feet apart from floor to ceiling.

Wow, I thought, looking at the contents. *Markasset does know how to dress!*

Arranged on the shelves was an enormous wardrobe of brightly-colored tunics, trousers, and belts. And boots and headscarves. And sandals. And pins and rings and metal chains that were either belts or necklaces.

I picked up a bright yellow tunic and shook it out. It had long sleeves and a high neck, and reached to mid-thigh on me. I looked back at the stack of clothes and found a bright green sleeveless jacket about the same length. It was heavier and elaborately embroidered and bordered with yellow—they made a beautiful match.

But I put them back. For one thing, the fact that their colors were deliberately coordinated set them apart from the ordinary street wear I had seen so far. They must be Gandalaran formal dress. For another, though I admired them and longed to wear them, they were a little too . . . obtrusive for me yet. I was learning more and more about this world, but I was still a stranger here. Best, I thought, to attract as little notice as possible.

So I selected a relatively plain blue tunic and set it out on the woven pad with some sandals. Then, with relief, I stripped off the clothes I had found myself in when I woke up in the desert. They had been carefully washed by the Fa'aldu at the Refreshment House of Yafnaar, but three days on the trail had thoroughly dusted them up again. The boots I shook off and placed on the floor of the closet with the other footwear. The clothes I dropped in a pile in the corner.

On one of the shelves was a short robe of a soft, thick fabric. It was well-worn, and obviously designed as a bathrobe. I put it on and went downstairs, the rough tile pleasant against my bare feet.

I went out the back door and along the path I had followed before, toward the back buildings. I looked in on Keeshah and smiled. He was sound asleep on the floor, lying on his side and twisted just enough so that one huge foreleg was suspended in mid-air. I had a strong impulse to go in and scratch the lighter fur of his chest, but I knew it would disturb him.

Rest well, Keeshah, I thought at him. *You deserve it.*

As though my thought had reached him dimly, he moved in his sleep, lowered the hovering paw, and curled around to rest his head on one extended hind leg. I left him then, and hunted for the bath-house.

It was only two doors down in a long series of outbuildings that formed the rear wall of the estate. It wasn't large, just a squarish room with a rectangular sunken pool long enough for a man to lie down in, and about as deep as the tubs I was used to. The tub was lined and bordered with pale gray tiles, each one decorated with fine blue traceries in an intricate design.

A ceramic pipe a couple of inches in diameter led down from the ceiling, evidently from a cistern on the roof. *No problem pumping water up there,* I thought. *The lake at the foot of Skarkel Falls is higher up the slope than the city—there would be plenty of pressure. And the water standing in the cistern would be sun-warmed.*

There was a rope hanging beside the pipe. I pulled it tentatively and was rewarded by a flow of water into the tub. On a ledge in the corner was a stack of scratchy-looking towels and several bars of soap. I took one—its scent was odd but pleasant—and climbed down into the tub. The water was comfortably warm, and I slid down the smooth tile until only my head was above water. I simply soaked for a while, really relaxing for the first time since I had awakened in the desert. I let my mind wander.

It was apparent that the firm of Thanasset & Son were in a jam. Thanasset was suspected, at least in some quarters, of aiding and abetting in the theft of the Ra'ira. At the very least he had, apparently, been negligent in his care of it, thereby contributing to the felony. And one person—one very important Chief of Police Zaddorn—suspected Markasset of complicity in the same crime. Markasset could even be said to have a motive: a certain rogueworld character named Worfit was very anxious to have a large loan repaid.

Markasset was better off than his father in one way: all he had to do was get on his sha'um and ride off to another city. To my mind, that was exactly what he had been trying to do when he took up the job with the caravan—though he had obviously had sense enough to travel incognito, with Keeshah following downwind.

Had Markasset been involved with the jewel theft? I just couldn't make up my mind about that. All the evidence I had seen assured me that Markasset had been a pretty wild young man—but I didn't want to believe that he'd pull off a robbery for which his own father would be blamed.

Besides, if he *had* been in on it, that meant that his job with the caravan had been part of the plan, and that the stone *was* going to Eddarta. That was more than robbery; that was treason. And I didn't believe that treason was in Markasset's character.

Or, no—*wait a minute! Suppose Markasset had helped steal the thing for ransom and then the crooks double-crossed him? If they had threatened him, that would explain his flight with the caravan.*

No. There hadn't been a ransom request. And anyway, I didn't want to believe that Markasset would run away from a fight.

But it seems certain that he was running away from a debt. What's the difference?

I couldn't tell. I was infuriatingly close to Markasset, but I still didn't know him. But something—maybe, I had to admit, my own hopes—told me that no matter how it looked, Markasset hadn't really been running away.

Could he have been chasing the stolen gem? I wondered suddenly, then instantly rejected the idea. *No, the only way he could have known it was gone was to be involved in the theft himself.*

And what about Worfit? Could he have demanded the Ra'ira as payment for Markasset's debt? Or is he somebody else altogether, unconnected with this whole mess?

After chasing everything I knew through my brain at least ten times, I gave up. My sole knowledge of detective work came from extensive reading of detective stories, which is something like trying to learn the Latin language by reading *Quo Vadis?*, *Spartacus*, and *Ben Hur*. That won't get you to *amo-amas-amat*.

I considered myself a rational, reasoning person with greater than average intelligence, and better than half a century of training in using my brain. It had been a long time since my undergraduate courses in logic, but some of it stuck with me. *All A is B; no B is C;* ergo *no A is C.* Perfectly true, but no help if you don't know what *A*, *B*, and *C* are. It's *impossible* to construct a chain of syllogisms when you don't know the subjects or the operators.

It all boiled down to the same thing which had been plaguing me since I came to in Gandalara. Lack of information. Except this particular information was absolutely necessary for my survival and Thanasset's. *Damn!*

Thanasset couldn't run from Raithskar the way Markasset could. The boy had been fairly footloose. But Thanasset's business, his career, his friends, his life were all here in Raithskar.

And I couldn't leave him.

I knew, then, that I had already made a commitment. Just when it had happened, I wasn't sure about. Probably when I first met Thanasset. But I knew now that, however I had arrived in Gandalara, I was here. Raithskar was my home now, and I had a life to live. I would sure as hell live it as honorably as I had lived my life before. That meant sticking it out with Thanasset, come hell or damnation.

I sat up in the tub, scrubbed myself down, and rinsed off. Then I climbed out, and while the tub was draining I reached for one of the towels. They were fuzzy and stiff, and they scratched away the water, rather than absorbing it. They left my skin tingling. I put on the bathrobe and returned to my room.

While I was dressing, I heard voices from below. One of them was Thanasset's, I was sure, but the others were higher-pitched. I couldn't make out the words. One of the higher voices said very little, then stopped altogether while the other went on talking to Thanasset.

Then there was a rap on my door, and the voice which had stopped downstairs said, "Are you dressed, young man? I'm coming in." I was startled—the voice might have belonged to my own father's mother, Gra'mama Maria Constanza!

"Dressed," I said, unnecessarily. She was already coming through the door.

For a moment, I froze. The thing that had come into my room was a creature out of nightmare.

The apish head was bald except for a black fringe around the edges, and the grayish skin was incredibly wrinkled. The deep-set eyes seemed to glitter evilly. The tusks in the half-open mouth gleamed whitely in the diffused sunlight from the window. An amalgamation of the Mummy and Dracula had somehow stepped down from the screen and into my presence.

The wizened horror spoke. "What ails you, boy? You sick?"

And the spell was broken. Ricardo's mind had been receiving that startling first impression. As Markasset's memories came flooding in, it was as though I turned from an image in a distorted mirror back to the original. And the person who faced me was a softly aging lady with a sweet, puzzled smile on her face. *Lavender and lace,* I thought, and smiled at her in real welcome.

"Milda, darling!" I heard myself say. "You startled me!" And I held out my arms.

She came forward in three quick steps and hugged me with a fierce strength. She was half a head shorter than I; she pressed her cheek to my shoulder as she very nearly squeezed the breath out of me.

"Oh, Markasset!" she said. "It's so good to see you again! I thought you'd be gone for moons—maybe years!"

"But I'm back now, as you can see!" I laughed, hugging her around her shoulders.

She pushed me away and tried to look stern. But the gentle old mouth still trembled on the edge of a smile. "Your father says to come down to the table as soon as possible. And *behave yourself*," she added. "We have company."

"Anybody I know?"

"I should hope to ride a sha'um! That girl Illia is here, and—for all her dizziness—she seems to be properly worried about you. Your father asked her to stay for lunch." She stopped, hesitated, and finally asked, "Nephew, you know I don't pry—" *That's true; she doesn't, bless her,* I drew out of Markasset's memory—"but . . . does that scatter-brained girl have any real reason to worry?"

I told her the truth. "I'm not sure—no, I'm not trying to put you off, darling," I added, as her face took on a look of hurt, "I really don't know. Maybe, after we've talked at lunch, I'll be more certain." I smiled at her again. "I'll let you know when to start worrying."

"Oh, *you!*" She said, and gave me another quick hug, then went to the door. "Hurry down now," she said. The door closed behind her, then reopened and she stuck her head back in. "I'm truly glad you're home again, Markasset." Then she was gone.

She was, I knew, my mother's father's sister. My great-aunt Milda. Or, rather, Markasset's great-aunt. *Will I ever get used to these double references?* I thought. *I'll have to work at keeping my two sets of relatives straight!*

But I knew that in Milda's case it didn't matter. She was such a dear old lady that Ricardo loved her already as much as Markasset did. In that moment, Milda became *my* Milda.

I went down the front stairs and into the room that opened from the midhall across from the parlor where Thanasset, Ferrathyn, and I had been sitting. This room was very light; the tall, narrow windows filled the wall that was the side of the house. There was a large square table in the center of the room that was set with china dishes finer, if possible, than the cups and pitcher I had seen at Yafnaar. They were worked in an intertwining blue and green pattern, with touches of yellow that seemed to suit the brightness of the room.

Thanasset and Illia were already seated at the table.

"Of course, I don't know if he really thinks that," Illia was saying earnestly, "or if he's only jealous of Markasset."

"What cause might Zaddorn have to envy Markasset?"

"Why—" she stammered, astonishment clear in her voice, "why, *me*, of course. I have told him that Markasset and I will marry soon, and he might—well, do *anything* to stop us!"

"Oh. I see," said Thanasset.

I wish I did, I thought. Then I said out loud, to announce my arrival in the room, "I see you've been filling in my father about Zaddorn's suspicions."

"Yes," Thanasset said drily. "And about your wedding plans."

I looked at the girl uncertainly. *I* hadn't heard anything about wedding plans, but I couldn't be sure what Markasset had said to her or agreed to. And I was a little annoyed that she had mentioned Zaddorn to Thanasset. She had seemed to regard his suspicions as a secret; I saw no need to worry the old man with them. *Or maybe,* I conceded, *I'm afraid they're right and wanted to spare him the truth.*

Illia was talking again, in a rush. She seemed to sense my displeasure. "I'm sorry, darl—Markasset. Perhaps I shouldn't have said anything, but I thought your father should know."

"About Zaddorn?" I asked her. "Or about our 'wedding plans'."

She looked very uncomfortable, and Thanasset was looking from her to me. *He's wondering the same thing I am,* I realized. *Am I really going to marry this girl?*

"Zaddorn, of course, silly," she said. "The other—well, he had to know sometime. Is it my fault you hadn't told him yourself before this?"

Now there she had me. If Thanasset were really as surprised—and not altogether pleased, I thought—as he seemed to be, why *hadn't* Markasset told him?

I sat down at the table and expressed my most fervent wish. "Father . . . Illia . . . I've had a long ride back, and I'm so hungry I could eat this table. Would you mind if we didn't talk about Zaddorn, or weddings, or *anything* while we have lunch?"

Illia opened her mouth to say something, but Thanasset interrupted smoothly and enthusiastically. "A fine idea." He beamed at me. "Milda!"

She came through a hinged door from the back of the house, carrying an enormous tray piled with food. She set it down in the center of the table, and we served ourselves. There was a large bowl of stew very much like the porridge I'd been served at the Refreshment House. We had each been given a utensil like the one I had seen at Yafnaar; we dipped our servings out of the large bowl into the small bowls before us, and filled our plates from an assortment of fruits. There was a fine-textured bread and a sharp butter-like spread. Milda filled three tall glasses with cool water, put the stoppered pitcher on the table, surreptitiously squeezed my shoulder, and disappeared back into the kitchen.

I didn't worry about manners. I really *was* hungry, and it was a great relief not to think for a while. The food was delicious, and I put away an enormous amount of it. At last I became aware that Thanasset and Illia had both finished eating and were watching me. Illia looked concerned; Thanasset seemed amused.

"It seems like ages since I've tasted Milda's cooking," I said, by way of explanation.

Thanasset laughed. "Milda will be pleased to hear that you noticed, Markasset. She did prepare the rafel herself in honor of your return. For my part, I'm glad to see that this business with Zaddorn hasn't dulled your appetite!"

There it was again, as though I hadn't put it off while we were eating. *I can't handle this,* I thought. *Not Illia and Thanasset together, with so many unknowns to deal with.*

"I feel like stretching my legs a little," I said. "Illia, will you walk in the garden with me? You will excuse us, won't you, Father?"

Thanasset caught on. He smiled. "Of course, son. Enjoy your walk."

We walked in silence. The garden was really a small park, with a stone-laid path leading from the house to the end of the row of outbuildings that formed the back boundary of the estate, along in front of the buildings and then back up to the house along the side wall. The area enclosed by the functional pathway was beautifully landscaped with slender, twisting trees, and flowering bushes which added fragrance to the cool, slightly misty air. Smaller stone pathways were part of the landscaping. It was a place to walk and be at peace.

We followed one of the narrow paths until it curved around a clump of trees and we were screened from the house. Then Illia stopped. Without a word, she put her arms around my neck and kissed me.

I was a full head taller than Illia; I could have resisted that kiss easily. But it was the most natural thing in the world for me to bend down to her and put my arms around her. Her mouth parted lightly under mine. I ran my tongue over her smooth, rounded tusks, expecting them to feel strange. But they seemed delicate in her mouth, perfect and erotic.

"Thank goodness!" she said, when she finally pushed me away. "The way you acted in front of your father, I was afraid . . . Markasset, I *am* sorry if I made trouble for you by telling Thanasset about . . . our plans."

"Plans?" I said stupidly, trying not to show her how shaken I was. She couldn't know how many years it had been since I

71

had been kissed in just that way—but I hadn't forgotten what a lover's kiss felt like.

Along with the new awareness of the relationship between Illia and Markasset, I had to deal with Markasset's physical response to the girl. Or mine. It was very confused. Under . . . less uncertain circumstances, I would have been delighted. But as it was, I tried to clear my head and think straight.

"Yes, plans!" she said. We walked over to a stone bench and sat down. "You haven't forgotten what you said to me—" she lowered her gaze to the ground "—*that night*, have you?"

That's just the point, I thought desperately. *I have forgotten. What did I say to you?*

I couldn't ask her. I was convinced that she loved Markasset, and that he might have returned her love. Looking at her here in the garden, with shade dappling the smooth golden fur on her head and her dark eyes shining in the fine-boned, alien face, I felt a physical echo of what must have happened on "that night." When I had accepted *being* Markasset, I had also accepted responsibility for anything he had done before I somehow acquired his body. That meant, I decided, accepting his promise to this girl. But not right away.

"Illia," I began—then found I didn't have the words.

She reached out and took my hand. "I know you're in trouble, darling, and this really isn't the time. But . . . I know Thanasset doesn't like me very much."

I started to object politely, but stopped myself. I thought she was right. Thanasset *didn't* like—or at least didn't approve of—Illia.

"All I want is—some assurance from you, Markasset," she said with dignity. "I know very well we can't marry before this nonsense with Worfit and Zaddorn is straightened out."

"Will it ever be?" I asked. "Oh, I'll pay Worfit what I owe him, that's no real problem. But Zaddorn is a powerful man, and rumor lasts a lot longer than the truth." *What* is *the truth, damn it!* "Are you sure you want to be married to the man who *might* have stolen the Ra'ira?"

"Is that what you're worried about?" She laughed and looked relieved. "Darling, you know very well that one day you'll be a Supervisor like your father. Nothing in your past can outweigh *that* honor." She moved closer and put her head on my shoulder. "And I'll be the *wife* of a Supervisor." Suddenly she sat up and looked at me squarely. "Won't I?"

Markasset had let her think so. Maybe it had been only a

good line, and it had obviously worked. But a promise—even an implied one—was a promise.

"Yes," I answered her.

After a while we walked back into the midhall of the house. Thanasset was standing in front of the sha'um portrait in wood parquetry, staring thoughtfully up at the sword mounted on the wall. He turned when we entered, and smiled.

"Well, there you are, children. Isn't the garden pleasant today?"

"It's lovely, sir," Illia replied. "It must be the most beautiful garden in Raithskar."

He turned and walked with us to the huge street door. "I'd like to think so, yes," he said. He opened the door for her. "Thank you for your visit, Illia."

"Thank you for your hospitality, sir." She turned to me and smiled radiantly. "Goodbye for now, Markasset." She started to leave, but turned back to face Thanasset. "Take care of him, sir. He's—" she looked my way with a slight smile "—not quite himself. I'm afraid that Zaddorn's suspicions have upset him more than we know."

"Rest assured I will see to his good health, my dear," Thanasset said. He closed the door behind her with a sigh. Then he linked his arm through mine and drew me back to where he had been standing.

Again he looked up at the sword and he said, almost offhandedly, "A nice girl, I suppose—but not terribly perceptive, is she?"

"I—I don't know what you mean, Father," I said. But I was afraid that I did know.

He moved to face me, and looked at me keenly from under his ridged brow.

"You're not my son," he said. "Just who *are* you?"

10

Surprisingly enough, I did not panic.

For one thing, there was no hostility in his manner or his voice. Wariness, yes. Curiosity. And something else—was it *respect*?

And I felt linked to Thanasset, committed to him. I was in his world, and in this world he had become *my* father. Somewhere along the line since I met him, I had realized I would have to confide in him eventually. But this soon? I wasn't ready.

Don't kid yourself. You'll never be ready, I told myself honestly.

Thanasset was watching me, reading the hesitation that must have shown on my face. "If you don't wish to tell me, I won't ask it of you," he said, with that oddly disturbing note of respect clearer now in his voice. "Any Visitor from the All-Mind is welcome. But . . ." He let his voice trail off.

"I do wish to tell you," I said, and knew it was true. It would be a tremendous relief to share even a little of this confusion with someone I could trust. And I *did* trust Thanasset. "I simply don't know where to start. Uh," I stalled, "could we sit down?"

"Certainly." He led the way back into the light, comfortable room where I had met Ferrathyn—was it only earlier that same day?

When we were comfortably seated with glasses of faen, "Who," I asked carefully, "do you think I am?"

"An Ancestor," he said, without hesitation. "A Visitor from the All-Mind who has chosen to grace the body of my son, Markasset."

I thought about that. Hell, for all I knew, I might be just that. Whatever it was.

Balgokh had said something similar—what had it been? *He said I had been touched with wisdom by an Ancestor.* I remembered. *And even he, who had seen Markasset for only a few minutes, had noticed the change.*

"Am I so different from your son?" I asked Thanasset.

He smiled at me, a little sadly. "Yes. You are courteous, well-mannered. You have a bearing of . . . confidence that Markasset lacked. He is a good man at heart, but rash and thoughtless, not given to thinking things through. He sometimes does foolish things."

Like helping to steal the Ra'ira? I wondered. *No, he doesn't even think that. He said "foolish"—not "criminal."*

Thanasset got up and walked over to the window. For a few seconds he stood there, looking out over the garden. At last he turned back to me, and what he said confirmed the brief inpression I had received when I met him for the first time.

"I confess that I do not always *like* my son. But he is my

only son, and I love him more dearly than my own life." His voice deepened, and for the first time I could see through his outward calmness to a core of grief and fear. "You need not reveal your identity to me," he said, with a dignity I admired more for having had a glimpse of its shaky foundation. "I have seen enough of you to be well content that your presence honors the body of my son. But I ask you, as a father, to tell me this: when will Markasset return?"

My brain seemed to freeze. *Return?*

Great God in Heaven!

The thought had simply not occurred to me before. I had accepted the fact that I had possession of a body that belonged to someone else. I felt no guilt for taking it over—certainly without its owner's permission. It had just happened. I hadn't planned it—hell and damnation, I had never even dreamed that something like this *could* happen.

That's not to say that I believed that reincarnation was impossible. As a child I had had the concepts of Heaven, Hell and Purgatory (and Limbo, which didn't concern me since I had been baptized) drilled into me. As I grew older, I began to question the truth of those teachings, and to consider other alternatives. Philosophically, Nirvana and the Final Blackout were equally unappealing to me. Reincarnation—well, it seemed like wishful thinking to me. The defining factor for my entire attitude toward an afterlife of any kind was the total absence of objective evidence. I decided fairly early to suspend belief. "Wait and see" was my personal policy with regard to eschatology.

And now, what I had seen fit none of the alternatives I had considered. Even reincarnation was supposed to be an entirely new beginning—not an interruption of someone else's life.

I had lived through a dizzying displacement. I had come to accept the change. I was prepared, after traumatic adjustments I haven't been able to describe adequately, to assume the identity of Markasset. And with his identity, his responsibilities. For Thanasset. For his possible involvement with the theft of the Ra'ira. For his obligation—one which Ricardo had never undertaken in his own life—to Illia. For his wonderful bond with Keeshah.

I had accepted Markasset's life. *The rest of Markasset's life.*

It had never occurred to me that I might only have borrowed it.

I felt suddenly like some indigent old drunk who has awakened from a rotgut binge to find himself in a fine house with no idea how he got there. He takes advantage of it, enjoys himself—clean silk sheets, caviar, and champagne—and then realizes suddenly that the owner may come back at any moment and throw him out. Or worse.

"When will Markasset return?" Thanasset's words echoed in my brain, stirring up a maelstrom of emotion. Not panic. Panic is unreasoning and unreasonable. It was logical, possible, even, I had to admit, *just* that Markasset might reclaim the place I had unwillingly taken from him. What I felt was a thundering, horrible fear.

Not fear of death. I had felt that before: when the doctor gave me the bad news, when I watched the meteor approach, when Keeshah rushed toward me out in the desert. This was far worse. It wasn't only that after having been given a second chance at life, it might be snatched away from me. It was . . .

The closest thing I had felt to it before was beginning a really entertaining mystery novel and misplacing the book. It's a poor simile, and only a shallow imitation of what I felt now, but it shared the sense of . . . leaving something important, something worthwhile unfinished.

I *cared* about this old man, about the town, about the Ra'ira. It terrified me to think that Markasset might return before I could straighten out the mess he had left behind!

I realized that Thanasset had said something to me.

I fought down the surge of fear, got it under control, and searched my short-term memory for Thanasset's words.

"Is something wrong?" came the playback. He was standing beside my chair, his hand on my shoulder. I was stiff and cramped, and I realized that I was clutching the arms of the chair as though holding on to life itself. Which I had been trying to do. With an effort, I relaxed my arms and reached for the glass beside the table. My hand was still shaking.

Thanasset picked it up before I could reach it. "I'll refill your glass," he said.

While his back was turned, I sat up straighter, shook my head to clear it. It would do no good to think of the future right now. I had to face a man who wanted to know about an intruder who had taken his son's place. I needed all my wits to be honest with him without frightening or alienating him.

Thanasset brought back my glass and sat down again across from me, obviously expecting an answer to his question. I looked at him directly.

"I don't know, Thanasset. Please believe me, I would tell you if I knew, but I don't."

His shoulders sagged, and I saw a brief struggle in his face. Then he smiled.

"A fair answer. Then—can you tell me about yourself? Who are you?"

Here, I knew, I needed caution. One of the things that had led me to be skeptical about reincarnation had been a uniform quality of silliness in the Westerners I had met who professed to "remember" past lives. The Hindu or the Buddhist of eastern Asia bears his belief with dignity. It is part of a religion. To so many Westerners, it was a topic for discussion at cocktail parties.

The "remembered" lives had always been exciting and ended in murder, execution, or dramatic suicide. Not one of them had been a potato farmer who died quietly in his bed after seventy years of monotonous hard work. I had heard the argument that only violent personalities survived intact, but I frankly saw more late-night television than actual memory in the "past lives" I heard retold. No, I had kept an open mind about reincarnation—in spite of those people, not because of them.

But if I had been unwilling to believe such stories about a world and a time within my experience, if even as history, what would Thanasset think of a man who claimed to have fought his way through the South Pacific in World War Two, had written fourteen well-received books on linguistics and three detective novels, and had died four days ago by being hit by a huge meteor?

My world had oceans, an abundance of wood and iron, horses instead of sha'um . . . Thanasset wouldn't even believe the world I had lived in—much less the role I had played in it. So what *could* I tell him?

Carefully, I said, "Before I tell you that, Thanasset, I—well, let me put it this way: I'm more than a little confused, myself. What do you know about . . . this kind of thing? Have you met cases like this before?"

"I?" he answered with surprise. "No, it happens but rarely. Maybe once in a generation in all of Gandalara. But I have read the accounts of most—if not all—of the Visitations. If I can help you at all, I'd be glad to try."

"I hope you can." *You don't know how much I hope you can!* "It's my memory, you see. It's . . . unreliable. I can 'remember' things that did not happen to *me*. I have some of

77

Markasset's memories, but not all of them, by any means." I smiled at him. "I remember you well, and Milda."

"And Illia? Is my son really planning to marry her?"

"That's one of the blank spots, I'm afraid. I didn't remember her at all at first. No one else I have met even strikes a bell." That wasn't quite true. I remembered Worfit all too clearly. But I didn't want to bring the outside story, so to speak, into this conversation.

He nodded. "According to the Recordings, that is not at all unusual for a Visitor. Enough memories remain of the displaced one to allow the Visitor to adjust."

"Well, yes, I appreciate what I have. But I still feel I'm missing some important pieces. That I don't know a lot of things I should."

"Such as?"

"Well . . . this All-Mind you mentioned. If I'm visiting from it I ought to know what it is. But . . ." My voice trailed off weakly when I looked at his face. "I—I don't."

He might have turned to stone, but his eyes widened. He stared at me with the same expression a devout Christian might wear if a radiant being with golden wings and a halo had said to him, "Pardon me, but who is this Jesus fellow you're talking about?"

After a moment, he relaxed. "I'm sorry," he said. "Your . . . ignorance startled me. But it was foolish of me to suspect you as one of the Nine." *Nine what?* "Even if I believed my son open to such evil—and he is not; he may be wild but he is basically good—the fact that Keeshah brought you home is perfect evidence of your worth.

"But . . ." he shook his head, obviously concerned, "not to know of the All-Mind? It's—well, it's like not knowing of the sky or the air."

"The knowledge may have been removed from my mind for a purpose," I said carefully. "Perhaps it is something I must learn . . . from you."

He looked up sharply, suddenly excited. "Yes, that may be it! Markasset had almost no conscious mind-link, and it was a source of bitter argument between us. I always contended that if he could bond with Keeshah, the other skills were there. I said he simply didn't want to try—" He shrugged and sighed. "Perhaps I was being unfair. But it seemed like a willful failing to me, and symbolic, somehow, of the other ways in which he hadn't become the son I wanted him to be. It was the main reason why I told him that I would not recommend him to the Council, should a vacancy occur."

"You *wouldn't?* Did he have a chance without your support?" I wasn't sure what the election process was for the Supervisors, but I was fairly sure of Thanasset's answer before he said it.

"Not the slightest. And he would have been the first son of the house of Serkajon to fail to qualify for the Council. He always seemed rather unimpressed with our family history—but I believe that he realized it, and felt a little shame over it."

"How long ago did you tell him this?" I asked. *The night before he left with Gharlas?* I wondered. *Have you just given me the true motive for Markasset's involvement—revenge?*

"Several moons ago. Our relations have not been . . . peaceful ever since." A wry smile touched the corners of his mouth. "You're thinking of Illia, aren't you? He didn't tell her."

"Maybe he didn't believe you'd really bar him from the Council."

"Maybe. But I prefer to think that it finally dawned on him that his future position meant a great deal to his romance with that girl, and telling her would diminish her interest in him rather drastically."

I think he's underrating her. Though she did say specifically "wife of a Supervisor." In any case, it explains Thanasset's disapproval of their relationship.

"But to get back to your suggestion of the purpose for your Visitation—I hope you're right. If I can help you understand about the All-Mind, perhaps Markasset will also learn. Then, when—if—he returns to me . . ."

Thanasset stood up, taking a small key from the pouch at his belt. He strode over to a wall cabinet, unlocked it, and took out a curiously-wrought bottle and two glasses. Special refreshments, obviously.

I was ready for it.

I felt a deep sense of relief that at last I would be able to discuss the situation, even in limited terms, with someone I could trust. And I was glad to notice that in Thanasset's attitude there was no trace of religious fear or awe. Respect, yes. But no more than that. For him, my situation was an individualized repetition of something that had happened before. I began to hope he might really help me to understand.

I couldn't help contrasting the present circumstance with the way such a thing would be treated in California. If a person I believed to be St. Michael or St. Francis came to my home, could I carry it off so naturally? Would I have offered him a shot of even my *best* booze?

That was, indeed, what Thanasset was pouring into the glasses. It smelled wonderful.

"Can you tell me something of yourself?" Thanasset asked as he handed me my glass. "What were your lifeskills?"

"When I was young," I said, choosing my words with much care, "I was trained as a fighting man. I was no great champion, but I learned to survive. In later life, I became a scholar and a teacher, adequate, but not famous beyond my own academic circles. I was not, I fear, a very distinguished person."

"A commendably modest answer." He sat down and looked me over critically, as though trying to see the mind inside his son's body. "Still, there must be *some* special quality about you, or the All-Mind would not have sent you to us."

"If there is, I don't know what it is," I said, honestly. "I am not even aware of what the All-Mind might have had in mind." He chuckled, and I realized what I had said. "Sorry; I didn't mean that to sound flippant."

"I understand." He waved a hand in the air. "You know, it's an odd feeling talking to someone you know, and yet you don't. I keep trying to call you Markasset, and reminding myself that you're someone different. It would help—may I ask your name?"

In Gandaresh, I knew, men's names always ended with a consonant, women's names with a vowel sound. I adjusted my own given name and gave it to Thanasset: "Rikardon."

"Rikardon," he repeated, thinking about it. "Rikardon. A very old kind of name. *He who leads upward.* A good name. But I confess that I have never heard it before."

I shrugged. "I told you I was not particularly distinguished." *Especially in Gandalaran history*, I thought. *I'd be very surprised if they had heard of me here.*

"Mmmm." He picked up his glass and sipped. I had been waiting for his opening; now I picked up my own glass eagerly.

The glasses were small; I could barely have fitted my thumb in one. After one sip, I could see why. The stuff had a rich flavor without being sweet, and an aroma that invaded the nose like a whiff of mint—but it was not mint. And there was power there. It wouldn't take very many slugs of that stuff to put a man flat on his face.

I liked it.

I learned later that it was *barut*, made by the Fa'aldu of

80

the desert from a secret mixture of herbs and fruits. An old family recipe, as it were, handed down through the generations. It was part of their trading stock, less plentiful but more lucrative than water. Ounce for ounce, its selling price was a hundred times more than that of water. How terribly, foolishly *human!*

The drinking customs were strong in Markasset's memory. After Thanasset and I had each sipped from our glasses, he lifted his glass to me and said: "Wisdom!"

I answered him, the words coming automatically, but I meant them: "And good health!"

We tossed off the remaining liquid in the little glasses in one swallow, and Thanasset went to refill them while I enjoyed the warm tingling which flowed gently through my whole body.

"There is so much to explain," Thanasset said while he poured from the bottle on the shelf. "I'm not sure where to begin."

He didn't even have a chance.

There was a sharp series of raps at the front door. Demanding. Authoritative. I looked over at Thanasset, the question plain on my face. He sighed and scowled.

"That's Zaddorn. I'd recognize that knock of his anywhere, anytime."

11

Thanasset replaced the bottle on the shelf and set down the glass he had been about to fill. He went through the doorway of the room and walked over to the large double doors that were the street entrance into the house. I followed him part of the way, and as he reached the door, he turned back. I thought he meant to say something to me, but the knock sounded again. He shrugged and opened the door.

The man who came through the door was dressed unlike any Gandalaran I had yet seen. He wore a long gray cloak of what seemed to be oiled linen, and on his head was a broad-brimmed gray hat of stiffened felt. He strode through the door and with a graceful, elaborate motion swirled the cloak from his shoulders and deposited it on a hook beside the door. Then his hat came off, and was placed on the same hook. Both were damp from the heavy mist outside, caused by the roaring falls behind the city. He had done all this silently and with an unconsciously theatrical flair, as though announcing his right to be welcome. But now he hesitated slightly, and I felt his cold, dark gaze on me—first on my face, then inspecting my waist. Then he lifted over his head the richly embroidered baldric which carried his sword.

He checked to see if I was armed! I realized, and I felt a stirring of anger that was partly Markasset's long-held rivalry, partly my own indignation. *In my father's house—does he think I would wear a sword here?*

Now I understood Thanasset's anger when I had, in ignorance, walked into his home wearing a sword.

"Good afternoon, Supervisor Thanasset," he said at last. "I must request a few minutes of your time." Again he glanced at me. "And of your son's."

"Certainly, Zaddorn. We were just having a drink. Won't you join us?" He bowed slightly and led the way back into the sunlit, high-windowed room. Zaddorn followed him and I followed Zaddorn, wishing that I had decided to wear the green-and-yellow suit I had found in the closet. For Zaddorn was wearing an embroidered gray tunic with a high collar and matching gray trousers. Somehow I knew that it was not a uniform, but merely his own conception of what the Supervisor of Peace and Security *ought* to wear. Fancy dress for daytime, perhaps, but not for a community leader who needed to be set apart from the crowd.

And I had to admit he cut an impressive figure. He was tall and broad-shouldered, and the belted tunic emphasized his muscular chest and arms. His voice was deep even when he spoke softly, as he had done to Thanasset. Yet I could imagine that, raised in command, it would stop a mad vlek in its tracks.

I found myself wondering what it was that Illia saw in Markasset.

Thanasset went directly to the shelf, but Zaddorn shook his head. "Ah, no. I thank you, Supervisor Thanasset, but barut is too heady for a man who needs all his wits about him. Please do not let me keep you from your pleasure, however."

Thanasset filled his glass, and brought it to me. Standing, we made the toast. "Wisdom!"

"Wisdom!"

"And good health!"

Thanasset replaced the bottle and glasses—apparently they

were used only for barut, and were thus self-sterilizing—locked the cabinet, and we sat down. Zaddorn wasted no time in coming to the point.

"I came here because I heard you had returned to Raithskar, Markasset. I presume," he said, glancing at Thanasset, "that you have learned of our loss?"

Zaddorn had a thinner, flatter face than most Gandalarans, with a longer, more normal-looking (to Ricardo) nose. But his eyes were still shadowed by the brow ridge, and they were dark and piercing. I could sense the intelligence behind them—and the subtle menace of an honest cop determined to solve a crime.

Perhaps it was his manner, smooth and deadly as a sword, which irritated me. Or perhaps it was some remnant of bad feeling between Zaddorn and Markasset. But I wanted more than anything to shake him out of his self-satisfied composure.

"Chief Supervisor Ferrathyn mentioned it when I arrived," I told him. "But it wasn't news by then." Zaddorn blinked, and I waited just until he was ready to say something before I went on. "There were rumors of it all through the marketplace."

Zaddorn was cool, but I had seen the well-controlled flashes of expression on his face. Eagerness, thinking it was going to be easy, after all. Disappointment when I didn't admit anything. And finally, awareness that I had staged it that way on purpose. A glimpse of anger then, before his face closed into a granite-hard expression of mild interest. I wouldn't be able to break through again—but I was delighted to have done it once.

"They must have upset you terribly," he said, "for you to have drawn your sword in Vendor Street."

"If you know about that," I countered, "you know why I did it."

He waved a hand negligently, as if to brush aside the reason. "I heard that there was a disturbance. Something about a couple of vineh attacking their foreman."

Zaddorn and I both heard Thanasset's sharp intake of breath. But we didn't take our eyes off one another. Beneath our normal-toned conversation was a declaration of private war, a contest of wills we both knew had not begun here, nor would it end now.

"I discounted it," Zaddorn continued. "Vineh do not behave in that fashion. They are never fierce."

"They certainly gave that appearance," I said.

83

"Perhaps. But I think it more likely that both you and the foreman misapprehended their motives. The theft of the Ra'ira is a most serious thing, and if—as you have assured me—everyone knows about it, it has created a general tenseness in the city, ready to be set off by anything unusual. You both panicked; that's all. And you drew your sword.

"You realize," he added, "that I could arrest you right now for waving a naked blade in the streets."

"Isn't it more important," interrupted Thanasset, "to find the Ra'ira? May I ask what progress you've made?"

Zaddorn looked at Thanasset, then back at me. We had been leaning forward in our chairs; now we both sighed and settled back—a temporary truce, a break before the next round.

"We are fairly certain that the gem has left the city. There is no trace or rumor of it in the city's rogueworld. It is my personal opinion that it left the city in the caravan of Gharlas. I have sent a guard command group after them, but it will be some time before that group returns with any information."

Again his eyes met mine, and I knew that this was the real reason he was here.

"I am in hope, Markasset," he said, "that since you have—ah, left your position with the caravan and returned early, you may have some useful news for us."

"I have already discussed this with the Chief Supervisor," I said, keeping my voice steady. Ferrathyn had merely been interested; this Zaddorn was out for blood. His voice slipped out of its impersonal tone into a deeper one which almost rang around the room.

"Well, you're discussing it with *me* now, Markasset. Why should I trouble the Chief Supervisor for second-hand information when I have the original source right here? Now tell me what you know about the theft of the Ra'ira!"

"There's nothing to tell, Zaddorn," I said. "During my time with the caravan, I neither saw nor heard anything that I can remember that would make me think there was anything odd going on."

"Why did you leave the caravan?"

"Personal reasons," I answered, and I couldn't keep all the anger out of my voice. "They have nothing to do with the theft of the Ra'ira. In fact, they're no business of yours whatever!"

He sat back with a smile and I realized, too late, that he had wanted to provoke me—and he had succeeded.

84

"No?" he said, all smooth steel again. "Perhaps not. But one can theorize, eh? I have been informed by usually reliable sources that you owe a certain Worfit some seven hundred zaks—a gambling debt, I believe. Is that correct?"

"I don't see how my personal finances are any of your business, either."

"You'd be surprised how little bits of unrelated information often come together at unlikely times," he said coolly. "For instance, I happen to know that you left town still owing him the money. He was quite put out to learn about it, according to my sources."

"He'll be paid," I said. He was getting at something, I could tell. And it worried me.

"Oh, I'm sure of it, since other—ah, sources tell me that you returned to town with enough and more to repay him. More, I daresay, than you would have earned from Caravan Master Gharlas, even had you completed the journey with him." He stood up, walked over to the window and looked out into the garden for a few seconds. Then he came back to his chair, placed his hands on its back, and leaned across it toward me. *Where did you get that money?*

I couldn't answer him for several reasons. First, I really didn't have the least idea where the large coins—twenty-dozak pieces, had Illia called them?—had come from. Second, I *knew* that the small coins had come from the money pouch of a man who had died horribly in the desert. And last, there was only one way Zaddorn could have learned about the money at all. Dear little Illia did not confine her confidences to me alone.

I was trying to digest the shock and come up with some kind of answer when my father said calmly, "My son is carrying twelve hundred zaks in the form of five golden twenty-dozak pieces. I gave them to him the night before he left. He told me about the debt, and I gave him enough to cover it and to provide him some spending money during his journey."

"But you still have all that money," Zaddorn said, still looking at me. "And Worfit is still looking for you. Why didn't you pay him, if you had the money before you left?"

Good question. C'mon, Markasset, tell me why, I thought, searching the elusive memory of the Gandalaran. To my surprise, he told me.

"I couldn't find him!" I answered, and I'm sure Thanasset and Zaddorn were both startled by the sound of triumph in my voice. "That kind of debt you repay in person, and . . ."

I almost laughed, "he had been arrested by one of your agents."

For the first time since he had arrived, Zaddorn's dignity slipped. He stood up and cleared his throat. I'm sure that, if he had been wearing the kind of necktie Ricardo was familiar with, Zaddorn would have adjusted it slightly at that moment.

"Yes," he said finally. "I had forgotten—Worfit was being questioned that night about another matter entirely." He gave Thanasset a long, hard look. "I can see that I'll get no more information here—but there are other lines of inquiry open to me. Perhaps they will prove more fruitful."

He strode out through the doorway, and we stood up and followed him. He was putting on his baldric and sword by the time we reached the door. He swirled the cloak to his shoulders with the same grace he had used in removing it and then, hat in his hand, he turned to Thanasset.

"Thank you for your time, Supervisor Thanasset. Markasset." He opened the door, then turned partway back. "I'm sure I'll see you both later." Then he put his hat on and was gone.

"Well, that's that," I said as Thanasset closed the door with a sigh. "There's no question that he thinks I stole the Ra'ira from you."

Thanasset shook his head. "You're only half right," he told me. "What he thinks is that you and I conspired to steal it."

"What? Where would he get such a foolish idea?"

Thanasset smiled at me with a tenderness that touched my heart. "Thank you for your faith in me, Rikardon. But Zaddorn reads people very skillfully. He knows that I lied about giving you—Markasset—the five gold pieces."

"Huh?" We were walking back into the "drinking room," as I had begun to think of it, with no help from Markasset. But the time had come for serious talk, and Thanasset did not offer, nor did I want, anything which might cloud our minds.

"Yes," he said as we sat down. "Markasset did tell me about his debt to Worfit. We both knew that thought of Keeshah would prevent Worfit from applying physical violence. We talked—no, argued, is a better word—on the evening before the theft, a few hours before I went to the Council Hall for Guardian Duty. I refused him the money, told him that I was tired of his irresponsible behavior, that this was one scrape he could get himself out of without my help." He had been looking at the floor; now he looked up at me.

"Don't think too harshly of me, Rikardon. I—I was angry. I would have given it to him the next day, probably. I guess I just wanted him to be frightened for a time, to teach him a lesson. When I read his note, I . . ." His voice trailed off.

I thought that the old man had done exactly the right thing—or it would have been exactly right if the complication of the theft hadn't come up. But I wasn't about to offer a personal judgment of how a father handled his son. Instead I asked the question that the new information raised.

"If you didn't give Markasset the money, why *do* I have twelve hundred zaks in my pouch?"

"It is the money I didn't give to Markasset. A few minutes after I went on duty, Markasset came to the Council Hall and went into my office. He carried his own key—which he left behind after he took the five gold pieces out of my cabinet."

"He left his key?"

"Yes." Thanasset smiled. "To show that he had taken it—he would not have wished that someone else be blamed for it. I have tried to explain—Markasset is an honest man, in his own way."

"I think I understand." And I was relieved. I wanted very much to think the best I could of Markasset. "It was more a forced loan than a theft."

"Exactly."

"And when did you learn about it?"

"After the excitement had died down a little over the *real* theft. I returned to my office, found the key there and the money missing."

"He took your money. Do you think he might also have been involved with the men who stole the Ra'ira?"

"NO!"

At last, the question I had dreaded had been asked, and answered. Thanasset's response was so immediate that I knew he had felt it hanging between us ever since I admitted that I knew little of Markasset's life.

"I do not entirely understand my son," Thanasset said, "but I know him. He would never betray me or Raithskar."

Another great weight had lifted from me. I didn't know much about Markasset, but I trusted his father. "I believe you," I told him, and relief and gratitude showed in his strong, craggy face. "Who *did* take it?"

He shrugged. "You have heard all that I know. Ferrathyn's theory about the Lords of Eddarta seems likely to me. But they would have needed information only available in Raithskar—someone here must have helped them. That is, if they

87

really *did* take the Ra'ira to help support their claim as the heirs of the ancient Kings of Gandalara."

"Tell me about them," I said. "The Kings of Gandalara." Thanasset's face took on a look of complete astonishment. I must have had the same look on my face as he suddenly stood up and bowed deeply before me.

"I am fortunate," he said. "If you know nothing of the Kings, you are one of the Very Ancients. And if you have no knowledge of Kä, then—" he paused, "you must not know about Steel."

I knew about "steel" in my world—but "Steel" in Gandalara was a mystery, especially as it was spoken by Thanasset. I could hear the capital "S" in his voice. I shook my head, though what he said had not been a question.

"Come with me," he said, and led the way out into the large central room. We walked over to the inlaid wall with the beautifully intricate sha'um pattern, and he pointed to the sword mounted on the wall above it.

"That is Steel," he said. "Its name is—" He stopped suddenly, and turned toward me. His voice was almost a whisper. "I should have known. Its name is *Rika*. Upwards."

I said nothing as he looked back at the sword and stared at it thoughtfully for several seconds.

"That sword was forged for Serkajon. It is one of the few swords in the world made of the Most Precious Metal." It was another Gandalaran term for Steel. "They stay strong and sharp for lifetimes of men, and they carry an imprint of the men who have wielded them.

"Serkajon was the first to hold *Rika*. In the generations since his death, it has been the duty of each father to judge whether his son was worthy to carry it. There have been only five, since Serkajon, strong enough in body and spirit that their touch on the hilt would not dishonor his memory." He smiled. "You will be the sixth."

Who, me? But . . .

Thanasset had turned away from the wall and was pacing slowly around the large room. I followed him, trying to think of something to say. But he was talking again.

"The Most Precious Metal came to Gandalara with the skybolt." He raised his heavy brows as he glanced at me. "Even as ancient as you are, you must know the legend. Back, far back, long before the first *written* history, a starbolt struck down from the sky, blinding everyone near it, killing many of our ancestors."

I bit my tongue; I had been about to remind him that if

they had died, there was a strong possibility they *hadn't* been his ancestors. And besides, the image he had given me recalled one of my own. A starbolt? A meteor, certainly. What else could it be? And I, Ricardo, had been killed by a meteor—or my body had. Yet that was in a different world. Why did it seem to me that the two events were linked?

"Yes," I told Thanasset. "I know of the starbolt."

He nodded. "I thought you would. The memory of it remains in the All-Mind, though dimly now. For it happened in the unthinkably remote past—a hundred hundred centuries ago."

A million years, I calculated. *And the All-Mind, whatever it is, still remembers it!*

"It struck here," he said, swinging one arm generally in the direction of the waterfall behind the city, "in what is now Raithskar. Some theorists believe that it brought the Most Precious Metal with it. Others say that the metal is a transformation product of its power. In either case," he shrugged, "it remains the only known deposit of Steel in all Gandalara." It seemed that the term for the finished metal was also applied to its main and indispensable ingredient: a chunk of nickel-iron meteor.

"Our Ancestors at that time were little more than animals, barely aware of their latent ability to think rationally and to anticipate the future. After the skybolt struck, those who survived began to use that ability. The trend was magnified threefold in their children, and, within two generations, the All-Mind had become fully aware."

It all made sense.

A huge chrome-nickel-iron meteor had come smashing in through the atmosphere in the distant past at somewhere between ten and twenty miles per second. At those velocities, plenty of hard radiation is given off during the time it takes to go through the atmosphere—between ten seconds and two minutes, depending on the speed and the angle at which it struck. That radiation would be lethal to those creatures near enough to barely survive the impact, and disabling to those who caught a smaller dose. And it was certain to produce mutations—most of them probably unfavorable.

But at least one favorable mutation had survived, and its descendants mined and worked the very fabric of their beginnings when they forged swords like *Rika* from the Steel of Raithskar.

"And the All-Mind?" I asked. "You were going to tell me about it, just before Zaddorn arrived."

89

"Yes, I was," Thanasset agreed, then hesitated. Suddenly he chuckled. "You'll have to forgive me, Rikardon. The All-Mind is so much a part of us now—I hardly know where to begin. But I'll try."

And so he did. We walked slowly around the beautiful parquet floor of the midhall as he talked, and I listened attentively, trying very hard to understand. But it was difficult. The meteor was a physical phenomenon which my world and Thanasset's, no matter how far apart, could share. But there was nothing in Ricardo's experience to help me now.

The concepts and vocabulary were strange to me—some of the terms Thanasset used simply had no equivalent meaning, and they were apparently so second-nature to Markasset that I got no help from his unreliable memory.

Besides, I don't believe that Markasset understood the All-Mind. And Thanasset, who was trying his very best to explain it to me in simple, logical language, didn't completely understand it, either. But both of them *accepted* it. For them, it was a basic fact of life.

But Ricardo Carillo had lived in a civilization where such notions were discounted by a large percentage of the intelligent population. Even those who did not discount them could not prove them. They could not even agree among themselves on terminology or basic theory.

But in spite of all the impediments to understanding, by the time Thanasset had finished, I did have a conception—my own, certainly, which probably didn't match Thanasset's—of what the All-Mind is.

12

The All-Mind is a *linkage* between Gandalarans. It is not precisely telepathic, but it seems to have some properties closely akin to telepathy. The Gandalarans believe that the All-Mind is the collective mind of all Gandalarans, both living and dead, with only a few exceptions.

They believe that each person is a new individual when he is born, but while he lives, and after he dies, his soul-mind (my word, not theirs) is part of the All-Mind, linked with it irrevocably, and so linked with every other Gandalaran, both living and dead. The webwork of those linkages, throughout the total four-dimensional space-time matrix which is the lifetime of the *race,* comprises the All-Mind.

I was surprised to find that Thanasset's attitude toward the All-Mind was respectful, but not quite reverent. Certainly it was implicit in what he told me that he believed in the survival of the individual soul-mind after death through its linkage with the All-Mind. Yet the All-Mind was not a god to Thanasset.

The Gandalarans have no temples, no rites or ceremonies, nothing even faintly resembling what I would call "worship" directed to the All-Mind. Each Gandalaran admires and honors it above all entities which are alive in his world, for he knows that the All-Mind is a greater entity, and that he is a part of it. Thanasset admitted, with a look of mild disapproval, that some radical thinkers believed that the personality—what I would call the soul—of the individual died with his body, and that only the integrated memories remained linked to the All-Mind. But whatever the actual nature of the survival, all Gandalarans are certain of their place in the history of their world. They will be remembered.

I have no opinion to offer as to which theory is correct. But I do understand why, though their regard for the All-Mind is the closest thing Gandalarans have to a religion, they do not worship it.

Thanasset didn't think of the All-Mind in the way I had been taught to think of God. I think it was Graham Greene who said something to the effect that he could not worship a God he could understand.

Gandalarans think they understand the All-Mind pretty well. They do not worship it, fear it, or try to win its favor. They do not even have faith in it or believe in it. It does not need faith or belief; it is merely a fact.

It is accessible.

Everyone is in continuous contact with the All-Mind. With most of them, however, that contact is largely subconscious. The few who can regularly operate that contact have a special duty in Gandalara. They are called Recorders, and it is their job to put explicit, carefully indexed knowledge into the memory of the All-Mind. And to tap it for stored knowledge.

In some ways the All-Mind functions like a giant computer-recorder. A non-Recorder can go to a Recorder to get information—history, law, customs, economics, and the like. From what Thanasset said, I got the impression that either the Recorder could establish his or her link and search out the information directly, or the inquirer could be put into something like an hypnotic state and his or her subconscious link could be raised to the conscious level.

Either way, it seemed, the answers weren't always there. Either nobody knew it to begin with, or for some reason it just isn't available.

In that one way, at least, the All-Mind resembles most of the deities I have ever heard of. It sees all, knows all, and tells what it damn well pleases.

When I said earlier that it was hard to understand what Thanasset was saying about the All-Mind, I omitted one large factor—part of the time I just wasn't listening. My skepticism was functioning in high gear, and while it stewed over one point, Thanasset covered two more.

Which just goes to show the stubbornness of the human mind. Here was I, who should be dead, living out of my own time and world, in the body of another being who wasn't even human—and I was discounting half of what Thanasset was saying because it seemed like the same sort of occult mysticism crap I'd laughed at all my life.

But if I gained little true understanding of the All-Mind from our discussion, at least I did realize at last why Thanasset treated me with such respect. To him, I was someone who had died long ago and had been an intimate part of the All-Mind—for how long?—and had come back or been returned by the All-Mind to a particular body for a particular purpose.

And that contributed to my skepticism, too. Because I couldn't buy Thanasset's theory about me. Rick Carillo of California, U.S.A., didn't fit into the matrix of the All-Mind in any way, shape or form. No matter how logical, well-reasoned, self-evident, or even *true* Thanasset's explanation had been up until that point, *I* tore a glaring hole in them.

What I believed, however, was far less important than what Thanasset believed. And that, at least, I could comprehend.

"If you know nothing of the Kings of Gandalara," Thanasset was saying, "it indicates that your own life-span antedated them. Do you know anything of the City of Kä?"

"Nothing," I admitted honestly. I didn't feel that the conversation I had heard, crouching behind a bush out in the desert in the middle of the night, could even be counted.

"What do you remember of the Great *Pleth*?"

Pleth? Markasset's memories refused to translate it.

"I'm afraid I don't know the word. Perhaps if you'd define it . . ."

"Ah, of course. It is little used these last twenty centuries. It is an extensive body of water. The Great Pleth was *very* extensive."

Oh sure, I thought. *A sea!* I was relieved to be able to say, for once, "Yes, I understand now. The—uh, Pleth was quite extensive in my day." I tried to frame a sentence which would say that I had even sailed the "pleth," but the vocabulary would not come to mind. Apparently there was no Gandaresh word for "sail" or "boat."

"Then you must come from some five hundred centuries in the past," he said, with a touch of awe in his voice. "This must be a completely different world for you!"

"Oh, it's all of that," I agreed wholeheartedly. Then I paused and thought about it for a few seconds. "Yet it is much the same in many ways. People still live and die, love and hate, succeed and fail. And the reasons behind the actions of men—motivation, emotion—are the same here as in my world."

Thanasset smiled sadly. "Do we progress so slowly, then? Are folk no more noble now than they were in your day?"

I realized that I had been speaking, thoughtlessly, of Ricardo's world; yet Thanasset interpreted my words as applying to his own history. And that brought the point home sharply to me.

We weren't so different, after all, Thanasset and I. And he was trying to understand me in the terms of my own world, even as I had needed to know about the All-Mind to understand Thanasset better.

I resolved to be as honest with Thanasset as I could. I had to mislead him, at least to the extent of allowing him to believe that my world *was* a part of his history. But I wanted his friendship, and I wanted that friendship to be based on truth. As much of the truth as he could accept.

"I received my training as a fighter because I had to oppose a group of people who intended to conquer all the existing territory."

"And did you succeed in preventing that conquest?" Thanasset asked.

"That one, yes. But fighting continued for most of my life, for various reasons and in different areas. I took a less active role in these later wars, training other fighters and making sure our own borders were well defended."

Thanasset was nodding. "Yes, that agrees with the few

93

records I have found of the time before the Kings. In spite of later abuse of the power he claimed, Zanek is often given credit for ending a period of continual, debilitating conflict between neighboring territories."

"Zanek was the first King of Gandalara?" I asked.

"Yes, it was he who united the Walled World. Led by the Riders, his armies reached out from the shores of the Great Pleth and first demanded, then won, the tribute and allegiance of city after city, until all of Kä was ruled by Zanek.

"For a long time Gandalara rested in peace. Zanek and his sons ruled wisely. But life became harder as the years passed and the Great Pleth diminished. The Kings began to demand greater tribute as their own fields failed to support Kä."

"Was that when Raithskar sent the Ra'ira to Kä?"

Thanasset looked at me sharply, but what he said was, "Yes. And it was shortly after we sent that single great prize to Kä that the Kings began to demand a different kind of tribute—slaves.

"Raithskar was spared that degradation because we had a more important gift—water. Our craftsmen built a carrier pipe to transport our clear, pure water to the great city, and that was considered tribute enough.

"But from everywhere else in Gandalara, slaves poured into Kä. They worked a few years—some only a few months—and then they died from the hardship and were replaced."

"That must have been shortly before the kingdom fell."

"Why do you say that?" Thanasset asked me.

"Because in my—time, men could not bear to be slaves. And any ruler who was dependent on slaves eventually became so weak that the slaves could break free of his rule. Did that not happen at Kä?"

"No," said Thanasset, with an odd flat note in his voice. "The slaves did not resist."

"Then—?"

"It was one of the Riders, the King's own elite guard, who destroyed Kä."

"Serkajon."

"Yes. The Riders were honorable men who served the Kings with absolute loyalty as long as they believed that their rule was good for all of Gandalara. But Serkajon knew—" Thanasset hesitated, searching for words—"he realized that the Kings were no longer ruling Gandalara; they were exploiting it. So he took the Ra'ira."

"Which had become a symbol of power?"

"Yes," agreed Thanasset. "When he brought it out of Kä, home to Raithskar, the Kingdom collapsed. The Riders came after Serkajon, of course. But he talked to them, explained what he had done and why, and they never returned to Kä. Instead they settled in Thagorn and kept their own traditions, in the hope that they might someday serve another king worthy of their loyalty."

"The Sharith," I said, remembering the conversation with Balgokh at Yafnaar. "Something was said about a 'duty' that is paid by the caravans."

Thanasset sighed. "They claim the right of tribute. To them, they are still the King's Guard, and entitled to a measure of support from the rest of Gandalara—even though there is no king, and hasn't been for hundreds of years. If it's not paid willingly . . ."

"They attack? That must be why Gharlas was hiring guards. Balgokh said that Gharlas planned to bypass Thagorn."

"Did he?" Thanasset asked, eyebrows raised.

"I don't know," I told him. "I woke alone in the desert. I don't know what happened to the caravan." I wasn't counting the corpse.

"Well. I regret what has happened to the Sharith. The Riders had a high and noble purpose when they settled in Thagorn. They deserted Harthim, the last King, because he used Gandalara for his own profit. Yet now—it seems to me they are doing the same thing."

"Is there no connection at all," I asked, "between the Sharith and the house of the man who once led them?"

"No. And I believe that Serkajon knew it would be this way when he elected to stay in Raithskar. It has been a kind of exile, really, though there was purpose in his choice, too. Yet every generation since Serkajon has contained a Rider, in spite of the expense of maintaining a sha'um in the city."

"Were the Riders also the Supervisors?" I asked.

"Often," Thanasset answered. "But not always. In some generations there were two and three sons. Only one boy in a generation felt the call of the Valley of the Sha'um, and it happened sometimes that the other sons had the skills necessary to act as a Supervisor."

"So the family of Serkajon has continued to lead—in Raithskar, if not in Thagorn."

"True, and I have never doubted Serkajon's choice. But I wonder what the Sharith would be today if Serkajon had gone to Thagorn. I have a strong memory of what they were. I mourn greatly for what they have become."

"They still ride," I said. I realized how important Keeshah had become to me. Even then, standing here and talking to Thanasset, the great cat was a comforting presence in the back of my mind.

Thanasset smiled at me. "True. It is a great honor to be chosen by the sha'um. Since they are still being chosen, there is still value in them."

He sighed, and went on more briskly. "I have answered my own question. We have not progressed. In Eddarta, those who claim the kingdom also claim the rights of kings. They keep slaves there still, starving and terrified tribute from the nearby provinces, which need Eddarta's water."

When Thanasset spoke of slavery, I thought about the vineh. My first impulse was to think of them as slaves, but as I remembered how they had looked, one moment docile and the next fierce, and how they had all three attacked their— what would you call it, their "keeper"? When I remembered the entire incident, I was glad that I hadn't mentioned the vineh in connection with Thanasset's discussion of slavery. They might be dressed like people, but I was sure they were not. They were work animals that happened to look like people.

"And we may not have 'wars'," Thanasset was saying, "but we honor and maintain the martial tradition. A man's sword is part of his family's history, to be passed on to his son at the proper age. The bronze sword you were wearing has been in our family for generations. Twice, when it became too damaged to be useful, it was melted and reforged."

I was beginning to understand why I felt guilty about leaving the dead man's sword out in the desert. I resolved to retrieve it someday, if I had the chance.

"Boys learn to fight more eagerly than to read, and compete regularly in training games. As men, they carry swords daily, with the implied purpose of defending their cities against attack.

"Granted, Raithskar has more reason than most cities to need such a force of fighting men—for the few times when the vineh have gotten out of hand, and,"—he barked a laugh—"for the protection of the Ra'ira. But I always thought it pointless and backward-looking, especially since I considered the Council sufficient security for Raithskar's treasure.

"That was another problem between my son and myself.

He excelled in the games, especially in personal combat, and I could never appreciate that as much as he would have liked."

Thanasset looked at the sword on the wall. "When I was a boy, I learned fighting skills because it was required, but I never struggled to be the best. *My* father told me that in all other ways I was worthy of Serkajon's Steel, but my lack of interest in our fighting traditions made him withhold it from me." He reached out a hand to trace the outline of the portrait. "And it was Markasset's enthusiasm for that, above all else, that made me feel *he* was unworthy."

He stood there for a moment, lost in thought, then abruptly shrugged off the mood.

"Well, back to the subject. No 'wars', as I said, but personal frailty and violence still exist. Every city has its rogueworld and its share of dishonest merchants, murderers,"—he made a wry face—"and thieves. No, we haven't really progressed. How very sad."

"If you really believe that, Thanasset," I said, "you're wrong."

"What do you mean?"

"Only that you shouldn't believe that it's a sad thing. It's a natural thing. People are like that. The trick is to learn to handle things so that the sort of people who want to take advantage of others have to work at it.

"Raithskar took the first step when Serkajon brought back the Ra'ira. Now, there may still be slavery in Eddarta and forced tribute to the Sharith, but here in Raithskar you live peacefully with only the violence of individuals to contend with. And it seems to me that Zaddorn has that pretty well under control.

"*My* world was torn with war and full of fear." Suddenly I wanted to stop talking. My throat tightened up, but I went on, saying things I had always known but had never spoken. "Terrorism and greed were the watchwords of my time. The world had learned to be cynical. To be trusting was to be a victim. To be fair was to be foolish. Virtue and corruption were at constant odds. Honorable men had to fight to be recognized, and still were doubted by other honorable men.

"I am not saying that I was personally unhappy in my world, Thanasset. I wasn't. But in Raithskar I don't feel so pressured and defensive. Sure, Zaddorn may believe that you and I have committed a dishonest act. But he suspects that only because something—mistakenly—leads him to believe it, not because he naturally suspects everybody's motives. And

97

when we prove him wrong, he will accept that proof and trust us as much as he did before all this happened.

"You asked if people had 'progressed' since my time, Thanasset. I can't really judge that. But I will tell you this—I believe that people are more naturally honest in Raithskar than in my world.

"I have never met a more honorable man than you are. Whatever brought me into Markasset's body, I am proud to be known as your son."

13

Thanasset stared at me, no less astonished than I at what I had said. I have never been one to confuse sentiment with emotion, and I know that that moment might have been one of the most emotional of my two lives.

But it was interrupted.

There was a loud banging on the door, followed just a bit too soon by Milda literally running down the front stairway to open the door. Illia fell through, sobbing, and Milda caught her around the shoulders. Illia reached out toward me, saying "Markasset" over and over again, until Milda shook her into silence.

"Now," Milda said, when Illia was under control, "I saw you running up the street as though Keeshah were after you. If you've got something to say, say it!" This was not the sweet old lady I had met earlier and loved almost instantly— this was a woman made of iron! And I still loved her.

Illia looked over at me. "They're coming after Markasset."

"What?" asked Thanasset. "Who is coming after him?"

"Zaddorn," she wailed, and I noticed that though she had all the human reactions of weeping, there were no tears. They would have been a waste of water.

"What *happened*, girl?" Thanasset demanded.

Illia calmed down, and twisted gently out of Milda's grip to walk across the floor of the large room toward us.

"Zaddorn sent a guard command group out after Gharlas's caravan."

"It couldn't have gotten back already!" I said. My computation of their travel time wasn't completely accurate, of course, but given the caravan's head start . . .

"How did you know about them?" Illia asked, looking at me sharply.

"The Chief Supervisor told me earlier today," I answered. "Anyway, does it matter?"

"It matters," she said. "A maufa just arrived with a message for Zaddorn. The guard group didn't catch up with the caravan—they met it on its way back to Raithskar. Or, rather, they met what was left of it. Two men and a vlek. The Sharith got the rest."

Maufa? I was asking myself, then a memory surfaced. *A trainable bird, like a pigeon, that carries messages! That must be what I heard in those cages when the posse passed me. Why didn't you tell me this sooner, Markasset?*

Thanasset grabbed Illia and turned her toward him. "What are you implying about my son?"

"*I'm* not implying anything, sir. But the men from the caravan said that when the Sharith attacked, Markasset—not by that name, of course, but Zaddorn figured out who it was—was nowhere to be seen. They're saying that your son was a Sharith agent, but now Zaddorn has some complicated theory about Markasset and the Ra'ira." She turned to me, her eyes pleading. "I know you didn't steal anything, Markasset. But your position as guard—why weren't you there when the Sharith attacked?"

She was hoping for a reasonable explanation. So was I. I was thankful when Thanasset interrupted again.

"What is Zaddorn going to do?"

"He's on his way here right now," Illia said. "He has legal grounds for putting Markasset into confinement on a charge of failing to perform a contracted service. But I know he's convinced that Markasset stole the Ra'ira."

O boy. And if I'm in the hoosegow . . .

"Father, I have to go."

Thanasset nodded. "I know, son. But not like that," he added, indicating my pantless blue tunic. "Take the time to dress properly."

"Where are you going?" Illia asked.

"To Thagorn. If the Ra'ira was on the caravan, it's in the hands of the Sharith now. Whether or not they were involved in the theft—" I glanced at Thanasset, who shrugged. It had occurred to both of us, I was sure, that the Sharith could have the same motives we had early attributed to Eddarta. "I couldn't say. But the trail leads there, and I can't follow it if Zaddorn is sitting on me."

"You didn't answer my question," she said softly.

I put hy arms around her and drew her close. She wasn't soft and yielding as she had been in the garden that afternoon. Her body was stiff, and she kept her arms between us.

"I promise you, Illia, when I get back to Raithskar, everything will be clear. But now I must go. Thank you for coming to warn me."

I lowered my head and kissed her cheek lightly, then released her and ran upstairs. I dressed quickly in the same sort of outfit I had been wearing when I woke up in this world. Then I ran downstairs to find the three of them still standing in the middle of the room. But Milda was holding a pair of leather bags tied together with three lengths of strong rope, and Thanasset was putting something into one side of the— they could only be saddlebags.

When they saw me, Thanasset said, "Be careful on your way to Thagorn," in an *almost* natural tone of voice. For an instant I was puzzled, then I knew what was happening. Thanasset was trying to tell me, without revealing to Illia that I didn't know a damn thing about Gandalara, where to find the Sharith. He must have been putting a map into the pack.

You're a smart old dodger, Thanasset! I thought to myself. Aloud I said, "Thank you, Father. I'll be as careful and as quick as I can." Without thinking, I stuck out my right hand. There was barely a moment's hesitation before Thanasset reached out and gripped my hand in both his own.

"Goodbye, son."

I turned to Illia, who was staring at the floor. I lifted her face with my hand and kissed her lightly on the lips. "Don't worry, Illia. Soon I'll be back and you'll know the whole truth."

"Why won't you tell me now?" she asked. "What are you hiding from me, Markasset?"

I couldn't say "nothing" because it wasn't true. I shook my head. "I am sorry, Illia. I just can't tell you now. But please believe me, it's not because I don't trust you. I—I simply can't tell you, that's all."

With a sob she fell toward me, and for a moment I held her.

"Hurry back, Markasset," she whispered. "Come back to me safe."

I released her and turned to Milda, who handed me the rope-linked packs, then tied a belt around my waist which had several small waterskins attached. They were already filled.

"There's enough food to last you for several days," she said. "And the water should go further, if you're careful with it. Markasset," she asked suddenly, looking up at my face and touching my cheek with one age-soft hand, "is it time to start worrying?"

Just then there was a knock at the door. A distinctive, emphatic knock. I had only heard it twice, but I recognized it now—Zaddorn!

"Never mind, nephew," Aunt Milda said. "There's my answer."

"Go now, son," Thanasset said. "I'll delay him as long as I can."

I ran to the back door and shifted the heavy packs to one arm. I grabbed my sword and baldric off the peg by the door and awkwardly drew it over my head. Then, with a last look into the room where Thanasset was standing beside the front door now—as I watched, the knock sounded again—I flung open the rear door, took two steps out, and stopped.

There were three men waiting for me with their swords already drawn. And from the worn look of their brown leather baldrics, I could guess that they knew how to use those swords. I could read that in their faces, too, in the scar along one man's right cheek, and in the looks they gave me. They were measuring, appraising me as only a fighting man looks at an opponent.

I was surprised. Not because Zaddorn had thought to place a rear guard, but that he had risked it with Keeshah in the yard. I glanced down the length of the yard. Even over the low mounds of the garden, I could see Keeshah's house. The heavy wooden doors which had stood open when we arrived were now closed and bolted shut with a length of bronze slipped through rungs on the outside of both doors.

Now that sounds like Zaddorn's planning, I decided.

"That's him," the man in the middle was saying. "That's Markasset. Grab him. The Chief says he has it on him."

I dropped the bags and drew my sword. They advanced slowly, and I tried to cover all of them at once.

I sent out an anxious thought. *Keeshah!*

I am here.

Can you break out?

No need. I heard them coming. I am up on the roof. I wait.

These men want to take me prisoner.

101

So far they hadn't really tried. They were circling, watching me, gauging me.

I kill, came Keeshah's thought, calm, with no anger.

No! I ordered. These were Zaddorn's men. *No, Keeshah, don't kill them. But—frighten them.*

They will shit.

In their place, I know that I would have. For Keeshah let out a roar that seemed to shake the ground beneath our feet. The three men whipped around to look at the cat house, where they thought the sha'um safely locked away, and saw the tall, lithe cat standing on the roof, his head lifted in that gut-wrenching roar.

Then he turned directly toward us, and fixed his gaze on the three men. He crouched down to the edge of the roof, and behind him we could see the tip of his tail, slowly lashing. He moved slightly, gathering himself, but even at a distance of some twenty meters, we could see that the pale golden eyes never blinked.

For a long moment—even I was holding my breath—Keeshah was absolutely still. Then he came down off that roof in a graceful leap that brought him five yards closer to us, and he was already running.

He stopped just short of the armed trio, snarling. He made feints at the men, leaping in and then back, staying just out of range of their swordpoints. Two of them were almost hysterical with fear, but they were holding their own. The middle one, whom I thought of as their leader, had more nerve than the other two—he turned his back on Keeshah.

"You guys take care of that fleabitten sha'um!" he ordered in his growling voice. "I'll take care of this filth."

He came at me with a high overhand cut.

Fencing with a broadsword is very different from fencing with a foil, a smallsword, or even a rapier. There is a lot more edgework and less pointwork. Besides, bronze is both heavier and softer than steel, so the blade can't be as long on a bronze sword.

Briefly, I wished I had grabbed the steel sword from the wall. But only briefly. Thanasset had said its name was *Rika*, but I had the feeling it was really Excalibur. I had enough troubles.

Right in front of me, trying to cleave me in two, was my biggest immediate trouble. I had learned broadsword work in Berkeley under Master Paul Edwin Zimmer, and I—that is, Ricardo—had never been anywhere near as good as my teacher. But it was not Ricardo who handled that sword now.

102

Markasset took over. Not his mind—I was still Ricardo Carillo—but his body. Markasset had been a far better swordsman than Ricardo could ever have hoped to be. He had been trained thoroughly. And his body remembered. In an emergency, reflexes take over. I was grateful to have Markasset's reflexes.

I parried the leader at *forte*, and as his blade slid off my quillon to my right, I swung around for a cut at his midsection.

My opponent leaped back to avoid my cut and started to lunge in with his point as my blade went by him. He barely parried me in time.

I was doing the fighting; I was in control. But it was a control the like of which I had never experienced before. My blade was placed with precision in space; my timing was accurate to the millisecond; my footwork was as beautiful and as automatic as that of a trained dancer.

I fought steadily, warily, waiting for an opening. I never took my eyes off my opponent, but I could sense Keeshah behind him, still keeping the other two busy, even enjoying the game.

At last my opponent let his blade drop just a fraction of an inch too low. I aimed a slash at his chest, knowing he would have to parry me by knocking my blade upward and to his right. He tried, but too weakly and too late. As his blade struck mine, I stopped the cut and lunged. If he had responded as I had expected, that lunge would have allowed the point of my sword to graze his right shoulder, and disable him enough for me to make my escape.

He had lifted my blade, but not deflected it. To my horror its point went deep into his throat. Blood spurted over bronze.

I withdrew and stepped back as he collapsed.

The other two were too busy with Keeshah to notice. Their backs were toward me. With two quick swings, I slapped each of them alongside the head with the flat of my blade. I didn't want to kill them.

Hell, I hadn't wanted to kill the first man.

I gathered up the pack I had dropped, and leaped onto Keeshah's back. I slung the rope between the bags across Keeshah's back, then crouched into position, lifting the heavy rope until it rested on my cloth-protected thighs rather than Keeshah's skin.

Over the wall, Keeshah.

But he had anticipated me, and was already running

103

toward the nearest wall, which joined Thanasset's yard to his neighbor's. An eight-foot wall is nothing to a six-foot cat, even with a man on his back. I felt his muscles bunch and release like steel springs, and we were on the roofs of the neighbor's outbuildings.

There were people out in the yard—they must have heard the racket Keeshah and the swords had been making. When they saw Keeshah jump down from their bath-house, they ran off in every direction. Keeshah ran through the yard, carefully avoiding trampling the infant who had been forgotten, and jumped the far fence. The next fence brought us to the corner, and now we were out in the street.

To the city gates, I urged him. *Don't stop for anything.*

We made quite a sight, the huge cat and his clinging rider, streaking through streets that had never before been ridden. It was almost dusk, and there were people out for strolls, walking through the warm early evening. We startled some of them, frightened others. Some laughed and pointed at us. Some watched us pass in silence, their eyes shining, and I knew they wanted to be where I was.

The gates of the city stood open as they had when we had entered that morning. It was incredible to me that only a day had passed since then!

The men at the gates had not been expecting us. Four of them, wearing gray baldrics like Zaddorn's, were standing close together, talking. Their attention seemed to be directed out the gate toward a group of farmers bringing in vleks laden with vegetables for the early morning market.

On the street, Keeshah's padded paws made hardly any sound, and while some people stared and others jumped back, nobody screamed. I was past the guards and out the gate before any one of them could get a sword out.

Keeshah went off the road to get around the small group of laden vleks. They became skittish, but their masters managed to keep them under control, for which I was thankful. No need in making matters any worse by dumping innocent folk's food all over the highway. We kept on going.

Soon there was no one on the road to be seen, and Raithskar was behind us, flowing slowly away as night descended around us.

I laughed aloud and hugged Keeshah's neck. I got a warm answering flow from his mind. We were safe for the moment, and together. I wanted to put plenty of distance between us and the city, and I knew Keeshah could do it.

After a mile or so, however, the flush of our success in escaping began to seep out of me, and a feeling of desolation began to creep in. I had just begun to realize that I could not return to Raithskar now unless I were willing to sacrifice my freedom, even my life, in order to prove Thanasset's innocence.

Was I willing? Yes. I knew that I would have to return. That commitment had been made a long time ago. Whatever it cost, I would prove the old man's honor.

If I had the time.

That's what bothered me—I was a fugitive now, in unfamiliar territory. If I didn't make all the right moves, I stood a good chance of being captured and prevented from finding the proof I needed. Keeshah was fast, but there could be delays.

And I had no doubt at all that I would be followed. As soon and as fast as possible. These people were not *homo sapiens*, strictly speaking, but they were utterly human. And throughout the human history of my world, no police force had ever given up on a cop-killer.

14

We stopped to rest a couple of hours before sunrise. I didn't wonder, this time, how I knew the night was almost over. Thanasset had explained that Gandalarans had a highly efficient internal warning system. It seemed logical that Markasset's internal awareness extended to his body's diurnal rhythms, so that I simply knew what time it was within fifteen minutes or so. They must use sandglasses or waterclocks in the cities for accurate timing, but they wouldn't be worth a damn on sha'um-back. So every Gandalaran in the desert conveniently carried a reasonably accurate clock inside himself.

I slept a little, stretched beside Keeshah on the salty desert floor. But I woke just before dawn, and I was facing east when the sun came up.

I have witnessed sunrises in most of the deserts of the southwestern U.S. I had never seen anything so beautiful.

I never saw the sun. The soft, mist-like cloud layer overhead began to glow with rich color. The same dramatic colors of any sunrise in Ricardo's world, but not as sharply defined. Red, orange, bright yellows in a random, shifting pattern, with no distinct break between them. The sky was filled with a gorgeous color show. The clouds seemed to absorb the colors from the east and diffuse them across all of Gandalara. The floor of the desert echoed the changing pattern of the sky, and I laughed to see Keeshah's face ripple from red to yellow to violet.

It was like watching a rainbow before it had been called to attention.

All too soon the sun tired of its coloring game and got on with its business of creating day out of night. As the desert grew swiftly lighter, I pulled out the map Thanasset had given me. I spread it out on the sand very carefully.

And saw absolute gibberish.

The big piece of glith-skin parchment was covered with a maze of red lines and black lines. Some were big scrawls of curves and wiggles, others were peculiar little angular squiggles that looked like a cartoonist's lighting bolts tied in a sailor's knots.

If that is a map, I thought, *I am Chesty Puller's maiden aunt.*

I turned the sheet of parchment slowly around, trying to figure out which way was up. The one obvious line on the thing was a firm black border line which ran along one side and off two sides of the square parchment. Obviously this was a map of only a portion of Gandalara, which could be matched up to others in the set for an overall map.

I looked around me and tried to orient the map. *That huge wall behind Raithkar should logically be this bold border line.* I turned to face Raithskar. *And there are mountains on my right. Yes, these markings might represent mountains . . .*

Suddenly a little group of the angular figures near the bold border line jumped out at me. There were only six of them in a row, but they read:

Raithskar.

After that, the whole thing suddenly made sense. It had simply taken a little time for Markasset's memory to come up with the reading skills necessary to understand the Gandalaran conventions of mapmaking. They weren't all that different, it seemed. North was the top of the map—once Markasset translated the squiggle-code for me, the rest was easy.

106

The bold line of the Great Wall ran irregularly on either side of Raithskar. It flowed to the southwest until it ran out of map. On the other side, it moved directly east until it made a sharp curve to southeast by south, then it disappeared off the edge.

Beyond the Great Wall, no landmarks were shown. The Skarkel Falls, which gave the city its water, were shown—but no source was even postulated, much less named.

There was indeed a range of mountains shown on the map. They were east of me and ran south by west from the Great Wall, making a sort of peninsula of high ground—the Mokardahl Mountains. At their southern tip was nestled a city marked by symbols:

Thagorn.

I studied the map carefully. Distances were marked in "days"—which meant the distance a man could walk in a day without killing himself. I figured that a sha'um could cover roughly three times that distance in a day—probably more.

I recalculated all the distances into sha'um-days. If we tried to go directly across the desert to the southern tip of the mountain range, it would take us three days. The Refreshment House of Yafnaar lay directly along that route, but I thought it best not to stop there. Zaddorn would be likely to check there, and, though he'd be several days behind, he'd then have definite proof of which direction I had taken.

No, we'd have to go straight across, if we chose the desert. And we'd be three days with too little water and—more importantly—no food for Keeshah.

I decided our best bet was to head southeast by east to the little town of Alkhum shown at the foot of the nearby mountains. Then we could travel almost due south past another little town called Omergol, to the southern tip of the Mokardahls. From there it was a straight shot—or so it looked on the map—east to Thagorn. It would be twice as long a trip as crossing the desert, and more dangerous in terms of being spotted along the way—but we'd have food and water, and our full strength when we reached Thagorn.

Sound all right to you, Keeshah? I asked. Keeshah had been right behind me, looking over my shoulder at the map. I didn't believe that he could read the map, but I was sure he had been following my thoughts. He dropped his chin to my shoulder and I pulled gently at one of his ears, scratching behind it.

Good, came his approving thought, but for a moment I wondered if he meant my plan or my scratching. He followed

107

it immediately with an image and a sense of appetite. It seemed there was game in that area that Keeshah remembered fondly. There was no name identified with the singularly unattractive animal—that sort of thing doesn't occur to a sha'um. I got only the briefest glimpse of it in Keeshah's mind, and it was more than I wanted. It was built something like a wild boar, but it had long, curving tusks and it looked trimmer and faster than any I had ever seen photographed. As a matter of fact, it looked mean and rather tough, but Keeshah remembered its taste with keen anticipation.

If that's what you want—at least I won't have to carry a side of glith slung nonchalantly over my shoulder when I leave town.

I mounted Keeshah and we set off for Alkhum.

I was relieved to know that Keeshah could find food easily for himself. Once I had formed the plan of following the mountains southward, I had immediately rejected the idea of riding or leading Keeshah into town, for the same reason I would not have stopped at Yafnaar if we had decided to cross the desert.

The people of a town might or might not remember a man traveling on foot. They would remember a man who left town with a huge hunk of meat slung over one shoulder—but they might not think it worth mentioning when Zaddorn came to call.

But a man on a sha'um would be a topic of conversation for days, and when Zaddorn asked about me—I could almost hear it:

"You see a stranger on a big golden palomino tiger?"

"Shore did, Sheriff. He went thataway."

So, when we reached the general area of Alkhum two days later, I cautioned Keeshah again about being seen.

Do not worry. What I do not eat, I will bury.

Like all the big carnivores in my world, Keeshah needed a regular supply of food. He seemed to have an internal system for processing food energy as efficiently as water usage. Nothing else could account for his tremendous endurance and the relative infrequency of his need for fuel. But his storage tank, as it were, had to be maintained at a minimum level and topped off now and then.

Right now, he was hungry. He had been looking forward to the imminent hunt with single-minded anticipation. And I had shared his thoughts until I was about ready to eat one of those evil-looking beasts myself.

I untied the rope that laced the packs together, stood up on

108

Keeshah's back and hung one of the packs and my sword and baldric over the gnarled branch of a tree. Then I jumped down, told him that I would meet him back • here, and watched him disappear into the forest. I turned eastward to where I figured the town should be, and started walking.

It was an odd sort of forest. It had grown up around us as we had climbed into the low hills that sloped toward the steep, craggy mountains still some distance away. There had been grass—real green grass, not the grayish, fluffy stuff that grew on the desert floor—and then scattered bushes, and finally this wooded area.

There were no tall trees such as Ricardo remembered from the California mountains. The tallest were no higher than three yards, and more than once in the last few hours, I had been forced to press myself to Keeshah's back to keep my head lower than the highest branches. To someone who might be standing on a hill, the head of a man jogging along at treetop level would be a remarkable sight indeed.

There were a variety of trees in the forest, but their one common feature solved a minor puzzle for me. I had thought, from the intricate parquetry in Thanasset's house, that there was a wood shortage. The forest proved me wrong—it was simply that there was no *straight* wood to be had, or at least it was rare in this part of Gandalara. I wondered, in passing, where Keeshah's scratching post had come from.

One of the common trees—Markasset's memory obligingly supplied the name *dakathrenil*—had a trunk which would have been twice as long if straight. But it twisted and curved, zigzagged upward in a ragged spiral until it was as tall as a Gandalaran. Then the trunk disappeared into a slightly mounded webwork of branches, forming a wide, flat umbrella. Its leaves were long and thin, and a rich deep green in color. They grew in clusters directly from the branches, spaced so that not a leaf missed the sunlight, and very little sunlight got past the leaves.

So dense was the shade cast by these trees that the ground underneath them was clear of any growth except the hardy grass which seemed to carpet these hills. Several times Keeshah and I had traveled almost in darkness through groves of dakathrenil trees. Their spacing had been so exact that I thought of them as orchards—as indeed they were. The tree in which I had concealed my pack and sword had been in full bloom with dozens of tiny blue flowers. The air around me was thick with their fragrance—a sweet pungence that re-

109

minded me of one of the fruits I had eaten at Thanasset's table.

I reflected, as I walked along, that I might be tramping through someone's apple orchard, and I wondered how the owner would feel about that. I decided not to let it worry me—I had plenty of other things to think about.

I wasn't sure what I would find in Alkhum—but I hadn't expected *not to find* Alkhum. The map had shown it located at the mouth of a pass—the Khumber Pass—and I had somehow expected a busy trade city at least the size of Raithskar.

When I finally came out into a clear area and saw the brick wall of Alkhum, I saw the reason why it had been hard to find. The "pass" rose behind the city in great craggy steps. It was clearly not easily negotiable for a man, much less a caravan. So I walked through the unguarded city gates into a sleepy farm town. It might still have been a trade center, I thought to myself, if Yafnaar didn't provide a comfortable stopover along the shorter desert route.

Obviously there was some foot traffic through the city, because no one I saw on the streets paid any attention to me. They lounged in front of stores or pursued their normal work. Just inside the gate, a man was molding the cupped tiles that seemed to be a universal roofing material. Women with bundles walked along, chatting together, and at the far end of what seemed to be the only street in the town, vlek-drawn carts were being unloaded. Baskets of greenish-brown grain were handed into a doorway by a line of men. Past them at another door, carts were being loaded with bulky sacks—a grain mill.

No one I saw was wearing a sword, and I congratulated myself on having had the foresight to leave mine behind.

I didn't need a sign to lead me to an eatery—a mouth-watering aroma was coming from an open door on my left. I went directly there, and stepped out of the bright sun into a cool dimness.

"Welcome to the house of Nasin, traveler," a raspy, friendly voice greeted me. My eyes adjusted quickly, and I saw the man who had spoken as he came out from behind a square window at the back of the room. He was the oldest Gandalaran I had yet seen. The top of his head was entirely free of fur, and the skin had darkened over his skull and clear down around his eyes until he looked as though he were wearing a close-fitting black mask and hood. He smiled at me broadly and without embarrassment, even though most of his front teeth were missing. The skin had wrinkled and shrunken in around his mouth, so that his one gleaming tusk, still solid and straight, hung outside his lower lip when he talked.

"A thirsty day out, sir. A glass of faen?"

"Yes, please. And some food."

"Right away." He went back through a doorway and appeared in the window again. I was just wondering if I should sit down at one of the small tables when he called out, "Here you are, sir." I walked over to the window. Its sill served as a counter—there was a rough clay bowl of delicious smelling stew and a glass of faen. I reached for my pouch, but the quick old man shook his head. "No, sir, thank you. You can pay me when you're through—you might be hungrier than you think!"

"If this stew tastes as good as it smells, you may be right!" I told him.

"The best to be had anywhere, sir! I make it myself."

I threw my pack under the nearest table and sat down with the dishes. The stew was indeed delicious, and both the glass and the bowl were refilled before I was finally satisfied.

"It's a pleasure to see a man appreciate good cooking!" rasped the old man. "Tell you what, I'll only charge you for the first bowl—that will be a zak six."

I opened my pouch and went cold all over. I had forgotten that Illia had bought a side of glith for me—she had used almost all of the smaller coins. Feeling like a man offering a hundred dollar bill to pay for a candy bar, I pulled out one of the large gold pieces. I said, "I'm afraid this is all I have."

The old man stared at me in surprise, tried twice before he was able to speak. "I couldn't change that for you, sir. Even if I charged you for the second bowl. Have you nothing smaller?"

"Only these," I said, and showed him the three quarter-zak coins Illia had left. The old man shook his head.

"That'd be only half your debt, sir. I hate to put you to the trouble, sir, but Lorbin the goldsmith has his shop just across the street. He'll be able to change that gold piece for you—at a fee, of course." The squinty gaze dropped quickly to my pack, where it still lay on the floor, and then back to my face. "You go on over, sir. I trust you to bring me my due."

"You're very kind," I said, and went out the door—leaving my pack.

Lorbin was a short Gandalaran, not fat but round-faced and sleek. His voice was smooth and rich.

111

"Ah, young man!" he said the moment I walked through his doorway. "How may I help you?"

"The proprietor at Nasin's can't change a twenty-dozak piece," I told him. "He said you could help me."

"Certainly, certainly." I handed it to him and he looked it over, measured it with a pair of calipers, and weighed it on a small balance. "Raithskar coinage—workmanship second only to Eddarta. Are you from Raithskar, young man?" He began counting out bronze and silver coins, still talking. "We get a little news here, and I've heard rumors of some trouble back there."

"I'm sorry I can't help you," I managed to get out, then went on with what glibness I could muster. "I am from Raithskar originally, but I've been away for a few years."

"Ah, yes, restless youth. Wanted to see more of the world."

"Yes—but I always knew I'd come home someday. That's why I've saved this coin through the years—for the trip home."

"Well," he said, stacking the coins on the counter between us and counting them again, this time toward me, "don't be troubled by what I said. Rumors are only rumors, after all.

"And Raithskar's a nice city. I've been there more than once—I'd be tempted to set up business there, myself, if the folk here didn't need me so much. But that's life, eh? Find yourself a niche and make the most of it."

He pushed the neatly stacked coins across the counter to me. "There you are, young man. Eighteen dozaks in silver, twenty-four zaks in bronze." I glanced over them. They were stacked by sixes, and easily countable.

"Correct," I confirmed. "And your commission?"

He carefully lifted two bronze coins off the top of a stack. "Quite right. Less two zaks for my trouble."

Less than one percent commission for money-changing? "A fair price. A pleasure to do business with you, sir."

"A smooth trip home to you, young man," he said, smiling. "And a happy homecoming."

I thanked him and went back to Nasin's to pay my bill and collect my pack. I insisted, because of the delay, on paying him for the second bowl of stew. And, since he knew I wasn't on my last dozak, he accepted, and wished me a happy day. I filled my waterskins at the well, and headed out of the village.

That's a great way to travel incognito, I said to myself. *Play the classic rich bum. Get a man to offer you sympathy and undercharge you, then flash a wad that would choke a vlek.*

Zaddorn knows I have those gold pieces. And Lorbin will remember me. He believed that homecoming story—but will Zaddorn? Sure he will—when Keeshah rides a vlek.

I had calmed down a little by the time I reached the tree where my other pack and my sword were hidden. Even if I had thought about those gold pieces earlier, what could I have done about it? There had been no time for moneychanging in Thanasset's house, and no opportunity between there and here.

Keeshah was waiting for me, radiating contentment. He sent me a welcoming thought and indicated that he was ready to move on again.

Not right away, Keeshah. Let's rest a little, and let our lunch settle.

Again I felt a sense of surprise from him. *Thank you.*

He allowed me to stand on his back to retrieve my things from the treebranch, then he wandered off into a shaded area, curled up and was instantly asleep. The way a cat sleeps, with one ear open.

I pulled the map out of the pack and studied it. If I were Zaddorn, what would I do? What would I think of Markasset? Where would I think he would go?

I thought back to the fight in Thanasset's garden. The cop I had ended up killing had said: *"The Chief says he has it on him."*

That seemed to mean that Zaddorn believed I had stolen the Ra'ira and was still carrying it around. Did he think I had taken it with me on the caravan and then brought it back to Raithskar, only to take it out of the city again? Going where? *Chizan*, and eventually Eddarta?

Neither city was on the map, but Markasset's memory told me that *Chizan* was ten days east southeast of Thagorn, and Eddarta some thirty-five days beyond *Chizan*, east and south of it.

No, Zaddorn was no fool and he knew Markasset wasn't one, either. But he might believe—*that's it!* I thought. *He must think that I stole the gem and hid it in Thanasset's house, then left on the caravan to make him think it was already out of the city. He probably thinks I did betray the caravan to the Sharith—to cover my tracks. I went back to Raithskar expecting him to believe that the Ra'ira had been lost with the caravan, so that I could stay home without being suspected.*

And do what with the Ra'ira? Pay off Worfit? And what would he do with it?

What does it matter? I asked myself. *If you're writing a fairy tale, don't quibble over talking bears.*

Why I would be confident of not being suspected, I couldn't imagine. Zaddorn might reason that I expected the entire caravan to be wiped out, and the two escapees had ruined my plan, making it necessary for me to grab the jewel and hightail it out of town.

But where? I thought irritably. *Damn it, where does he think I'm going? Where will he go in order to catch up to me in the shortest time possible? He knows I'm days ahead of him already, riding Keeshah. What the hell is the man thinking right now?*

He could have decided that I would head west—the map didn't show me what lay in that direction, and Markasset's memory was not cooperating. But I couldn't count on that. I'd have to assume he figured I would head southeast. And whether I was going to Eddarta to turn the Ra'ira over to some Lord who had paid me to steal it or whether—and this was a new possibility—I was going to collect it from the Sharith, whom I had paid to steal it—whichever he thought it was, I would have to go through Thagorn.

So Zaddorn is heading for Thagorn, too, I decided. *And he'd take the quickest route with the best chance of finding definite traces of my passing, knowing that he can't hope to catch up with me until I stop somewhere—maybe in Thagorn itself.*

I drew my finger across the map from Raithskar to the Refreshment House at Yafnaar. *He'd go there first, looking for me. If he doesn't find news of me there—which he won't—would he go directly to Thagorn?*

No, I decided. *Because he still wouldn't have any proof that I'm heading for Thagorn. He'll know that if I don't stop at Yafnaar I'll follow the mountains down to Thagorn. But he won't bother to backtrack to Alkhum—he'll cut across the Omergol and look for me there.*

I did some quick calculation. Ten days for Zaddorn to travel from Raithskar to Omergol. I had been two days on the road, so that made it . . . eight days from now, Zaddorn would reach Omergol.

Keeshah, I called. He was instantly on his feet and trotting toward me.

I replaced the maps and retied the packs, mounted Kee-

114

shah, and slung the packs across my lap as I had done before. As we started southward, I was thinking:

Zaddorn will be in Omergol eight days from now, and I'll be there tomorrow. That gives me a clear seven-day lead on him.

So why am I still worried?

The answer to that was readily summed up in one word. *Zaddorn.*

15

I might have made better time if I'd been able to use the road that ran along within a few miles of the towering cliffs, but I didn't dare. The next town of any size was Omergol, a good day's ride on sha'um back, and four days by shank's mare. Any traffic I met would remember me. There were disadvantages to being partners with a sha'um, though the advantages outweighed them by twenty to one.

Like the ancient Roman roads of Europe, the highways of Gandalara don't need repair very often, and when they do, the job is fairly easy and the materials close at hand. They're built of rock salt, which is just about as hard as marble. In some places, I found out later, the road is simply a smoothed ribbon over a natural bed of rock salt. In a place where it never rains—*never*—there was no need for the ancient road-builders to take drainage or seepage into account.

There should be an old saying here, "There's only two kinds of weather in Gandalara—hot and dry." There should be, but there isn't. There is no word for "weather" in the language. The concept doesn't even exist, because the condition doesn't exist. Climate, yes; weather, no.

Does a fish ever talk about humidity?

The most widely-traveled roads are those that run near the Great Wall, where the water is. So when a rut or a pothole develops in the surface of a road, the locals get a few buckets of sludge from the edge of the nearest salt swamp and fill the defect carefully. When it dries, you have rock salt again.

Since it is only the roads and the caravans that keep trade going, and since only the roads will take wheeled vehicles, the local folk do a pretty conscientious job of keeping them in repair.

Near dusk of the second day the sounds on the highway grew more frequent, and the cheerful voices of men greeting friends blended with the inane bawling of the vleks. I rode low on Keeshah's back, and we moved carefully through the trees, watchful for the occasional cottage. We had reached the outskirts of Omergol, and it was obviously far different from the sleepy farm village of Alkhum. From the amount of traffic flowing from it, I decided it must be a good-sized city, and I was overcome with a need for a hot meal and a cold beer and a night's rest on something softer than the salty earth. Surely one more traveler would not be noticed.

I dropped my saddlebags over a nearby limb then slipped off Keeshah's back.

Stay out of sight, I warned him, and received an answering flow of scorn—did I think he was stupid? I laughed and scratched his forehead in apology.

Back when? he asked.

Tomorrow. Dawn—no, I hesitated. I wasn't sure, after all, how far away the city was and how long it would take me to get back here on foot. And Milda's pack of supplies was running low—it might be a good idea to wait until the shops opened and replenish my food rations before I left Omergol.

Tomorrow noon, I decided.

Here?

Yes. Feed well.

I watched his tawny form move silently through the trees away from the road. Then I set out on foot, still following the road, but some distance from it.

That is, I thought I was moving parallel to the road—until I almost stepped right out on it. I caught myself in time and made sure I was screened from the flow of traffic while I took some time to think.

This was a wide and busy highway, with traffic moving at a steady pace going both ways. To my left—toward the city, which was hidden from me by the trees—groups of men moved on foot, laughing and talking. They were dressed in the same kind of coordinated outfits I had seen in Markasset's closet—not as rich, perhaps, but obviously these were young men all set for a night on the town. Carts traveled in that direction, too, mostly farm carts laden with produce, and men dressed in simple clothing who looked as eager for the city as their better dressed counterparts. But, as I watched, a

116

dusty caravan groaned and waddled by, weighed down with cargo well-wrapped against the dryness of the desert. I thought I recognized in the colored cloth covering the carts one of the merchant banners I had seen in Raithskar.

That's what gave me the clue that solved the puzzle. When I had looked at Thanasset's map, I had judged that Zaddorn would cut straight across the desert from Yafnaar to Omergol. It hadn't occurred to me, then, that the same route might be used as an alternative to the hot, dry march across the desert from the south. The road I was watching was not the one I had been following, but one which intersected it at Omergol.

Any caravans which took this route must follow the Great Wall south—through Thagorn? Under the noses of a band of Riders who raided the desert travelers to collect their just "tribute"?

Tribute—of course. The Sharith probably charged these caravans a high toll for safe passage near Thagorn. And they would pay it—for the privilege of a more comfortable trip, for the safety of the remainder of their goods, and for the assurance of getting to their destinations alive. The Sharith probably regarded anyone who dared the desert route as traitors trying to evade their taxes.

But as I said, I had seen only one caravan going *toward* Omergol, and its role as a trade route stopover would not account for the high volume of traffic. The city itself must have some attraction of its own.

One thing more I learned, watching the traffic moving by. Nine out of ten men on that road going in either direction were wearing swords. And the rest wore long knives at their belts. Well, when in Rome . . .

I wore my sword. I stepped out from behind the bushes as though I had stepped behind them for personal reasons, and joined the parade. Nobody looked twice at me. I returned the courtesy.

But I did glance at the carts coming from Omergol. They were larger and sturdier than the farm carts, which were wood frames mounted on a single axle with wooden spoke-wheels rimmed with bronze. All the carts I had seen up until now had beds and sides of interlaced rope, which had seemed eminently reasonable to me, considering the time and expense it must have taken just to laminate the long bars of wood together which make up the cart frame, axle, wheels, and tongue.

The carts coming from Omergol were wagons, really, with

double axles and beds strengthened with long slats of wood interwoven with rope. It took four vleks to pull the ones I saw, and they were *working* at it. I was finding myself more and more curious about what Omergol produced that had to be hauled away with so much effort.

The road turned a slight corner, and I had my answer. Boy, did I have my answer.

I was looking into the intersection of the two roads, and past that through the gates of the city straight up its throat. I say "up" because Omergol climbed the foot of the Great Wall in huge terraces. I could distinguish five levels, and straight through the center of the city ran a continuation of the wide highway on which I was standing. Stairsteps as wide as the broad avenue climbed between each level.

To the right of the city, further up the slope, which was gentler here than behind Raithskar, I could see a fine mist which meant a river. I could hear it, too, and it was not falling, as the Skarkel did, but rushing down the side of the mountain.

To the left of the city was a huge pit, which had climbed the hillside at about the same rate of the city. A stream of men and women was flowing from that worksite back into Omergol.

And between the pit and the river gleamed the beautiful city of Omergol.

I was to learn later that Omergol was primarily a mining town, digging and polishing semi-precious stones from underground mines further up the slope of the Wall. But it had a second interest which had to be hauled away in double-axle wagons, and which it flaunted. Between its high-demand goods and its place along the trade route, Omergol was a rich city—and it wore its wealth proudly in a mantle of pale green marble.

It took all the control I had not to stop in the middle of the road and just stare at it. Every building, large and small, was faced with smooth, polished marble. The westering sun cast soft shadows into the streets and across the lower buildings. The murmur of the river in the background added to the whole effect. The city looked clean and cool; its wide avenue was an open invitation; and the crowds of people moving along that avenue amid peals of laughter made me conscious of being alone and very tired.

It was hard to keep my eyes on the road, but I tried. I didn't want to draw attention to myself for looking like a classic case of hickdom. But I needn't have worried—the city had the same effect on the people around me. In tacit agreement we all began to move a little faster.

As I watched the city draw nearer, I wondered about the odd color of the marble. I decided that there must be a vein of copper in those hills somewhere. Basic copper carbonate, in adequate quantity, might account for the soothing pastel green of Omergol's walls.

Had the first builders of this city planned to build it of the beautiful marble they found nearby? Or had some Gandalaran analog of Augustus Caesar found a wooden city and transformed it into this cool green elegance? As I passed through the gates, I felt again that sense of antiquity I had experienced when Thanasset and I had too briefly discussed the history of Gandalara.

The wall and gate had been recently refinished with a fresh surface of marble, but just inside, the buildings wore their original faces, which in some places were scarred and rounded by erosion. In rainless Gandalara, only the wind could have accomplished that slight damage. And, even throwing a dust-storm or two every year, my mind simply couldn't grasp the enormous amount of time these buildings had been standing.

To either side of the wide avenue just inside the city wall were open areas which served as the city's marketplace. Beyond them the stairs began their ascent, and the wide avenue was edged with open doorways. From them came the savory smell of cooking meat and fresh-baked bread, and a heady mixture of sound. The clatter of dishes and coins and the wooden rectangles used for gaming spilled from the doorways. Music from string and wood instruments, here in a light tune, there offering steady, stirring rhythms, and occasionally acting as accompaniment for voices. Other voices, men's and women's, were laughing and talking, in one case, at least, quarreling. In that one case I managed to dodge past the doorway just before two young Gandalarans, farmhands by their dress, and smelling strongly of faen, fell out into the avenue and rolled, struggling together, down the stairway. Several people followed them, shouting with excitement. Roughly half, I guessed, were trying to stop the fight. The other half were betting on their choice to win. From somewhere appeared another group of men with the efficient look of cops.

I had been trying to decide where to stop for the meal and rest I wanted so badly. At that point I decided to move on;

the neighborhood seemed a little rough, and the last thing I needed in Omergol was trouble.

So I mounted the rest of that flight of stairs, ignoring my clamoring belly. The second level of the city was less crowded and somewhat quieter. I considered going further up, but rejected the idea. The higher levels were undoubtedly the newest; the business districts would be more expensive and a common traveler would be more conspicuous there.

Just about then I saw it. It was on the other side of the street, its open door inviting me. And above the door, carved in bas relief out of the deepest green marble I had yet seen, was a large and somewhat stylized image of a sha'um. It was passing to the left, but its head was turned out toward the avenue, and it looked quite fierce. Under the carving, set in gold lettering, were Gandalaran characters: The Green Sha'um Inn. It looked like just the place I wanted.

I walked through the door into a narrow lobby. Stairs led upward on my right; a door opened on my left and I hesitated at the cheerful sound of voices and the unmistakable aroma of a bar. First things first, I told myself.

A man was seated at a desk just beyond the beginning of the stairway. As I started toward the desk, he stood up and bowed. "How may I help you sir?" he asked.

"I need a room for the night," I said.

"There is a room available," he replied. "The charge will be ten zaks."

I did some quick figuring and decided that it was a reasonable sum for a night's lodging. I fished a dozak piece out of my pouch and put it on the desk.

He didn't take the money immediately. Instead, he brought a huge register book from somewhere behind the desk, a thin brush, and an inkwell. My throat went suddenly dry as I realized that I had never written a Gandalaran word. But my fear passed as the man opened the register book, dipped the pen in ink, and looked up at me. "Your name and home, sir?" he asked, poising the brush above the page.

I was ready for that. I hoped my relief didn't show as I gave him the alias: "Lakad, Mildak's son, of *Chizan*."

He wrote. Then he took the coin, put it somewhere in the desk, and gave me two zaks change.

"I hope you enjoy your stay with us, sir." He handed me a key. "Room eight; up the stairs and to your right."

"Thank you. I-uh-sure need a bath." Did the rooms come with one? I suspected they didn't, but I didn't want to come right out and ask a stupid question.

120

"Ah. Koreddon's Bath-house is just around the corner to the east—almost behind us. You can't miss it. But they're closed for the dinner hour. Won't open for a while yet. Why not have a bite yourself, while you're waiting? Or a nice cool drink?" I looked at him and he knew he'd made a sale and smiled. "The Onyx Room," he nodded toward the doorway I had passed as I entered, "is always open. Welcome to Omergol."

"Thanks."

The Onyx Room ran the length of the building back from the street. To my right, as I entered, a bar of shiny black marble stretched along the far wall. Behind it were two burly bartenders, each serving half a dozen people of both sexes. I hadn't realized just how thirsty I was until I saw one of the bartenders serving up a mug of faen. He caught my look and grinned. He was missing a couple of lower teeth, a silent testament to the hazards of tending bar in a neighborhood that could turn rough. I guessed he must have served his apprenticeship on the first level of the city.

He poured a mug of faen and handed it across the bar to me. I took a deep drink. "Thanks. Can I get some dinner?"

"The best in town," he answered, and the smoothness of his voice was a surprise. "Make yourself comfortable and I'll inform the kitchen the dinner crowd is starting to arrive."

The room was fairly wide, with tables and chairs scattered across the marble-tiled floor. Against the wall opposite the bar was a regular pattern of tables and high-backed benches which created a booth-like effect. The tables had mosaic surfaces of green and black marble shavings, the visual effect very similar, though more dramatic, to the wood parquetry I had seen in Raithskar.

I drained the mug and handed it back for a refill before I walked over to a small booth and sat down. I was facing the rear of the large room, and I watched the bartender go to the far end of the bar, open a door and say something, then return to his work. He grinned at me again and said my dinner would be ready soon. I nodded and smiled my thanks, but I could feel my mind drifting. Whether it was fatigue or the faen I had downed so quickly, I couldn't tell, but I suddenly felt completely relaxed and free of worry.

For the first time since I had left Raithskar I began to wonder, in a comfortably detached sort of way, what I would do when I did reach the stronghold of the Sharith. I had little doubt that arriving unseen would be impossible. From all I had heard, they were too well-trained to forego an effective sentry system. And if it were somehow possible for me to slip through the "human" guards, how could I elude the sense of smell of their sha'um?

I floated in a sort of limbo, separate from the noise of the growing crowd in the bar, aware of my surroundings, but only peripherally, as if they did not concern me at all. I thanked the bartender, who personally brought my dinner, and I was not too detached to enjoy a well-cooked glith steak and a rich assortment of fruits.

At times I watched the people around me, and I was vaguely surprised to see that not everyone was enjoying the same meal I had been served. In fact, now that the crowd had arrived, there were waiters and waitresses taking orders for specific dishes. The bartender, obviously, had chosen my meal for me. I was somehow deeply flattered that he considered me a steak-and-potatoes type.

I had several more glasses of faen, and I took my time over the meal. The entirety of my experiences in Gandalara wandered through my thoughts. Yafnaar. Keeshah. Thanasset. Zaddorn. Illia. Keeshah. The Ra'ira. The Sharith. Kä. Milda. And always Keeshah.

People came and went around me; I overheard scraps of conversation and was comforted by their triviality. I was nursing what I had decided must be my final glass of faen when there was a general movement in the room. People standing up, chairs and benches scraping. At first I thought, *There must be a very specific dinner hour here, and it's over*. But that was disproved by the voice of my bartender friend, speaking in the doorway behind me.

"Good evening, gentlemen. Where will you be seated?"

But it was a small mystery and not worth my attention. I stared into my faen and thought about the greater mystery. What had happened to the Ra'ira?

The room had grown quiet, but I assumed that most of the people had left. I was thinking that I, too, should be going, when a deep voice sounded at my shoulder, crashing through my preoccupation.

"I think we will sit *here*," it said.

I looked up, then. Two men were standing next to me. They were dressed in a manner I had not yet seen in Gandalara. Their trousers and tunics were a finely-woven fabric exactly the color of the desert sands. Their boots and wide-brimmed hats were a darker tan, and tied around their

122

waists were long sashes of a pale yellow muslin. They wore baldrics, swords, and an arrogant manner.

To one side of them stood the bartender, looking at me, his expression one I could not read.

16

I blinked up at them, trying to will away the fog. I was bewildered by the fact that the room hadn't cleared, after all. It was still full, but everyone was standing up, away from their tables. Everyone except me.

As I struggled to grasp the significance of that fact, the newcomers glared at me. One of them put a hand to his chin and slid a wooden bead down a slim string. Then he thumbed his hat back from his forehead and it slid off to hang from his shoulders, held around his neck by the string. It was a curious hat, stiff-brimmed with a rounded top.

If it were red instead of tan, I thought crazily, *that hat would do a nineteenth-century cardinal proud.*

"Well?" the stranger asked.

"Well?" I repeated, feeling as though I had just awakened. I was confused. I was beginning to be frightened.

"Stand up, you son of a flea!" he yelled. Both of them took a step backward, and they drew their swords.

Suddenly everything seemed crystal clear to me.

Those are uniforms! They must be local cops. How the hell did Zaddorn get word here so fast?

The effects of the faen and the calmness of my brief reverie faded away from me. I was back in focus, sharply alert, and there was one driving thought uppermost in my mind.

I can't let them take me now—not when I've come this far. Thanasset's future depends on my getting to Thagorn and finding the truth.

I've already killed a cop. They can't hang me twice . . . and I can't go back to Raithskar without some answers.

The glass of faen was in my right hand, still half full. I tossed it into the face of the nearest man—the one who was still wearing his hat. At the same time, I stood up and launched my empty dinner plate at the other one. He ducked.

123

I had knocked over my bench and the one behind it. I kicked them away from me, and drew my sword.

The bartender moved then. He went behind the bar and with steady, practiced movements, began pulling breakables down from the shelves.

Some of the customers left hurriedly out of whichever door was nearest. Most of them just pressed back away from the three of us, me and the two hats. They looked on with great interest.

I decided I had misjudged the bartender. He needn't have worked the lower level of the city to have earned those broken teeth.

As the two uniformed men squared against me, my perception shifted the same way it had done when Milda had come into my room the first time I saw her. In one timeless instant, it was as though the film of life had stopped and I was looking at a single frame frozen on the screen.

The title of the film should have been *Tarzan on the Planet of the Apes*.

I was faced by a couple of mad bull apes clad in comic khaki uniforms. The one on my left, who had pushed his hat back, had a snarl on his face that revealed a snaggled right tusk that somehow looked more dangerous than the normal one.

The one on my right had a neat scar that ran down his right cheek from the inner corner of his eye to a point about an inch from the corner of his mouth. You might have called what he was doing a smile—if you were feeling generous.

The film started moving again.

Snaggletooth came in with an overhand cut that was meant to cleave me from guggle to zatch. Scarface came in with an underhand thrust to my belly. These two boys knew how to work together.

I brought my own sword up from my left in a backhand slash that slammed Snaggletooth's sword aside and brought its edge dangerously close to his partner's nose. Instinctively, Scarface leaped backward, and his thrust missed me by inches.

As Scarface's sword arced upward without meeting any resistance, I reversed my own slash and slammed my blade against his. The weapon spun free of his hand and looped to my left, spinning. It clanged point-down on a tabletop, fell over, and skittered off the edge.

That marble surface can't have been any good for the

point of that bronze sword, I was thinking. *In fact, I hope he'd have trouble roasting a marshmallow with it now.*

Snaggletooth recovered from the deflection of his overhand chop and moved in to protect the disarmed Scarface. For a few seconds it was cut, parry, thrust, and parry while Scarface ducked around behind his partner and snatched up his sword.

I was beginning to tire, and I knew that I couldn't handle both of them for long; I had to put one of them out of commission, and fast.

I picked on Snaggletooth because he was closer, and because he was doing his very best to slice off whatever of my body he could get at. I backed him a little, waited for an opening, and aimed a thrust at his midsection. As he was recovering from that, I whipped the sword up in a backhand slash at his head. His blade came up in time to deflect mine a little. My wrist turned—instead of the cutting edge, the flat of my blade slammed against Snaggletooth's temple.

He dropped his sword and crumpled to the floor.

I whirled to find Scarface aiming a low, shallow slash at my legs. I jumped the swinging sword and chopped down with my sword, drawing blood from a gash on his forearm.

He stepped back toward his partner, watching me. Snaggletooth was rousing; he rolled and started to get up from the floor. Scarface misjudged the distance, collided with his partner, and fell over him, knocking Snaggletooth back to the floor.

I suppose I could have killed both of them right there, but it didn't occur to me. Ricardo had done his share of scrapping, but always in self-defense. So I retreated down the room, moving backward to keep both of them in sight while I caught my breath.

I glanced behind me; the kitchen door at the end of the bar was blocked by spectators. The two sand-uniformed men were between me and the front door, and they were recovering fast. Snaggletooth seemed groggy still, and Scarface had shifted his sword from his bleeding right arm into his left hand. But they were getting to their feet and they looked, if possible, even less friendly than before.

I was about to make up my mind to try a surprise dash between them when the front door was blocked.

An angry sha'um squeezed through the man-sized door and filled up that end of the room. He padded toward us, and another one came in after him. They knocked aside tables and ranged themselves on either side of the uniformed men.

Then, almost in unison, they let out snarling roars and started across the littered floor for me.

I suddenly felt sorry for the men who had faced Keeshah in Thanasset's garden.

Nobody was more surprised than I was when they stopped. The men walked forward and stood beside their cats, glancing from them to me and back again.

They sheathed their swords.

"We have other business, stranger," said Scarface.

"But we will see you again," said Snaggletooth. "Next time save yourself some trouble—show the proper respect."

The big cats got themselves turned around and padded softly back out the front door. One of them looked back at me one last time. It had eyes the color of gold, and they shone with hatred. It growled softly—*That's a promise if I ever heard one*—then went on out.

Before the men could follow their sha'um, the bartender moved his bulk to block the doorway.

"What about the damage to my place?" he asked.

Scarface jerked his hat in my direction.

He never lost his hat! I noticed. *Shades of Roy Rogers!*

"He started it," he said, and now he was holding his right forearm with his left hand, applying pressure to stop the bleeding. The right leg of his trousers was decorated with vertical red streaks. "Let him pay."

"He's a stranger here," defended the bartender. "And he didn't draw the first blade." He smiled. "Though he did draw the first blood."

Scarface would have backhanded him for that, but Snaggletooth grabbed his shoulder and squeezed. Then he opened his pouch and drew out some coins. "This cover it?" he asked, and dropped them into the bartender's hand.

The bartender hefted the coins thoughtfully, then stepped aside. "That's fine. Come again anytime."

The two men glared at him and walked out. There was a heartbeat or two of stunned silence, then the crowd descended on me in a rush of noise. I was backslapped and congratulated and bought more faen than I could have drunk. I caught fragments of conversation:

"Never saw anyone better with a sword."

"Standing up to them alone. Imagine! *And* their sha'um. That takes real guts."

"Stupid, if you ask me."

I agree with you, buddy. I just wish I'd had a choice.

126

"Maybe they'll learn they can't push everybody around, the arrogant . . ."

"They'll be back, and he'll be gone. What then? I'll tell you what," the voice rose in pitch, "they'll take it out on us, that's what."

"Worth it, I say, just to see them taken down a notch or two . . ."

In the end—and it didn't take very long—they all wandered away to spread the legend I had fumbled into being. All at once I was almost alone with the bartender.

I looked around the wrecked room and said, "I'm sorry for all this."

"Don't be," he grinned his gap-toothed grin. "You've made me famous."

Yeah. Great way to travel incognito. I sure as hell hope I'm a good long way ahead of Zaddorn. He's not going to have any trouble at all following this trail.

I reached for my pouch. "How much do I owe you for that delicious dinner?"

He waved his hands. "Forget it. What they paid will cover your tab, too." He shook his head. "Beats me what happened. I'm not complaining, mind you. But that's the first time I ever saw any of the Sharith walk away from a fight."

"I can't help you," I told him. "I figured it was all over when those sha'um showed up."

The bartender looked at me sharply. "You didn't know they were Sharith? That explains a lot."

"The man at the desk said something about a bath-house," I changed the subject.

"Koreddon's?" I nodded. "Out the front door to your left. At the end of the stair level there is a side street that comes around back of the inn. Korredon's is the third door on the opposite side of the street."

"Thanks."

He grinned again, and I decided that, on him, the missing teeth had a certain charm. "My pleasure."

I found Koreddon's with no trouble, and I was delighted to learn that it had some of the qualities of a Japanese bath-house. It was run by a large family. The youngest boy brought me towels and soap and filled a marble-lined tub in a large, ornate room. As I soaked, I listened to some beautiful minor-toned strains produced by a mature woman I took to be Mrs. Koreddon from what looked like a rectangular harp.

And when I was clean, an almost toothless old man dried and massaged me with iron-strong hands.

So that's what the Sharith are like, I was thinking. *Not very appealing, are they? But not foolish, either. Their cats brought a message about something more important than an upstart stranger who didn't know enough to offer his seat to the Riders, and they listened.*

At least Zaddorn didn't send them. I still have some time. What happened today could cause trouble in Thagorn—but I'll face that when I come to it.

I feel as though I should be worrying about Zaddorn, I thought as I relaxed under the old man's soothing fingers. *But I'm too tired to do any more worrying.*

The old man had to wake me when he was finished. He solemnly accepted the extra zak I offered him when I settled the bill. From the boy I got a shy smile of thanks.

I went up to my room and settled down on a fluffy floor mat such as I had seen in my room at Raithskar. It had been a long, eventful, confusing day, and I was pooped. I reached out with my mind to touch Keeshah's—he was already asleep, but he responded to the contact with the mental equivalent of *Mmph?*

Nothing, Keeshah. Sleep well. I'll see you in the morning.

Mmph, he agreed.

Still lightly linked with Keeshah, I dropped gratefully into sleep.

17

I woke well after dawn, feeling refreshed and eager to see Keeshah again. I ate breakfast in the Onyx Room, and was surprised when the bartender from the night before brought out two plates of food and sat down to join me.

His name, as it turned out, was Grallen. Throughout the delicious breakfast, I was entertained by stories about the bar's regular clientele and the odd and sometimes funny confrontations between different types of people which occur in hotels.

When we were finished, he gathered up the dishes and seemed to be ready to leave.

"Going off duty now?" I asked him. "You work a long shift."

"Have to," he said. "It's my place."

For a moment I thought he was referring to class status of some sort, and I had to struggle to fit such a self-effacing statement into the frontal-assault personality I had already observed. Then it hit me.

"You mean you *own* the Onyx Room?"

"And the Green Sha'um Inn. And a good chunk of real estate on this side of the street." He grinned. "Surprised?"

"Yes," I said, laughing. "Sorry, but you sure *look* like a bartender."

"Not at all strange, since that's what I am. But I figured out early on that there's no profit in pouring someone else's faen." He settled back into his chair and devoted a few seconds of concentration to scraping and stacking the plates. "I don't usually make any noise about having a little money and some weight to throw around."

"Why are you telling me?" I asked him.

"Last night."

"You mean the two Riders?"

He nodded. "Let's just say I owe the Sharith a little aggravation, and I feel as though you've paid part of that debt. It's a service I won't soon forget."

He looked *into* me with dark, knowing eyes. I wondered how I could have missed seeing the wisdom behind the battered face.

"I know people, my friend. You're not just an ordinary stranger. I don't care what you're up to. I just want you to know that Grallen's behind you if you ever need help. And I thought you should know the value of the help I could offer.

"Breakfast," he finished briskly, "is on the house."

He stood up, and so did I.

"Thank you." It was all I could think of to say, and he understood that I wasn't just referring to the free breakfast.

Grallen carried the dishes back into the kitchen, and I walked out into the morning.

I made my way slowly down the central stairway toward the city gates. I stepped into several shops along the way to make small purchases: cured strips of meat, fresh and dried fruits, and a tasty loaf of coarse-grain bread that looked as though it would keep well. I also bought a few sweet bakery treats and I munched them happily as I walked out of Omergol.

Instead of retracing my steps exactly, I turned right as I left the city and walked north along the road which followed the foothills. The morning smelled fresh and new, and the people I passed greeted me with cheerful good humor. After last night's massage, my body felt loose and strong and ready for anything.

A suspicion nibbled at the back of my mind. *You shouldn't be feeling this good,* it warned me. I slapped it down and told it to shut up. *Feeling good feels wonderful for a change!*

When I had walked about as far north as I had traveled south the day before, I stepped off the road and headed west. I hadn't gone far when that annoying suspicion sat up and said *I told you so.*

I saw them at the same moment Keeshah's warning sprang into my mind.

Markasset. Sha'um. I am close. I come.

"Them" was Snaggletooth. Riding the mean-looking, golden-eyed sha'um. I heard a soft sound behind me. I didn't have to turn around to know that Scarface and the other sha'um were back there.

No, Keeshah, I ordered, and grappled with my own fear so that I could better control the cat. *Are you downwind? Do they know you're nearby?*

Yes. No. He sounded puzzled.

Snaggletooth slid off his sha'um's back and walked slowly toward me.

Keeshah, stay away unless I call. Please. If they see you, they'll know who I am. These guys could be my ticket into Thagorn—don't spoil it. Please stay hidden. I promise I'll call if I need help.

I felt Keeshah hesitate, wonder, grumble. He was primed for a fight; I sensed his conflict as he tried to obey my wishes above his own instincts.

Yes, he agreed at last, then added: *Don't like it.*

I didn't have time to thank him because Snaggletooth's bruised face was only inches away from mine. It was no more attractive from such a close view.

"We got a score to settle," he said. His tone told me that there would be no reprieve this time—the score *would* be settled.

I wasn't quite sure how these two men could help get me into Thagorn. The possibility had only occurred to me when they had shown up just now. But I had already settled on step one of the unknown plan: *Don't get yourself killed.*

"So now you're going to let your sha'um finish the job you couldn't do yourselves?" I asked. Snaggletooth's face turned dark.

It was an old trick, a challenge of honor by ridicule. Like

130

when an unarmed man challenges a man with a gun to a fist-fight. *Yeah*, I thought uncomfortably, *and the man with the gun laughs in the other guy's face and blows his head off*.

Either it worked in this case or they had never had any intention of letting their sha'um interfere. Because Snaggletooth waved his hand and the sha'um ahead of me moved back and lay down. I heard Scarface slip down from his cat's back, and that cat, too, move away. Scarface appeared at my right elbow. I took a step backward as they drew their swords. Scarface was using his left hand now; his right forearm was tightly wrapped with a length of linen.

I drew my sword. "Two against one?" I asked hopefully. But that honorable they weren't going to be.

"Same odds as last night," Scarface said. And they came at me in a double rush.

I ran through a short, wordless prayer to Markasset.

We were standing in a young grove of dakathrenil trees. They had grown taller than our heads, but their umbrellas of branches were still narrow and lacy enough to admit a lot of light.

I dodged to my left, evading Scarface's overhand slash and blocking Snaggletooth's thrust. Scarface turned and deftly shifted the momentum of his chop into a vicious two-handed swing at my midsection. I jumped backward and the edge of his sword whacked a good inch into a tree trunk on my left. Snaggletooth had anticipated the move. He grabbed the tree and swung around it to my left.

He very nearly skewered me. I saw him just in time, twisted to get my sword between us and deflect his aim; the edge of his blade dragged a long, stinging cut across my chest.

Markasset hurt, came Keeshah's raging thought. *I come now.*

No, not yet.

Please.

No. Stay downwind.

I could feel him seething, eager to join the fight. The fire I sensed in him seemed to flow into me until I felt stronger, quicker, more alert.

Snaggletooth roared at the sight of my blood and began to press me back. I needed all Markasset's skill and more to keep his bronze blade away from my skin.

Through the clanging of our swords, I heard the soft snicking sound of Scarface's blade being drawn out of the

131

treetrunk. I looked over Snaggletooth's shoulder; Scarface had disappeared.

I began to worry about where he was.

Snaggletooth leaped forward with a grin of triumph. Had I retreated, as he expected, I'd have been chopped in two by Scarface's sword. But I smelled him behind me and jumped, instead, to the right. Snaggletooth had to pull up short to keep from catching Scarface on the point of his sword.

They were beginning to stink of frustration, and I knew they would start taking chances. So I stayed close to the trunk of a tree, using it for a shield. The lowest branches were eye-ridge level, but I always knew exactly where they were. The other two weren't as lucky, and several times narrowly missed knocking themselves out.

Finally Scarface used his bandaged arm to swing around the treetrunk as the other one had done earlier. He aimed low, and he had a lot of momentum in his thrust.

I knocked the point of his sword into the ground and brought my knee up under his chin. He went down.

Snaggletooth was behind me. I jumped over Scarface and ran for another tree, Snaggletooth following me. From the sound of his heavy breathing, I judged the distance. I whipped around the tree to face him, leaped to catch the highest branch I could, and swung my weight on the springy tree, legs extended. Both feet connected with Snaggletooth's midriff.

He dropped his sword and doubled over, gasping for air. I landed on the ground, sheathed my sword, and walked up close to him. Ricardo delivered a sharp, satisfying right cross and Snaggletooth collapsed in a heap.

The two sha'um came up roaring, and I backed off. They didn't come after me, but stood guard over the unconscious men, now and then nuzzling and licking. I was reminded of Keeshah and me out in the desert.

Keeshah. I could feel him fading, and for the first time I realized what had happened.

You were with me, weren't you Keeshah? I could smell and hear better. You did help me fight this battle, after all, didn't you?

Tried, he answered. *Hurt?*

I looked down at the blood on my tunic, pulled it away to examine the cut. It was a bad place and might take a while to heal, but it wasn't deep. I was suffering more from the fading link with Keeshah, and I realized that his splendid fighting spirit had kept me going far past the point of my own

132

endurance. I felt let down and shaky now, and I leaned against the tree I had swung on, because I didn't trust my legs.

I'm all right, I told Keeshah. *That's a very special trick. You and Markasset must have made quite a fighting team.*

No.

What?

First time.

I didn't have a chance to wonder about that. Scarface and Snaggletooth were coming to.

Scarface's arms came up around the great wedge of his cat's head and held it, stroking and soothing the sha'um's concern for its master. Snaggletooth woke up choking and holding his gut; his cat lay down beside him, watching me with its golden eyes. Snaggletooth recovered enough to throw an arm up around the cat's neck. The sha'um stood up slowly, helping Snaggletooth first to sit, then to stand up.

Maybe these two wanted to kill me a few minutes ago, I was thinking. *But as Thanasset said to me in different words not too long ago, anybody a sha'um loves can't be all bad.*

I stood up straight and came out from under the tree. I was tense until I was sure neither one of them would reach for his sword.

Scarface moved to stand beside Snaggletooth. They touched their cats, who roared and complained, then quieted and sidled off unhappily.

If that means what I think it does . . .

It did. Snaggletooth worked his mouth, spat out a tooth, and spoke with a quiet dignity that I wouldn't have expected—but which somehow suited him.

"They won't hurt you now."

"I don't want your lives," I said, understanding and impressed by what he had meant. "I do want some information. First your names."

"I am Bareff," said Snaggletooth, "and he is Liden."

"Why did you quit so suddenly last night?"

They glanced at each other. Scarface—that is, Liden—answered.

"We thought you were one of us."

"Sharith?" I was beginning to see, but it wouldn't do to understand too easily. "What made you think so?"

"When our sha'um came in, they said you smelled of sha'um," explained Bareff.

I did, I thought. *But I bathed and had my clothes washed.*

133

And I haven't touched Keeshah yet this morning. I'll bet their cats are confused.

"Then why all this hassle today?" I asked them.

Liden spoke up. "We're supposed to be told where our agents are, so that this doesn't happen. We sent a message to Thagorn last night, and the answer arrived this morning."

Handy things, those maufa, I thought. *Fast, too.*

"The Lieutenant told us we didn't have a man in Omergol," said Bareff. "He said to bring you in just to see what was going on."

"Then you weren't supposed to kill me?" I asked them.

Scarface rubbed his swelling jaw. "Not that it wouldn't have been a pleasure."

I laughed then, and I caught a facial twitch from Snaggletooth that might have been the start of a smile. Or maybe not.

"Well, Bareff and Liden," I said finally, "I demand that you never raise sword to me again. But that's all I demand. Your lives are restored to you; the debt is settled."

They looked at each other, waiting for the catch. I let them stew for a few seconds, then I laid it on them:

"I need to go to Thagorn." I just let it hang there.

"Why?" asked Bareff. He bent over and picked up his sword; Liden walked back a few paces to retrieve his. They both looked at me thoughtfully before they sheathed the bronze blades.

"A personal matter," I said. "It's important to me that I have a chance to talk to—" What had they called their leader? "—the Lieutenant."

"The Lieutenant don't talk to groundwalkers," sneered Bareff.

"You'd have taken me back to Thagorn as a prisoner, right?"

Liden nodded, the scar showing white against the bruise flowing upward from his chin.

"If I had wanted it, I could have taken you back as my prisoners, right?"

Another nod. I didn't need their facial expressions to tell me that every member of the Sharith would have despised me for doing it. I, too, was a Rider. I'd have felt the same way.

"Neither way suits me. Your Lieutenant—he might talk to me if I came to him in the company of two of his best men." That wasn't flattery; I was sure they were exactly that. "Not as prisoner or master—but as a friend."

They chewed that over, staring at me. Finally Bareff said: "I've never met a groundwalker I'd call friend."

I felt a temptation to call in Keeshah, to prove my kinship to them and end this bickering. But Balgokh had said that Markasset was the only Rider not connected with the Sharith. They already knew that I wasn't one of their own. Seeing Keeshah would identify me positively—and I was still plagued by Markasset's lack of knowledge about the Sharith. They might welcome me as a long-lost brother. Or they might think me a traitor, a maverick, and refuse to have anything to do with me. I couldn't take the chance.

I felt Keeshah in the distance, getting ready to come in as he sensed my almost-invitation.

Sorry, Keeshah, I told him. *Stay where you are.*

To the two Sharith I said: "I'd say most groundwalkers feel the same about Riders. But I've had a taste of your honor—" I waved vaguely at the sha'um "—and of your swords."

I waited. Ricardo had been a military man for a large portion of his life. As a Marine, I'd had the occasion to convince a few wetfeet that mudsluggers were worth something, too. I was hoping I'd just taught the same kind of lesson to these two members of the Gandalaran cavalry.

"Well," said Liden. His sha'um came up to him, and he put out a hand to stroke the smooth brow. "Well, let's get moving, then."

I sighed.

It's not hail-fellow-well-met, I decided, *but it's a start.*

18

The two sha'um knelt beside their masters. Liden mounted; his cat soood up and ambled a short distance southward. Bareff swung his leg over the cat's broad back, then turned to me and grinned. There was a gap in his lower left jaw.

"Come on, groundwalker. See how it feels to Ride."

I just stood there, looking at the flattish, dark-furred head of the kneeling sha'um. It was watching me, hating me.

"Or have you changed your mind about going to Thagorn?"

Bareff's voice sounded dimly in my ears. I could spare no attention for him or for his cat. I was paralyzed by the icy rage that swept through me from Keeshah's mind.

YOU RIDE ONLY KEESHAH!

I could barely breathe through the onslaught of emotion. Keeshah's anger, yes—but my own reactions, as well. Love for the great cat. Awareness of our unique partnership, guilt over this necessary betrayal. I knew he was coming closer and was ready to attack Bareff's sha'um. I was desperate to stop him for Thanasset's sake. I was desperate to make him understand the need for this ugly deception, to win his forgiveness and cooperation.

Wordlessly, I reached out to him. I pushed against the violent waves of disappointment and pain and outrage and fury. I seemed to push *through* a barrier—and we were linked as we had been during the fight. Only now I shared his perceptions more completely. I could see the trees passing, feel the ground thudding by underneath me/him.

I pushed further, and another barrier yielded. I felt Keeshah slow and stop. I had touched the center of Keeshah.

It was not a union, precisely. We were each aware of ourselves and of the other as separate entities. But in that intense moment of contact, we shared something more than communication, something far more intimate and revealing. The best term I can find for it is *understanding*.

It lasted a bare instant, a closeness so pure and complete, a joy so sharp that we could endure it only briefly. Then we slipped back to the less complete, but more comfortable, communication pattern we had always shared.

You must go, Keeshah agreed reluctantly. *I will follow.*

No, I told him gently. *There are too many sha'um in Thagorn. You couldn't hide from all of them. Will you wait here for me? A few days?*

Yes.

Keeshah. I felt I had to say it. *This one I ride means nothing to me.*

I know. A rumble of impatience. *Go.*

Keeshah's presence left me abruptly, and I felt empty and vulnerable. But my sight cleared and I looked at Bareff, who was enjoying what he took to be my hesitation.

"*Have* you changed your mind, groundwalker?" he asked.

The cat's golden gaze had never left me.

"Your sha'um doesn't like me much," I told Bareff as I finally moved toward the pair.

136

He uttered a short, scornful laugh. "He hates your tusks, groundwalker. But he'll put up with you for my sake. Hurry up."

"My name is Rikardon," I told him as I swung a leg over the cat's back behind Bareff. I didn't have to pretend to be awkward. The sha'um surged upward before I had my balance, nearly dumping me off on my keister.

I grabbed at Bareff's tunic for support. The sudden movement jerked open the cut on my chest, and it started to sting and bleed again. I hauled myself into position and held on, suffering the laughter of the men without comment.

It was a nightmare ride.

Bareff occupied the space I would have taken on Keeshah, lying along the big cat's back and moving with its rhythm. But I was riding almost on the cat's hindquarters. Even though I lay forward as far as I could over Bareff's back, I was still almost sitting up.

My spine jarred with the cat's every step, and its pelvis ground painfully into my inner thighs. I couldn't help thinking that it wasn't very comfortable for the cat, either. So I pulled on Bareff's hips with my hands and used what pressure I could from my legs to ride more lightly.

It wasn't until we stopped for a light meal that I remembered the parcel of groceries I had dropped when the fight started. Not that they were needed; while I had been fighting Keeshah's jealousy and mounting Bareff's sha'um, Liden had retrieved their saddlebags from somewhere nearby, and they were well-stocked. I recognized some of the items from the same shops where I had bought my purchases—except that the Sharith had the finest the shops could offer, and I'd have bet my shirt they never paid a cent for any of it.

We traveled south for the rest of the day, stopping frequently to let me shift from one cat to the other. The sha'um hunted while we slept that night, and in the morning were fresh again. At midday we rounded the southernmost point of the Mokadahl range, marked by a sheer, looming cliff, then headed eastward.

We had been following the road from Omergol, through semi-cultivated areas dotted with grainfields and orchards. When we turned east, the ground began to rise and go wild. The curly-trunked trees I had seen so often on the way south had been cultivated and trained to their upright stance and umbrella of branches. Here the same trees covered the hillsides, twisting closer to the ground and all overgrown with branches.

The low trees, tall grass, and other types of brush made the hillsides ideal for the concealment of small animals. As the sha'um passed by, the creatures concealed near the road panicked and fled, and I amused myself by trying to classify the types I saw.

None of them were identical to the animals Ricardo had known, though there were similar body configurations. I asked Markasset's memories for the names of the animals I saw; it gave me a few, but not many. I gave up fairly quickly and simply watched the activity and listened to the hoorah stirred by the passing cats. There seemed to be a huge bird population in these foothills, and some of them had very musical voices.

A poet might say I was watching a living symphony. But I'd have to be more truthful and admit it sounded more like Spike Jones' band tuning up. In a hurry. Loudly.

But it made the day pass quickly, and I was surprised, that afternoon, when the cats reached the top of a long slope and stopped to catch their breath.

I slid off the cat's back—Liden's—and stretched as I looked up at a fortified wall made of stone and packed with earth. It had been built as a dam is built, filling a narrow depression between two steep hillsides. It was perhaps a hundred feet long, and at the deepest point of the valley it stood at least thirty feet high.

There were men stationed at intervals along the level top edge of the wall, but just now their attention was focused on the gate at the center of the wall. A caravan master was supervising the payment of his toll fee. He was talking to a man wearing the same type of uniform as Bareff and Liden, except that the sash tied around his waist was red. They conferred over a list and checked things off as items were laid on a low stone shelf that had been built, apparently, as part of the wall.

It was a noisy scene. The caravan vleks were hysterical with the smell of sha'um all around them. Those men who weren't actually unloading goods were busy swearing at the vleks, trying to control them. The actual appearance of Bareff's and Liden's sha'um was hardly noticed by the frenzied animals.

So this is Thagorn, I thought. *The wall must guard a sheltered valley—a strong defense position. Even if you discount the cats, it's easy to see why nobody wants to take on the Sharith.*

I just hope I can find some answers, get out of here with my skin intact, and get that skin back past Zaddorn.

I looked up at Bareff and Liden, who were still mounted. The heads of the cats were turned toward me, nodding slightly with their heavy breathing. Was it my imagination, or had the gleam of hatred I had seen in the eyes of Bareff's sha'um faded somewhat?

He's just tired, I decided. *And he deserves to be. It wasn't an easy trip for them, either.*

"Your sha'um," I asked the men, "what are their names?"

"Their names?" Liden sounded surprised. His jaw had returned to normal size, but the bruise had turned so black that the white of his scar looked like an open wound. He reached forward and stroked his hand along the cat's right jaw. "Cheral."

I looked at Bareff.

He made the same gesture and said: "Poltar."

I moved to stand in front of the two huge cats. Poltar was much darker and shorter than Keeshah; Cheral had a rangy look, and splashes of slightly varying shades of tan, giving his fur an indistinct color. They were standing, still carrying their Riders, and I had to look up into their faces.

I raised my hands to my waist level, palms upward.

"Poltar, and Cheral—thank you."

The two great heads lowered, and my upturned palms felt the very lightest touch of their furred muzzles.

I turned away and started walking toward the gates, trying to clear a tightness from my throat. I would have given everything, at that moment, to have Keeshah with me to ride through those gates as the unquestioned equal of the Sharith. But if I couldn't ride Keeshah, I'd walk.

I had taken only a few steps when I discovered that I had company: Bareff and Liden on either side of me, Poltar and Cheral following them. I glanced quickly at their battered faces, but they stared straight ahead and didn't look at me. So I turned my eyes forward and the three of us marched abreast toward the city gates.

We approached the man with the red sash, stopped, and waited. He glanced up at us, his face almost hidden by the brim of the hat which shaded his eyes, and nodded slightly to acknowledge our presence. Then he gave his attention back to the caravan master and his tally sheet.

The man with the sash seemed satisfied, and he signed one of his men to hand over a colored cloth, which was tied to the pack of the leading vlek. Then he turned to us.

139

"Bareff. Liden." He didn't even look at me. "Come inside the gate; the fleabitten vleks will not pass while your sha'um wait out here. And though Shaben is one of the few who pay their fair duty willingly, I have had enough of caravaners for one day."

We walked through the gate, and I had another surprise. I had not yet seen any city gate in Gandalara closed, even at night—but the heavy wood-and-bronze gates of Thagorn swung shut behind us.

Now he looked at me. I couldn't see his eyes, but the hat brim moved up and down in my direction. "Is this the man you sent the message about?"

"Yes," answered Bareff.

"He wants to talk to the Lieutenant," added Liden.

I was relieved to learn that red-sash wasn't the Lieutenant. I hadn't gotten a clear look at his face, but I was sure he was fairly young. Something in his slimness or the slight swagger in his walk, the effort audible in his speech to make his light baritone voice convey authority.

"*He* wants to talk, does he? Well, talk, groundwalker."

"To the Lieutenant," I said quietly.

The boy took a deep breath—to calm himself or to swell his chest, probably a little of both.

"I am Thymas, Dharak's son. Anything you have to say—"

"He'll say to the Lieutenant," Bareff interrupted. "After he's had a chance to get cleaned up."

"And what say do you have in this?" the boy asked, seething. "He's a common groundwalker—"

"He's not a *common* groundwalker, Thymas," Liden said, "and he's here as our guest."

"Tell your father that *we* need to talk to him. Tonight, if possible. We'll come to the Hall after supper," said Bareff. He nudged me and the three of us, followed by the cats, started off toward some large buildings to the right.

Behind us, we heard a sword leave its scabbard. "You need a lesson in manners, Bareff," said the boy's voice, shaking with anger. "I am the Lieutenant's son; no one gives me orders!"

Bareff stopped and turned slightly, talking over his shoulder. "You make me draw my sword, I'll have to kill you, boy. Now no groundwalker, even an *uncommon* one, is worth this kind of fuss. Ask Dharak. Let him decide. *But ask him.*" We started forward again. My back itched until I heard Thymas put away his sword and move off in the opposite direction.

I also heard muffled laughter and whispering from the ramparts of the wall. *Public humiliation,* I thought, *is no way to make a friend of the boss's son.*

The large buildings turned out to be barracks, with a dining area and individual, fairly comfortable apartments. Bareff pulled out some of his own clothes for me—"civvies," I was relieved to note, instead of a tan uniform—and directed me to the common bath-house near the river which bisected the valley. Then he and Liden went off to attend to their cats. They joined me later; we returned to the barracks and were served a flavorful rafel by a girl of an age equivalent to thirteen or fourteen human years. Then we walked back to the main thoroughfare which led from the gate, crossed it, and climbed a gentle hill toward a big square building which topped it.

I had expected an ornate audience hall such as I had seen in European palaces. Instead, we went through one of many sha'um-sized doors into a HALL.

It had a high ceiling, walls of wood parquetry polished to a high glow, and a floor inlaid with thousands of small marble tiles that must have come from Omergol. It was the size of half a football field, and in its exact center a huge block of pale green marble served as a speaking and review platform.

There were two men standing on the platform. One was the boy who had met us at the gate. He wasn't wearing his hat now, and the light from oil lamps suspended from the ceiling washed over a head of pale golden hair, lighter even than Illia's.

And the halo seemed drab compared to the white crown the other man wore. While the boy seemed only to be waiting for us, the man beside him was compelling us, drawing us across the marble floor toward him like a magnet.

He was wearing tunic and trousers of desert tan like the others, but the cloth was a tighter, finer weave. The tunic draped softly, and was cinched to the large man's trim, muscular waist with a blue sash of a material that resembled shiny brocade. The trousers were tucked into the tops of sueded leather boots, and the upper edges of the boots were reinforced and trimmed with leather stitching on the outer edges.

He was an elegant, commanding figure: the Lieutenant.

Bareff and Liden and I had marched, shoulder to shoulder, in silence across the huge room. There had been only the whisper of cloth against cloth and the reassuring swish of my sword against my pantleg as we walked. I had dared only one quick glance at the other two: the rough, marginally sloppy men I had encountered in a bar in Omergol had been transformed into soldiers.

As we halted neatly in front of the dais, I called up my own military training. I needed every inch of it to stand at attention under the penetrating eyes of the Lieutenant.

"Why is a groundwalker brought before me armed?" he said at last. His voice was rich and deep, resonant in the empty Hall. If there had been a thousand troops around us, every last one of them could have heard him clearly.

Beside me, Bareff spoke up. "His name is Rikardon." There was respect in his voice, but no fear or tension. "He won our life-debts, and freely gave them back. He said he needed to talk to you."

"And you think I should listen?" the Lieutenant asked. "What do you say, Liden?"

"I say he's not afraid of sha'um. By the time we got here, he was riding second place with respectable skill. Poltar was carrying him willingly."

"Cheral, too, Lieutenant. I don't know what he wants with you," Bareff said, "but I'll stand for him while he's in Thagorn."

"So will I," added Liden.

The Lieutenant stepped down from the dais to stand in front of me. Thymas moved to the edge of the platform, his hand on the hilt of his sword.

"Rikardon," the Lieutenant said, nodding slightly at me. He was taller than I, with a narrow face well-lined with age. The bristling shock of snow-white fur which swept back from his prominent forehead seemed anomalous to me—everywhere I had been so far, age had darkened the Gandalaran brow.

"Dharak," I said, and nodded back at him.

For a few seconds we just stared at one another.

"You bring a high recommendation, Rikardon," he said at last. "Say what you have to say. I'll listen."

19

"Someone I care about is unfairly accused as a thief, Lieutenant," I said. "I believe that the stolen article was on the caravan of Gharlas and I know that the Sharith—uh—acquired the goods on that caravan. May I look through them?"

"The goods we—uh—acquired," he said with the hint of a smile, "have already been distributed among the families. Perhaps if you'll tell us what you're looking for. . . ?"

I cupped my hands close together and called up Markasset's memory. The men around me faded and I spoke to them through a vision of the Ra'ira resting in its glass case. "A gem about this size, Lieutenant. Irregular, clear blue if you look through the edge, darker and twisting toward the center—"

"The Ra'ira!" Thymas shouted, startling all of us. "Father, if the Ra'ira has left Raithskar—"

Dharak whirled toward his son, and Thymas' voice choked in his throat. "Bareff, Liden," said the Lieutenant as he turned back to us, "you've done well, bringing Rikardon to me. I understand I owe you, Bareff, another vote of thanks for not taking Thymas up on his challenge this afternoon."

"Father!"

The Lieutenant went on as if he hadn't heard the furious outcry. "If you wish it, Thymas will apologize publicly for his rude treatment of your guest and his disrespect to you."

"I'll do it when Eddarta frees the slaves!" The boy jumped down from the platform and started to draw his sword.

Dharak caught Thymas's sword hand in one of his, and forced the sword back. They stood there, eye to eye, a tableau of the struggle between generations. Then Thymas relaxed, lowered his gaze, and stepped back a pace. The muscles along his neck stood out with the force of his anger. The old man seemed outwardly calm, but the torchlight reflected from his eyes with an odd shine.

"The boy needn't apologize," said Bareff. "It's all past the gate now, anyway."

"Thank you," said Dharak. "Again. You're training the cubs tomorrow morning, aren't you?"

143

Bareff nodded.

"Then I'll let you get on with your preparations. You brought Rikardon here, left him, and didn't hear a word he had to say. Understood?"

Liden and Bareff both nodded, then turned to me. "I hope someday we find out what this was all about," said Liden.

"I don't know all the answers, myself," I told them. "Thanks for your help."

Bareff barked a short laugh. "Sure. Anytime you need more help, just kick our teeth out again."

He slapped me on the shoulder, and he and Liden started back toward the door through which we had entered. The Lieutenant waved at me, and he and I, followed by Thymas, walked around the dais toward a door in the opposite wall.

"As you can guess, we would have recognized the Ra'ira if it had been with the caravan," the Lieutenant told me. "No man or woman of the Sharith would keep it from its rightful place in Raithskar. That would be breaking the pledge made by the first Lieutenant to Serkajon during the time of the Last King."

We had reached the door, and we stepped outside to find it already dark. Thymas and Dharak reached to either side of the doorway for torches, and I looked out over the valley of Thagorn.

Across the stream which divided the long valley, single-family homes had been built in clusters of six, with a community cooking area in the center of each. I had noticed that much as we had climbed to the Hall. At night each cluster cast a soft glow upward into the blackness, the inner walls of the homes reflecting and channeling the cheerful light of the cookfires.

It looked as though someone had lit giant candles and placed them with pleasing randomness on the floor and around the edge of the valley.

Through the silence surrounding the empty Hall, we could hear distant laughter, and catch strains of music from a stringed instrument. Children screeched and were hushed. Sha'um roared and were quieted. The sounds came to us clearly, if faintly, from across the stream.

It was so beautiful that I wanted to share it. I reached out for Keeshah.

Yes, came the acknowledgement instantly, eagerly. The touch of that warm and familiar link made the beauty of the night complete.

Can you see, Keeshah? Through me? Can you see this?

144

There was a moment of silence, then a question so wistful that I felt my chest tighten with physical pain.

I come there?

Not now, Keeshah, I told him. *What I'm doing here is too important to my father. But one day we'll come back together. I can't promise,* I told him, thinking about the horrible moment when the point of my sword sank into a man's throat, *but if it's possible at all, we'll return to Thagorn together one day.*

Light sparked beside me and I jumped, breaking the contact with Keeshah. Thymas had lit a torch with a small contraption that looked like a pair of tongs. The arms were twisted as well as curved, so that their tips would pass one another. In the tips were mounted a piece of flint and a very small piece of steel. This, I reflected, must be Gandalara's primary use of Raithskar's rakor. No wonder a *sword* made of steel was so rare and highly prized.

We turned away from the peaceful scene on the other side of the stream and went back down the hill toward one of the barracks buildings.

"Some of the caravan people are still with us, waiting for the arrival of Eumin, the slave trader from Eddarta," explained the Lieutenant. "Perhaps one of them has information which will help you find the Ra'ira."

A recent memory crossed my mind. "Is there among them, by any chance, a man with four fingers on his left hand? The smallest finger missing?"

"I have seen too little of them to know," said Dharak. "Thymas? Have you seen such a man?"

"Yes, Father," said Thymas, who had remained strictly silent after the confrontation with his father. There was a note of controlled excitement underneath the subdued tone he used now. "A man called Hural. He has been very quiet since his capture, hardly eating."

"We'll soon find out what he knows about this," the Lieutenant assured me grimly. "I blame myself in part; I should have known that Gharlas, flea though he is, wouldn't have come to us just for the reasons he gave me. He—"

Just then a shout of laughter rang out from the guards on the wall, which lay now to our right. We had reached the main avenue and had clear sight of the gate area, which was ablaze with light activity. Four men on each side swung open the huge doors of the gate, and two men rode through it. A shapeless bundle was suspended between them in what looked like a rope net; the supporting lines for that cargo net were looped around the men's hips so that they, and not their cats, would bear the chafing.

The bundle was moving and shouting. I felt every single hair on my head stand at attention.

It was Zaddorn's voice.

There flashed through my mind, finally, that memory of Markasset's which had been warning me vaguely but eluding me as to specifics. It was the end of a foot race, an annual event by the size of the crowd cheering as Zaddorn was awarded the cash prize. He looked much younger in the memory, and Markasset felt much younger—and exhausted. He had come in a poor second to Zaddorn, who wasn't even breathing heavily.

In a world where most people traveled on foot, Zaddorn was an endurance runner. The memory gave me another piece of information, too. Clearly through the years came the special smirk of triumph Zaddorn flashed to Markasset from the awards area. Their rivalry had not begun with Illia.

The Lieutenant called to the two Riders, and they swerved toward the sound of his voice. Their cats stopped barely two yards away from us and sidled closer together so that the bundle slapped to the ground; they released brass catches at their hips to loosen the carrying ropes.

I felt a sweeping relief. Had things happened differently, I was certain that I'd have arrived in Thagorn in exactly this manner.

Zaddorn quieted until he had been unrolled and untangled from the net. One of the Riders leaned down to help him up; Zaddorn grabbed one of the man's legs and jerked him off balance, delivering a knee into his midsection as the man fell. Zaddorn twisted on the ground to face the other Rider, but stopped dead still. The point of a bronze sword hovered just above his throat.

"You put your groundloving feet in the dirt and stand up, you," the Rider said. He moved his head toward us, and I stepped back a pace, out of the torchlight. "This is Dharak, Lieutenant of the Sharith, and his son, Thymas. Show some respect or I'll gladly give your blood to the ground."

Instantly the snarling, fighting animal who had been hauled into this place as a potential slave was transformed into the elegant city official I had met in Thanasset's house. He stood up and bowed gracefully to the Lieutenant, then a little less deeply to Thymas.

His clothes were dusty and torn, and his handsome face was swollen along one side of the jaw. His skin was abraded

146

from the friction of the rope; one muscular shoulder was completely bare, crusted with blood.

"Gentlemen," he said. I could almost see the soft gray of his suit, the swirl of his cape. "May I introduce myself? I am Zaddorn, Chief of Peace and Security for the City of Raithskar. I have come in friendship, seeking only information. I am looking for—"

I had been quiet long enough. "The same thing I am," I said, interrupting and stepping forward. Zaddorn wasn't surprised to see me; rather, he smiled with satisfaction. "A man with four fingers on his left hand."

Zaddorn stared at me, considering. It was obvious he knew I hadn't told the Lieutenant who I was, and that identifying me would prove me a liar. I was standing, armed, in the company of the leader of the Sharith and he had been dragged into Thagorn like a load of glith skins. He wanted to expose me; I could see it in the way his jaw tensed.

But his jaw relaxed. *You're a good cop, Zaddorn,* I thought at him. *The crime—or the mystery—comes before your personal feelings. Thanks.*

"Have you found him?" he asked.

"Not yet," I answered, and gestured vaguely toward the barracks buildings. "But he's here. A man named Hural."

The Lieutenant had been following our exchange, looking from me to Zaddorn.

"Is this man a friend of yours?" Dharak asked me.

In the silence that followed, I watched Zaddorn. We both knew what the situation was. In Raithskar, I was a suspect in a robbery and a possible candidate for the Gandalaran equivalent of second degree murder—of a cop, no less—and his main rival for an attractive woman. In Thagorn, he knew he needed me. And how he *hated* it.

I'm no saint. I let him worry for a few seconds. I even enjoyed it a little.

"He is not my friend, Lieutenant. But he's telling you the truth. He's an officer of the government of Raithskar." I remembered the phrase Bareff had used. "I'll stand for him while he's here."

"Good enough," said Dharak, and waved away the guards.

"My sword—" began Zaddorn.

"Will be returned to you when you leave," said Dharak. "Now listen well. Rikardon has given his life as bond for your good behavior."

Is that what it means? Holy—!

"In Thagorn, that means silence except when you're spoken to," Dharak continued. "Understand?"

Zaddorn nodded, and Dharak grinned.

"All right. Thymas, go find this Hural and bring him here."

There were several people sitting and standing around the cookfire near the barracks. Thymas went over to them, spoke to one of them, then approached a dark bundle lying against the wall of the building. He said something, grew impatient, then leaned over and dragged a small man to his feet. The man coughed raspily, jerked his arm out of Thymas' grasp, and staggered toward us. He came into the circle of our torchlight; I was holding the torch Thymas had carried down from the Hall. When he saw me, he lurched forward and peered up into my face. His breath smelled foul.

"You," he whispered, and spluttered through a choking cough. "You were supposed to guard the fleabitten caravan! Where were you when the Sharith attacked?" His eyes narrowed. He laughed insanely, his voice rising, then gurgling into another racking cough.

"That's enough out here," said Dharak. "Let's go inside. Bring him, Thymas."

Dharak led the way into another barracks, this one apparently empty. He lit a lamp and placed it on the largest dining table, and we sat down around it. The little man had worked himself into a regular fit, and he lay half across the table, coughing and gasping for breath.

I was glad of the short break. I could almost hear Zaddorn thinking it, and my own mind echoed his question: *That's right, Markasset, where were you when the Sharith attacked? And what is your connection with Gharlas?*

20

The lamp was a thick, smokeless candle placed inside a beautifully faceted glass chimney. It cast a remarkable amount of illumination over the faces of the others at the table: Hural and Thymas across from me and Zaddorn, Dharak at one end of the table.

"Awright," said the four-fingered man at last. "Whattaya

want with me?" His words were slurred and hurried, as though they were being chased by a cough.

"Answers," I said. "You helped Gharlas steal the Ra'ira. How did you get into the security room? Where has Gharlas taken the gem?"

"You'll ride a thaka before I tell you anything, you filthy, sneaking—"

Thymas caught the man by the back of his neck and nearly lifted him from the chair. "Show the proper respect," he grated, "or you'll be missing more fingers."

He let Hural down. The little man rubbed his neck and looked hatefully at Thymas, then over at me. For the first time, he noticed Zaddorn. "Hey, ain't you the Chief of Security from Raithskar?"

"I am Zaddorn, yes," he answered.

"Keeping low company, ain't ya?" he sneered.

"That will be enough," said Dharak, the command in his voice making Hural cringe back from him. "Answer the questions."

"Why should I? You gonna give me my freedom and make me healthy again? Eh? What you got to offer?"

"Revenge," said the Lieutenant. "You've no need to keep silent out of loyalty to Gharlas. Rikardon, here, did not betray the caravan to us. Gharlas paid us handsomely—not only to raid the caravan but to kill everyone on it."

"Kill—?" Hural assimilated it rapidly, and his face stiffened. "Then why didn't you?"

"It seemed wasteful. Obviously Gharlas never wanted to see you and the others again. We could accomplish that as effectively by assuring your presence in Eddarta's copper mines as by destroying you. And make a tidy profit."

"Why?" I asked. "Did Gharlas tell you why he wanted this?"

The Lieutenant frowned. "As I said before, I blame myself for not seeing through him at once. He gave me a complicated story about the trip having been funded by a man he hated. It would be an amusing vengeance, he told me, to use his rival's money to pay for his rival's ruin." Dharak shrugged. "It sounds patently stupid repeated like that. All I can say is that Gharlas in person is a very persuasive man. I agreed to it, though I couldn't tell you, at this instant, why I did."

"I'll tell you why," spoke up Hural, and there was bitterness in his hurried whisper. "You said he's persuasive. He's all of that and more. Gharlas has the ancient power—he can

149

control minds!" This last was almost shrieked, and set off another bout of coughing. When he had recovered somewhat, he stared across at me.

"Yes, I'll tell you; why not? You asked about the security room. Gharlas used his power to make the old man *believe* he locked the door—he didn't. We walked right in!" A shrill giggle, choked off by fear of more coughing.

"Why did Gharlas want the Ra'ira?" asked Zaddorn, and Dharak and Thymas were too interested to rebuke him for speaking out of turn.

"Now that's the weird part. I been overseeing Gharlas's caravans for a long time. I've known he's not quite right up here." He tapped his temple with a finger of his mangled left hand. "I've always thought it pretty strange that he always—and I mean *always*—got his way around people.

"This trip seemed pretty ordinary until we got to Raithskar. We stopped here, paid the tribute, Gharlas worked his deal—but I didn't know about that. After we've set up in Raithskar, he calls me to his room one night and confesses that he is—get this!—*the rightful King of Gandalara*. And he's going to prove it by taking the Ra'ira back to Eddarta with him.

"I ask him how he plans to get away with that, and he gives me the news about this power he's had all along. His eyes are shining and strange and I *know* he's gone over the Wall."

Hural stopped, cleared his throat, and spat on the floor—to the obvious disgust of the Lieutenant and Thymas.

"But—you know—we been together a long time. And he scares me with that power stuff—maybe he was using it on me, I don't know. But anyway, I went along; I helped him steal the filthy thing."

"How was this man involved?" Zaddorn asked, pointing at me.

"Him?" The little man grinned. "What was it you called him? 'Rikardon'? Well, that's not the name he gives me. He tells me he's—"

My body went completely tense; I could feel a similar movement in Zaddorn beside me.

"—Lakad. Says he's from *Chizan*."

That's why the alias I used in Omergol came so easily, I thought. *I—Markasset—had used it before.*

"He comes to me the night before we're scheduled to leave and wants to hire on as a guard. Well, I already know there's going to be a special, important cargo this trip, and he looks

150

strong enough, so I says yes. But the next morning, when we're packing and this guy shows up for duty—at the last minute, so late I'd given up on him—Gharlas has a regular fit! He don't say anything to you, but to me he says plenty. Don't I know Sharith agents are everywhere? Didn't I have more sense than to hire on a stranger? And so on. And later, when the Riders came in without any warning, and you had been on guard duty, I figured Gharlas was right."

"What happened to Gharlas?" I asked. "Where was he when the Sharith attacked?"

"Didn't see him. Figured at the time that he was one of the lucky ones to escape," he said wryly. "Now I guess he just left us during the night—some old friend, eh?"

The cough had been suppressed long enough, and now it shook him again. The thin shoulders jumped violently as he doubled over the table. When he sat up, still panting heavily, there were flecks of blood on the table and around his mouth. He looked at me with eyes that were glazed with pain.

"Cheated two kinds of fate," he said, and allowed himself a thin, gasping laugh. "First the Riders don't kill me like Gharlas wanted, then they don't get to sell me, either."

"What do you mean?" I asked, but I was all too sure what he meant.

"I'm dying," he said. "Known it since this morning. Wanted it." He looked up at the Lieutenant. "Lost finger same place I picked up this nuisance cough—copper mines of Eddarta. Cough goes away if I eat right. Stopped eating when I came here. *Never going back to those mines.*" He said it with such force that he began to gasp. He was too weak now even to cough. Thymas had an arm around his back, supporting him.

"Please, Hural," I asked him, horrified by what was happening but desperate for some answers at last, "where is the Ra'ira? What happened to it?"

His eyes turned to me, focused with great effort.

"Gharlas . . . has . . . it," he said.

It was the last thing he said.

Some hours later, I was standing outside the door of the Lieutenant's richly appointed home. It was situated on a rise near the river, the only single-family dwelling on the barracks side. I had been there for several minutes, watching the candle-flames of the cookfires dwindle, one by one, and die down.

We had turned Hural's body over to the Sharith guards,

and had come here. A gracefully aging, smiling woman had greeted her husband and son with warm affection, and had served us faen as we sat around a tile-topped table. The conversation had remained neutral until Shola excused herself, which she had done as soon as she had realized we were all thinking about something else.

"Do you believe what he said?" I had asked Zaddorn as soon as she had left. "About the mind-power Gharlas claims to have?"

Thymas had spoken up before Zaddorn could answer. "Such power exists," he said excitedly. "We have seen it used."

"Indeed?" Zaddorn had inquired. "By Gharlas, you mean?"

"No, I don't mean Gharlas," Thymas had said impatiently. "I'm talking about Tarani."

"An illusionist with a traveling show who stops by here now and then," Dharak had explained. "The illusions are so perfect that no other conclusion is possible. And Tarani admits to holding the power, tells us in every show that it is being used, and challenges us to see through the illusions. We can't.

"Yes, I must agree that the kind of power Hural described is possible. There is no evil in the illusions cast by Tarani for our entertainment. But the idea of Gharlas with such power and, if Hural again is to be believed, with such ambition—" He had shuddered. "The old words are true: 'To crave power is to be ruled by madness.' Surely Gharlas *must* be mind-ill."

"Oh, I wouldn't argue that point at all," Zaddorn had agreed. "But what *Rikardon* wants to know is whether I believe that Gharlas has that power and used it to steal the Ra'ira." He had looked at me thoughtfully for a long moment, fair repayment for the few seconds I had let him squirm before I spoke up for him to Dharak.

"Yes," he had said at last, "I believe him. He was dying; he had no reason to lie. And it explains some puzzling things: how he learned about the security system, for instance, as well as how he got into a supposedly locked room—without the aid of the Supervisor on duty.

"I believe him," he had repeated, "and that's what I'll tell the Council of Supervisors when we get back to Raithskar."

I had let out a sigh of pure relief. Thanasset was safe.

The Lieutenant, too, had seemed to relax from the edge of tension. Thymas, however, had reared back indignantly.

"Back to Raithskar?" he had repeated incredulously. "Aren't you going after Gharlas, to get the Ra'ira back?"

"My duty is in Raithskar," Zaddorn had explained quietly, stifling a yawn. "I'll send discreet messages to the security people in the other cities; I'll be notified when Gharlas turns up. We'll get it back, don't worry."

"Don't worry?" Thymas had repeated again. "The Ra'ira *belongs* in Raithskar. You can't just—"

"That will be enough, Thymas," Dharak had cut him off abruptly. "For the second time today," he had said to Zaddorn, "I must apologize for my son's manners." Zaddorn had nodded; the boy glared at his father but had said nothing. "It's getting late," Dharak had said then, "and we all need some rest. You'll want to leave for Raithskar tomorrow, of course."

And the group had separated. Zaddorn and I had excused ourselves and left father and son together to talk things over. Zaddorn had accepted an earlier offer of the use of Dharak's private bath-house, and I had stepped outside to be alone with my thoughts for a few minutes.

Thanasset was in the clear at last—that was the most important thing. I thought about the man I had killed and regretted it, sharply, again. Not because of the possible consequences now, but because I hadn't wanted it to happen. And because I knew Thanasset well enough to know that a death in his service must have grieved him.

I let my thoughts wander through the time I had spent in Gandalara. Idly I counted the days and was astonished to realize that it had been less than two weeks. I felt a strong life-investment here. I had met people I respected, some of whom I also loved. I had begun to get a feel for Markasset, though I still didn't know him. Hural's information hadn't explicitly cleared Markasset of any involvement—I still didn't know how he wound up in the desert, or who the dead man . . .

I had been leaning against the wall of Dharak's home. Now I stood up straight, startled.

Could that have been Gharlas? I wondered. *I searched him thoroughly and he didn't have the stone. Can it be that the precious Ra'ira is wandering out in that desert right now, riding Gharlas' masterless vlek?*

I was so occupied with this new line of thought that I barely noticed a young boy run up to the front door to my left, knock, and go in.

Come on, Markasset, I pleaded silently. *What did Gharlas look like? Was he that dead body? It will look queer for me to ask about a man it's been proven I knew—but if I have to, I will.*

I was distracted, then, by the appearance of Dharak

153

through his front door. He looked first to his left, then turned to his right and saw me. He was holding a strip of cloth in his hand.

"Oh, there you are, Markasset. I have news."

"News?" I asked. Then it hit me. "You—you called me—"

"I've known all along who you are," he said calmly. "Come, step away from the house and I'll explain."

We walked down the hill toward the river, which made a constant rushing noise—not loud, but soothing. Away from the lighted windows of the house, it was pitch black. Only the sound of Dharak's voice told me where he was.

"It's quite true that we Sharith have 'agents everywhere', as it is whispered in every marketplace," he said, laughing lightly. "They are people who owe us loyalty for one reason or another. And they do not, as most people seem to think, merely spy out the caravans which do not pay their proper portion to the Sharith.

"We are isolated here in this valley," he continued. "By choice, it is true, a choice made long ago, a bond sworn and kept by generation after generation. But isolated, none the less. Our agents tell us what is going on in the world.

"Naturally, as soon as the Ra'ira was stolen, we heard about it."

"But Thymas—your son seemed surprised," I said.

"He was. All communications come directly to me. I was the only one who read that one, and I didn't tell Thymas about it. For that matter, I didn't tell anyone."

"Why is the Ra'ira so important to him?"

Dharak sighed. "It is important to all of us. You, of all people, must know the story of Serkajon."

"That he took the Ra'ira back to Raithskar, that the King's guard followed him there for vengeance, but instead abandoned the King and settled here in Thagorn."

"That's essentially it. Serkajon convinced the first Lieutenant that the Ra'ira was a symbol of power, and that the Kings had outlived their right to power. That first Lieutenant had sworn loyalty to Serkajon and to his purpose: to keep the Ra'ira surrounded with honorable men so that no single man could ever use its beauty to call to himself power over other men."

I was beginning to understand. I thought of the gemstones in Ricardo's world which had carried "curses" of ill luck and evil fates. All of them that I could recall had been coveted for their beauty as well as for their value. The Ra'ira was a compellingly beautiful stone, the kind to attract legend. Origi-

154

nally a symbol of a city's loyalty to its King, it had changed hands again during the social upheaval associated with the end of a monarchy. It may have been only coincidence; it may not. But certainly, if it had not already acquired its reputation when Kä fell apart, that event, following so closely the removal of the Ra'ira, had stamped a mystic aura of power on the beautiful gem.

"I am merely the Lieutenant. Because Thanasset no longer rides, you are, by right of heritage, the Captain. Originally, I kept silence out of a sense of duty to your family.

"Among the Sharith, rank must be earned. The messages said only that you had fled, but I refused to prejudge you as a coward. When you *walked* into Thagorn, you proved several things to me. First, it took a great fighter to win the respect of Bareff and Liden. Second, it took a great commitment of loyalty to deny yourself the companionship of your sha'um for any man's sake. Third, Zaddorn didn't race out here merely after the information Hural had; he was chasing you. Yet you have treated him with honor, and you will return with him to Raithskar to set straight whatever he holds against you.

"So, after I had the chance to know you, I kept silence still out of a sense of duty—to you. As far as I'm concerned, you *are* the new Captain, and in spite of Thymas's impatience, I will await your orders about the Ra'ira."

I began to breathe again as Dharak continued talking, a disembodied voice in the darkness saying incredible things. *Not me,* I was thinking frantically. *No Captain here, I'm just an NCO. Don't call me "sir"!*

"Of course, you must settle things in Raithskar first, and that brings me to the news," he was saying. "Rumors about the theft have spread widely through Raithskar until there has been a general demand for answers. Tonight's message tells me that the Chief Supervisor has had to yield to public pressure and suspend Thanasset from the Council."

"What?" I was jolted from my momentary panic. "Thanasset suspended? When?"

"Only today. But the message says things are getting ugly. The public has begun to believe that Thanasset did cooperate with the thieves. They are calling him a traitor and asking for the forfeit of his property."

I felt a chill crawl up my spine. "A mob."

"I'm afraid so. From what I've seen of Zaddorn, I'd say he could control them, but he's not there now." He hesitated. I could almost hear him deciding whether or not to tell me what I had already guessed. "You and Zaddorn need your rest tonight, Markasset—but tomorrow, I suggest haste. The people are asking for more than Thanasset's rank—

"They are demanding his life."

21

I was glad to find Zaddorn already asleep in the room we were to share. I lay down on the fluffy pallet on my side of the room, called Keeshah and arranged for a meeting place the next day, and tried to blank out my mind. I thought it would be impossible—but it seemed only a moment later that I woke to sunlight streaming in through the latticed window.

Zaddorn and I said our farewells at the gate of Thagorn. Thymas was still sour and resentful, but his words were courteous enough. Bareff and Liden grinned and waved at me from a distance; I called to them to say goodbye to their sha'um for me. The Lieutenant exchanged a few polite words with Zaddorn, then turned to me.

"I have no doubt you will return to Thagorn soon, Rikardon. It will be my pleasure then to greet you personally, and show you more of the life of the Sharith."

"I'd like that very much, Lieutenant," I said, ignoring Thymas' startled look as best I could. I fell back on Ricardo's customs once more and offered my hand. "I can't promise I'll be back, but I'll try. I'd like to get to know you and your people better."

Dharak hesitated only briefly, then gripped my hand so strongly that I felt a sudden surge of affection for him. I knew I wasn't the man he thought I was—but just for a moment I wanted to be. He carried a tremendous burden of leadership.

He and Thanasset should meet, I decided at that moment. *They'd understand each other. They both have slightly inappropriate sons.*

I was warmed, then, by a feeling of kinship with Thymas, and impulsively I offered him my hand, too. He looked surprised, then took it. Dharak smiled at the look of puzzlement on his face.

Then Zaddorn and I set out at a jog for the place where I

had asked Keeshah to meet me this morning, the stream which had been my last stop on the trip to Thagorn. I had given Zaddorn the news about the developments in Raithskar. He had agreed, grimly, that we had to hurry back. But he had been quietly noncommittal when I assured him that Keeshah could carry us both.

So we traveled in silence, expending all our energy in covering distance. It suited us both, I think—as I had told Dharak, we weren't friends. As Gra'mama Maria Constanza would have said, if you can't say something nice . . .

Shortly before noon we left the road and headed for the appointed spot. Keeshah was already there, and he could wait no longer. He came running to meet me. He was still some distance away when we could hear him crashing through some thick brush. Zaddorn stopped, but I paid no attention. The trees were taller here, and the ground generally less overgrown, than was usual in this area; I caught a glimpse of Keeshah's tawny head and I started running, too.

The one with you? Keeshah asked. *Friend?*

Yes, I called. *Thank you for being patient.*

It was hard, he told me, not griping or boasting, just stating the truth.

I know. I've missed you, too.

When we were about three yards apart, I caught the glimmer of joyous mischief from him—it wasn't enough warning.

Keeshah came straight at me, bent his neck downward, and rammed me in the stomach with his forehead, knocking me off my feet. Still running, he lifted his head and flipped me up and over his back in a dizzy somersault. I crashed into a tall cluster of the curly trees and grabbed desperately at branches as I fell. I managed not to break my skull when I hit the ground.

That's where I stayed, because Keeshah was right on top of me, grinding his muzzle into my chest. I grabbed his head and twisted, trying to wrestle him down to the ground. He roared and began to scoot backwards, shaking his head to dislodge me. He dragged me a good, scratchy ten yards before I gave up.

"Enough, Keeshah," I gasped out loud, out of breath from laughing.

He nudged my chest again, this time almost tenderly.

Together, he said. *Glad.*

Then he lay down beside me, panting a little from the run and the playful struggle, and rested his chin on my out-

157

stretched arm. A few minutes later, Zaddorn's voice penetrated our peaceful communion.

"I couldn't see what was happening," he said, "but that *sounded* like a lot of fun."

"It was," I said, ignoring his sarcasm, and stood up.

Home now? Keeshah asked me.

Yes, I told him. *All three of us must go, Keeshah. I know it will be hard for you to carry two all that way, but it's important.*

I can do it, he said, almost scornfully. *I won't. Not him. You don't like him.*

I felt a deep sense of sympathy for Bareff. But if he could convince his sha'um to carry a man who had beaten him senseless . . .

As I had done then, to convince Keeshah of an urgent need, I reached out to him now. I felt his mind quiet expectantly, and this time it was easier to achieve that intimate bond that conveyed understanding without the need to compose communication symbols.

And Keeshah agreed to carry Zaddorn.

He will mount first, I said to Keeshah, and forestalled his objection. *It will be easier for you; I have learned to ride second.*

Zaddorn had been watching us quietly for the few seconds required for the exchange. Now I turned to Zaddorn and said: "Watch." I sat on Keeshah's back and slid into riding position, then sat up and got off again. "Like that. I'll mount behind you."

Zaddorn didn't move.

"Well?" I said impatiently. "You know how important time is. Get on!"

"I—" It was the first time I had seen Zaddorn lose his composure. There had been a certain style even in the way he had come up fighting from the cargo net in Thagorn. Yet now his face, thinner than ever from the long run across the desert, was ashen white. His dark eyes reminded me of something . . .

"I don't think I can do that."

That's the way I looked in the mirror at Yafnaar, I realized. *Scared right down to my toenails. It's not just that Keeshah's a big, dangerous cat. Zaddorn has spent all his life with both feet on the ground. At least I was accustomed to the idea of riding an animal—he has never even considered it.*

I was learning something else about the relationship between Zaddorn and Markasset. No matter what other triumphs Zaddorn had scored, Markasset held the ace: he had Keeshah.

Well, sympathy won't help him now, I decided.

"Either you get on Keeshah's back," I said aloud, "or he'll carry you through the gates of Raithskar by the seat of your trousers."

The challenge stirred him up, as I had hoped. Zaddorn glared at me, then the muscles along his still-pale jaw twitched with determination. He walked up to Keeshah, sat down on his back as I had done and slid into an approximation of the position I had shown him. I checked both sides, moved his hands a little higher on Keeshah's shoulders, then mounted behind him. He was stiff as a salt block.

He's terrified, I explained, and I had to smile at Keeshah's disgusted agreement. *Stand up slowly and walk around. Let him get used to you.*

There was no direct response from Keeshah, but I felt him getting impatient and stubborn. I had just barely enough time to warn Zaddorn.

"Close your eyes and don't pinch Keeshah's shoulders," I shouted as Keeshah leaped up and set off at full run. He found the road and headed for Raithskar. I was very glad that I couldn't read Zaddorn's mind.

Keeshah tired quickly, of course, and gradually Zaddorn thawed out. We followed the mountain trail, the route by which Keeshah and I had made the trip out. It would have been faster to cross the desert, but Keeshah needed food to sustain him through the trip. There was game for him along the hills.

But we used the same travel pattern Zaddorn had adopted for the sake of speed: travel four hours, rest for one. We took a longer rest occasionally, to allow Keeshah to feed and rest more thoroughly. Zaddorn didn't complain—in fact, our tacit agreement to silence held except for the purely mechanical communication relating to food and rest stops—but I knew he was approaching the end of his endurance by the end of the second day. He had worn himself thin on the way *to* Thagorn, and this constant application of a different kind of strength was telling on him quickly.

For all our sakes, I called a halt near a stream in the late afternoon. I didn't wake him on time, but let him sleep an extra three hours. Keeshah, too, accepted the extra resting time. But though I tried to sleep, I found I couldn't. My head was buzzing with thoughts of Thanasset—what was happening to him? A mob—would they even listen when we got there? Always assuming we would get there on time?

"You let me oversleep," Zaddorn's voice spoke to me from the dark.

"You needed it," I said, then called "Keeshah!" We heard him stand up, stretch and shake himself. "And I need you."

After we had all taken care of some necessary body functions, Keeshah knelt and I waited for Zaddorn to mount.

"You take the front position for a while," he said. "Fair trade for the extra sleep."

"You'll be sorry," I told him, and asked Keeshah to let me know if he were too uncomfortable with Zaddorn riding second.

"Probably," he agreed drily, and we mounted.

It's all right, Keeshah told me after a few minutes. *He learns.*

Gratefully I gave up my weight and my troubled mind to Keeshah's soothing rhythm. I slept clear to the next stop.

After that, we traded positions every time we stopped. Zaddorn, too, learned to nap while Keeshah carried us.

It was noon of the fourth day since we left Thagorn that we rode up to the gates of Raithskar. The last leg had been a long one, Keeshah as eager as we to get back. He pulled up short, snarling, as a cordon of armed men flowed out the gate and surrounded us.

I slid off Keeshah's hindquarters, lifting my hands to show that I had no intention of drawing my sword. Zaddorn sat up, still on Keeshah's back, and the effect on the men was electrifying.

"Zaddorn?" said one of the men, stepping forward and dropping the point of his sword. "We didn't expect you back for another week." He grabbed his gray baldric with one hand and replaced his sword in its sheath. His face said plainly what he wouldn't put into words—certainly they didn't expect Zaddorn to arrive on the back of a sha'um.

Want home, Keeshah told me. He was panting heavily. *Rest. Want home.*

As soon as possible, Keeshah. I promise.

Zaddorn swung his right leg over Keeshah's back and slid to the ground with his characteristic grace. "Well, I'm here now, Klareth. What's the situation?"

"You know about—?"

"Thanasset, yes. Now answer me, man!"

"It's bad, Zaddorn. We've had to put the Supervisor into custody in his own home. The tension had been building ever

160

since he—" he nodded in my direction "—rode out of here. The people took that as an admission of guilt for him and for the Supervisor." His voice dropped almost to a whisper. "I've never seen the people this stirred up about *anything*, Chief. Things could get very nasty any minute now."

"Let's go," Zaddorn said, and started for the gate. I followed him, my hand on Keeshah's neck. The cordon of men fell in around us in a double rank.

There was a lot of whispering in the marketplace as we passed, but nobody challenged us. The crowds got thicker as we approached Thanasset's house, and I felt a coldness in the pit of my stomach.

The street in front of Thanasset's door was packed solid with people. Word of our coming had been shouted ahead, and the crowd turned its attention in our direction.

"There he is," someone yelled, "the traitor's son! How dare he come back to Raithskar?"

"Zaddorn, too!" someone else called. "Zaddorn's with him."

"What news?"

"It's the traitor Markasset!"

The tide of people swept toward us, tumultuous, curious, demanding, abusive. The noise was incredible; even those who merely wanted information wouldn't have been able to hear us. The cordon of men was pressed back by the sheer weight of people until Keeshah—though he wouldn't have phrased it this way—was beginning to feel like a furry sardine.

Home close! he told me impatiently. *I go.*

"I can't hold him back much longer," I shouted in Zaddorn's ear.

"Let him go," he yelled back. "He'll get us some room."

I let him go. By then I didn't have any choice.

Try not to kill anybody!

He shouldered his way between two of the guards and announced to the crowd that *he wanted to move.* A climbing wail of panic began around him and rippled outward. His claws and teeth damaged the nearest people, but the far reaches of the crowd still didn't know what was going on. Many more people were hurt by being crunched between the edge of the mob, still pressing inward, and the center of it trying to get away from Keeshah.

Zaddorn and I followed Keeshah closely, with four men around us guarding our rear. The rest of the cordon got separated and swallowed in the crowd. There were guards

161

around the house shoulder to shoulder, all of them standing tense and quiet until we got close to the garden gate. Then they came forward and formed a protective V around us until the gate was opened and we got through.

I have never felt a sense of relief quite like I felt when that gate had closed behind us.

Keeshah started off for his house, but Zaddorn said: "Call him back. Only for a minute."

I did, and he came grumbling.

"We can't leave that crowd without some information; they'll tear down the house," Zaddorn told me. "Ask Keeshah if I might mount him once more and climb to the top of the wall."

Keeshah knelt for us at my request, and in a few seconds we were both standing on top of the garden wall, a tapering structure of gray brick. The edge was narrow; Zaddorn overbalanced and I caught his arm to steady him. It trembled slightly.

He's about ready to collapse, I thought.

But once he had his balance again, he stood rock-still and waited while the crowd noticed us and roared, realized slowly that Zaddorn was waiting for quiet so he could speak, and, more slowly still, gave him what he wanted. We stood above the silence for a full two minutes, looking over the mass of jutting-browed faces.

Young, old, and in between—they all carried that same terrifying expression. The look of an individual who had discovered the power of many. These groundwalkers were riding now, riding a high sense of strength, and to support that insidious addiction they joined each with his neighbor to keep the power directed. Some of them, I knew, didn't even care *where* the mob's energy was directed; they only wanted to be part of it, to maintain that heady sensation of a current of power flowing through them.

Enough of them had been legitimately concerned—at least originally— that the target for their threatened violence was still what it had been: Thanasset's house. They were quiet, now, waiting. But they could be set off at any moment, and there were far too few of Zaddorn's men to control them.

We need riot guns and tear gas, I thought desperately. Then: *The hell we do! Didn't I tell Thanasset that I liked his world better, where violence was a personal matter rather than a group activity? I'll be damned if I'll let this crowd of misguided fools prove me wrong!*

162

They had quieted to listen to Zaddorn. But they heard from me first.

"How many of you," I asked, using my best drill-sergeant voice, "know what this is all about?" I didn't wait for an answer, but went right on. "I'd be willing to bet that most of you were on your way to the market, or to school, or back to work, when you saw a crowd starting here and came on over to see what was happening. Some people are angry, they say that a crime is going unpunished—maybe the people you talk to are *strangers*, even, and yet you accept their word for what has happened, and join in, adding to the noise and confusion.

"Well, I want you to *think*, now, about what you're trying to accomplish. Does any of you, individually, want to kill me or my father?" There was a rumble, a couple of affirmative shouts that died when the shouters didn't get immediate support from the people around them. "Then why," I asked them, "would all of you want to do such a thing?

"Oh, you don't want our deaths, you say?" I began to walk along the narrow rim of the wall. "All you want is justice? Fair punishment for whoever stole the Ra'ira? Well, *who made you the judges?*" I shouted at them.

"The theft of the Ra'ira is a crime against Raithskar. It's especially a crime against the Council, and because Thanasset is *under suspicion*, the Council has suspended him until his involvement could be proved or disproved.

"This man," I pointed back to where Zaddorn stood. He had placed himself with a hand against the wall of the house for stability when I started pacing. "This man has worn himself out looking for that proof. He has it. But he doesn't owe it to *you*. You're not concerned citizens of Raithskar—you're a howling, mindless mob! Let him give his evidence to the Council, and let the Council judge us. Raithskar has thrived for generation after generation under the administration of the Council—give them your trust again. Let them decide."

There was a restless movement and a murmur as they became people again instead of a crowd.

Then someone shouted: "Fine words from a man who turned a sha'um loose on us!" He had a point, and the crowd could see it. "And who will it be good for if we turn away now? *Him*, that's who! He wants to save himself and his father. The Council will never rule against them! He said it himself—Thanasset's been a Supervisor too long!"

"That's where you're wrong," said a voice from my right. The door of the house had opened quietly and Ferrathyn stood in front of it now, his slight old body clothed with dig-

163

nity. The small porch was a couple of steps up from the street level; the crowd could see who it was.

"The Council will judge fairly, with the interest of Raithskar at heart. You know that Thanasset is an old and valued friend to me, but that would not stand in the way of any action, should be Council decide he is in any way to blame for the theft. If you have no faith of your own in the Council, then will you accept my personal guarantee that the matter will be decided according to the evidence, no matter what it may show?"

He's got them, I cheered to myself. *He's turned the tide in our favor!*

"I did not send Keeshah against you," I said quietly. "You pressured him until he couldn't be controlled. And surely, after seeing what he can do, you can have no doubt that I have returned to Raithskar willingly. I mean to stand beside my father as we face the Council's judgment."

"Now," Zaddorn said at last, "all of you go on about your business. And be glad no one was seriously hurt. As soon as anything is decided, an official announcement will be made in the square. Now stop blocking up this street!"

They started to move. Zaddorn and I jumped down into the garden. Keeshah had long since gone into his house.

"You go in and join the others," I told Zaddorn, who looked ready to fall over. "I'll draw some water for Keeshah and come right in."

He nodded wordlessly; we walked toward the back of the house and he turned left while I continued on toward the back buildings. Keeshah was already sound asleep on his ledge. I drew some water for him and spent a few seconds just standing near him. Then I went up to the back door of the house, comparing how I felt now with the way I had felt that first time.

I had been confused then, frightened of a world I didn't understand, uncertain of my future here. I had a lot to learn, but I was gaining a feel for this world. Ricardo had made his own connections with the people Markasset knew; he had made *Ricardo's* presence mean something in Gandalara.

I paused at the door, assimilating the way things had changed since that other time. While I hesitated, the door opened. Thanasset stood there, smiling a true welcome—for me, and not for Markasset. I was so touched that I couldn't say a word.

But Thanasset, too, had seen the parallel.

"Don't just stand there, son," he said. "Come on in."

22

With exaggerated care, I removed my baldric and hung it on one of the pegs beside the door. Thanasset laughed and slapped me hard on the back, then somehow he was hugging me, quick and hard.

I turned from him to the others, who were all standing in the great hall. Milda said, "Oh, Markasset!" and ran over to me. I wrapped my arms around her and lifted, swinging her around until she was breathless with laughter. Then I set her down and opened my arms to Illia.

"We've been so worried, darling!" she said, and rushed into my arms. Zaddorn or no Zaddorn, I let myself enjoy that kiss. Then, with one arm around the girl, I walked over to where Ferrathyn and Zaddorn were tactfully not watching us.

"Your timing was perfect, sir," I told Ferrathyn. "Thanks."

"Don't thank me, young man," he said, a smile wreathing his face with more wrinkles. "You displayed a gift for oratory your father tells me he never suspected. Without your groundwork, my words would have had no effect.

"Zaddorn has just been giving me the evidence you spoke of. I have no doubts that the Council will reinstate your father with full pay for his missed time." He shook his head. "It's a frightening thing, the reappearance of mind-power in an ambitious man. Gharlas could make trouble for all of Gandalara."

"What's this?" asked Thanasset. "What about mind-power and Gharlas?"

Zaddorn repeated what Hural had told us for the others, who had been busy greeting me while he reported to the Chief Supervisor. Thanasset was horrified.

"And it was used on me? Without my knowledge? Great Serkajon, Ferrathyn, Gharlas must be impossibly strong." He was pale. "You know, now that I know the truth, I almost wish I *had* forgotten to lock the filthy door!"

"You musn't feel that way, Fa—Thanasset," Illia corrected hurriedly. "After all, this clears you of any blame. And it proves Markasset wasn't involved, too, doesn't it, Zaddorn? Doesn't it?" she repeated when he didn't answer immediately.

"Yes, Illia," he said tenderly, and sighed. "I'd still give a week's pay to find out just what did happen—where he got the money, why he was on the caravan in the first place (and under an alias at that), and why he wasn't around by the time the Sharith attacked. But I've learned enough, about the theft and about our friend," he said, waving a hand at me, "to convince me that he wasn't involved in the theft. Unfortunately, that makes the rest of it none of my business. Oh, he might be chargeable for leaving his post on the caravan, but I doubt that Gharlas will be willing to confront him according to the law.

"So—yes, as far as the office of Peace and Security is concerned, Markasset's name is clear."

"Of involvement with the theft," I corrected him.

"Isn't that what I just said?" he asked.

"I *killed* a man on the way out of Raithskar," I said, thinking: *If they've forgotten, don't remind them! Keep your mouth shut!* But I was too surprised to follow my own advice. "One of your officers."

"One of my—" Zaddorn began. "You mean the man out back, don't you?" He walked over and stood eye to eye with me. "Those men worked for Worfit." He said it quietly, then waited a few seconds, staring at me closely. His words and his attitude were good news and bad news. I waited for the other shoe to drop.

"Markasset would know that all peace officers wear gray baldrics. Who are you?"

"Why—why, he's Markasset, of course!" Illia said and tried to squeeze herself between us, defensively facing Zaddorn. I took her shoulders, stepped back a pace and turned her to face me.

"Illia, I'm sorry you had to find out about this so abruptly, but Zaddorn's right. I'm not Markasset." She put a hand to her mouth and began shaking her head, her dark eyes wide.

I heard a gasp behind her and I looked out at the others. Zaddorn had a calculating look on his face. Milda had made the sound; Thanasset had moved over to her and put an arm around her shoulders. He'd had some time to get used to the idea.

Ferrathyn's face was so gray with shock that I was alarmed. But his sharp mind had worked it all out in a flash, and had come to the same conclusion Thanasset had reached. Only he had gone a step farther, and chosen a logical candidate for the alleged Visitor.

"Are—are you Serkajon?" he whispered.

"No!" I said hastily. "Oh, no." *Don't call me "sir"*, I thought again. "I'm—well, I'm nobody special."

"Rikardon," said Zaddorn. "The name you used in Thagorn?"

I nodded.

"Rikardon?" repeated Illia. "Then w-what happened to Markasset?"

"Please tell us," begged Milda. "I know the boy had his problems, but—but his heart w-was good." She looked tiny and frail in the circle of Thanasset's arm.

I let go of Illia and walked over to take Milda's hands. "Milda darling," I said, and she made a little sobbing sound. "I have some of Markasset's memories—not all. But some of the strongest and happiest concern you." I reached down into Markasset's memories and tried to separate the warm feeling for Milda into separate images. "The sound of your voice singing over the cookstove. The neat way you stitch when you're mending things." I smiled at a memory. "And you never complained when he teased you—did he really unravel your weaving every night for a half a moon?"

"Yes, he did, the scoundrel!" she said with a giggle. She glanced up at Thanasset and said, "I never told you about that, Thanasset—I was afraid you'd really get after the boy. But he unraveled *most* of what I'd done during the day. I went to the loom next day convinced I was crazy because I remembered doing more than I really had done. And once I caught him, I told him he could just learn to do what he'd undone. Your sleeping pallet was woven by your son!" She said it with such triumph that we all laughed and for a moment the tension was broken. Then she looked at me seriously again.

"Thank you for bringing back those happy memories, young man. I want to say that I have no fault to find with you—you've done a great thing for our family, and I'm grateful. But I—will Markasset—is he—?"

"I don't know, Milda," I said gently. "I don't understand what has happened; it might *un*happen at any time and it might not.

"But I want you to believe something. I know how much Markasset loved you, and I love you, too."

"Th-thank you," she said in a shaking voice. I released her hands and she turned her face to Thanasset's shoulder.

"What did happen?" Zaddorn asked.

I shrugged. "I woke up out in the desert with a lump on my head. Everything I know about Markasset—except, as I

167

said, a few scattered memories—I've learned since then."

"So you don't have the answers either?"

"No. I can't remember anything about the night the caravan left, or the night Gharlas disappeared. I can't even remember what Gharlas looks like!"

"And were you," Zaddorn asked in a low, tight voice, "going to marry Illia in Markasset's place?"

"I felt an obligation to complete Markasset's life, since I had somehow borrowed his body. That included keeping his promises."

I walked back over to Illia, who was looking wildly from me to Zaddorn.

"But it's different, now, dear," I told her. "I expected to have to hide behind Markasset when we talked in the garden that day. It's really better this way. I'd like to think that I'd have told you before the wedding, anyway, to give you a fair choice. Let's just leave things for a while so you can get to know the person I really am. And take my advice—give Zaddorn another chance, too. We've been through a lot together these past few days. He's a man I'd trust my back to."

"I—oh, I'm so confused!" she wailed. She looked at Zaddorn steadily for a moment, then turned her dark eyes up to mine. "In the garden that day, and just now—it was *you* kissing me, not Markasset, wasn't it?"

"Yes," I admitted. "I'll admit I appreciate Markasset's taste, and maybe I took advantage just a little. But I don't *know* you yet, and you don't know me. Give it some time. Please."

"Yes," she said at last. "All right."

"Thank you," Zaddorn said, and came toward us, holding out his right hand. "This is your custom, but it's one I like. Welcome to Raithskar, Rikardon." I took his hand gratefully. "I hold nothing of Markasset against you," he said. "And for what it's worth, I think you'll be rougher competition than he was." He glanced at Illia, who lowered her eyes in sudden embarrassment. "But I'll be trying harder."

"Friends," Thanasset drew our attention to him. He came over to me and put an arm around my shoulders. "I'm glad that there is no need of deception among us any longer. I have known about Rikardon since the day he returned to Raithskar from the desert. I saw no need to worry you, Milda," he added.

"I regret the loss of my son," he said, and had to pause for a second or two. "But in Rikardon I have found qualities Markasset lacked: steadiness, confidence, a strong feeling for

168

what is right and the conviction to stand by it. Whatever brought him here, he awoke into a mess not of his own making. He accepted and fulfilled Markasset's obligations.

"We cannot tell if Markasset will ever be returned to us; we must accept Rikardon in his place." He walked over to the portrait of the sha'um, stretched up and brought down the sword of Serkajon. I realized, suddenly, what he was going to do. I would have objected if my voice had worked, but I was trying to swallow a tennis ball.

He faced me, holding the long, gleaming sword across his body. It had been recently polished.

"Rikardon, few men of our family have carried the Steel of Serkajon. It has been the tradition for father to judge son; I found Markasset lacking, a fact which did nothing to draw us together. But I must change that judgment now." He offered me the hilt of the sword.

"Please accept from my hands not only the great sword of Serkajon, but the love and respect I would feel for Markasset, could he be here. Whatever he might have asked of me is now yours."

There were a lot of things I wanted to say. I looked at Thanasset and I knew *he* understood. I could explain to the others later, when that tennis ball finally moved.

I gripped the hilt of the sword and lifted it from Thanasset's hands.

I felt a strange sensation, like the jarring crawl of an electric shock, but without any pain. There was a sweep of images through my mind, so swift and varied that I felt myself reeling.

Thanasset was there, as a younger man, riding the sha'um whose portrait decorated the wall. Laughing. And Milda, too, was younger, softly sad over the death of a man she had loved.

She changed into Gra'mama Maria Constanza, who patted my hand and dried my tears over a torn book page. And there was Julie, the first time we were together—sweet and wonderful. The war marched by and there she was again, weeping in shame because she hadn't had the strength to wait for me. I kissed her and shook her husband's hand and walked away. . . .

Illia was there, near me, naked, eager. Zaddorn, a boy, losing a sword trial to me. Illia was watching, Zaddorn was angry, I was laughing.

Two lives paraded through my mind and mingled. A wall had dissolved and the stacked-up contents of two rooms crashed together and bounced around.

Ricardo's life moved quickly through. School, reserves, students, summers, women . . . the doctor . . . the meteor. I viewed them lightly, as though I were watching an old movie so familiar that I could quote the next line at any given time.

I tried to cling to Markasset's memories, to absorb them, make them part of me. But they, too, slipped by, one by one, giving me barely time enough to recognize the people in the images. I learned to let them go easily, sure now that I could call them back when I wished. I lived through Markaseet's life up to a night not long past . . .

Then I remembered the night the Ra'ira was stolen.

23.

"It's only seven hundred zaks, Father!" I pleaded desperately, hating him because I knew he was right. "I promise it's the last time, and I'll pay it back."

"How?" he demanded. "You've applied yourself to the mondea tables, but to nothing else. You might have been a scholar, a teacher, an administrator. You might have learned a craft. Never mind this debt; how will you support Keeshah after I'm gone? Will you go and live in the wilds and share the game he kills?"

"Don't start that old argument up again," I warned him. "We're talking about a single debt—my last gambling debt. I'll find a way to pay it back. But Worfit wants his money, Father. And I do owe it to him."

"Now you've hit the right word," he said grimly. "You owe it to him. So you pay him."

"It's the last time!" I repeated again, appalled that he didn't believe me. I meant it. I'd never made that promise before; I meant it now. Why wouldn't he believe me?

"It's one time too often!"

I left, then, slamming the back door hard enough, I hoped, to break the latticed glass panel. I sat with Keeshah in his house, rubbing his stomach and thinking.

Father was right about one thing: I had no way to earn that money myself.

Or had I?

"I do have one skill," I told Keeshah. He looked at me with one eye still closed and told me to keep rubbing. " I can fight. I'll hire on as a caravan guard."

The more I thought of it, the better it sounded. It would get me out of Raithskar, and out of Worfit's reach for a while. If the caravan went far enough, and was rich enough, and if I caught another caravan back, I could pay Worfit off completely. That would show the old man I could pay my own debts, make my own way.

And the promise was still good, I decided. I'd never gamble again. I didn't have a hope in the world of becoming a Supervisor until I quit the rogueworld and really tried to study city administration. And I'd been letting Illia think that Dad would put me up for it next opening, which would probably be when Ferrathyn fell over at last. So—when I got back from wherever it was, NO MORE GAMBLING.

I gave Keeshah's chest a final scratch and headed for the marketplace. On the way I revised the plan a little. I had been going to hire out me and Keeshah, then find Worfit and tell him what I'd done, promise him his money as soon as I got back. But I had a better idea—I'd hire on as a footguard, and use a phony name. Nobody'd get hurt; Worfit would get his money; and meanwhile, Markasset would just mysteriously disappear. The only bad thing was not riding Keeshah—but he could follow the caravan, and I could see him every night. He wouldn't like it, but he'd do it.

I was in luck when I reached the marketplace. A big caravan, owned by a man named Gharlas, was leaving the next morning and going all the way to Eddarta. I hadn't really wanted to go that far; the little man with only four fingers on his left hand said if I'd go as far as Chizan, that would get the caravan past the raiding territory of the Sharith. They didn't expect trouble; they'd paid their duty on the way in; but it didn't hurt to be extra careful. If I wanted the job, I had it.

I took it.

It was dark by then. I thought about going home. Father would still be there, since he wouldn't go on duty tonight until dayend. I thought I should tell him I was going, then decided just to let him worry. It was his fault I had to go. But if I went home, we'd only argue again.

So I went to say goodbye to Illia.

She came to the second-floor window when the pebbles hit it. "I can't come out now, Markasset!" she whispered. "Mama's

171

in the front room; she'd see me and we'd fuss over me going out this late."

"Jump down from there," I told her. "That slim waist of yours will fit through. I'll catch you."

There wasn't much light except what fell from her room. She stared down, deciding. "Are you sure you can catch me?"

"Yes, you don't weigh anything! Jump!"

All right," she said, a little breathlessly. "Here I come!"

And she jumped. I felt a twisting in my chest. Illia believed in me competely. If I said I could do a thing, I could do it. She trusted me.

She nearly pulled my arms off when I caught her, but I kept on my feet. I could tell I had impressed her, but for once I didn't care about that. I had realized, for the first time, how good it felt to be trusted.

"Put me down," she said, but I kissed her instead. She was wearing her sleeping shift, and her body was soft and warm underneath it. Her breathing quickened to match mine, and I carried her out into her father's garden. There was a place, near the bath-house, that was blocked from the house but open to the sky. The song of the Skarkel Falls seemed especially beautiful right there.

We had made that place our own. That's where I took her to say goodbye.

"You really ought to tell your father where you're going," Illia said later. "He'll worry something fierce."

"You're right," I said. "But if I see him again, we'll only yell at each other over this, too."

"Write him a note," she suggested. "I'll take it to him tomorrow." Her parents had gone to sleep by then, not even missing their daughter. She went quietly into the house, brought out brush and parchment, and I did write a note. "Leaving this morning on caravan to earn money for Worfit. Back when I get here. M."

"That's not much of a note," she said when she read it.

"It's all he'll get. Listen—I'm going to miss you."

"I'll miss you, too, Markasset. Terribly. Hurry back."

"When I get back, you'll see, loye. I'll dig in, and I'll be ready to be a Supervisor in no time. And then—"

"Yes?"

"Will you marry me, Illia! After I'm a Supervisor?"

"You know I will."

When I left her, it was less than an hour before dawn, the time set for the caravan to depart. I realized that I hadn't planned things too well—I had no extra clothes, and no money to buy extra food for Keeshah on the off chance that he couldn't find game in the hills while we crawled across the desert at vlek pace.

So I stopped by Dad's office. It was closer than going home, and he had never objected when I used my own key to the drawer where he kept extra money. That is, he hadn't started to complain until I started gambling against money not yet in hand, and began losing. He had forbidden my use of that money, but hadn't asked for my key back.

Well, this wasn't for gambling, so I went into the building and up the stairs to Dad's office. He would be in the security room now; it was some four hours into his scheduled shift. I unlocked the drawer—and found five twenty-dozak pieces.

It was the money Dad had had at home, in the wall niche. He had brought it down here and locked it up—why? Because he knew I knew there was never much money here. And he also knew I knew he had that money at home. He had been afraid I'd steal the money from him to pay Worfit!

If that was all he thought of me, so be it!

I reached in and took the money. I'd pay off Worfit before I left, I'd take the rest for travel expenses, and I'd come back when I was good and ready, not before. I'd come back to Illia.

I threw the key down on top of the desk. I wouldn't be needing it again.

I went to Worfit's largest gaming house, where he usually spent his dusk-to-dawn office hours. Marnen, his one-eyed assistant, told me that Zaddorn had ordered Worfit's testament about a disturbance in another of his houses the night before—a "scuffle" that had resulted in two dead men.

"I can't wait," I told Marnen. "Tell Worfit that I've got his money, but I have to leave town for a while. As soon as I get back, I'll pay him what I owe him."

Marnen nodded. "Sure, Markasset. You always been good for it before. A little slower than usual this time, maybe. You'll be back when?"

"I can't say for certain. Two moons, on the outside."

The one-eyed man shook his head. "He won't like that."

"Tell him if he kept better security in his places, he'd have been a richer man tonight."

Marnen hooted with laughter. "I ain't gonna tell the Chief that, not me!" He wouldn't try to stop me; he understood the peculiar code of honor that demands personal payment of gambling debts. "See you soon, Markasset."

I had to leave with the caravan in only a few minutes—I

173

had *signed a contract. As I hurried through the streets toward the marketplace, I considered this new twist of events.*

The effect would be the same, I decided. I'd just keep the money until I got back, then pay off Worfit. If he got impatient meanwhile, maybe he'd go directly to Dad and show him what it's like to owe money to the rogueworld. They wouldn't hurt him any more than they'd hurt me—because of Keeshah. But they could annoy him a lot.

I reported to the caravan and the little man—Hural—yelled at me for being late. He introduced me quickly to Gharlas, a tall, thin man with a piercing stare that made me uncomfortable. Then we were on our way.

I let the first few days of the caravan flow through my mind. The caravan passed through Yafnaar, and I understood Balgokh's comment about the "change" in Markasset. He was unhappy with the choices he'd made, and he was curt and aloof from the people on the caravan. I skipped along to the caravan's last night on the trail. . . .

It was shortly after moonrise. As usual, I had met Keeshah a goodly distance from the caravan to keep his scent away from the vleks. The wind tonight was southerly, so we were out ahead of the caravan.

Keeshah warned me someone was near, and we flattened out on top of a mound to see who it was. Gharlas! Leading a well-packed vlek. What was he up to?

I had watched him a lot since the caravan started, and I had met many men I liked more. There was something odd about him—that piercing stare, the way he sometimes went all vacant, as though he were living in a dream world. He had been snappish and unpleasant the entire time; I'd come to the conclusion he was nervous about something.

And now he was sneaking off in the middle of the night?

"I'm going to follow him," I told Keeshah. "You keep out of sight and be sure to stay downwind of that vlek."

I did follow him. For about half an hour. Then there was a blinding, crashing pain in my head. . . .

"Markasset is dead," I told the others. "Touching the sword—I remember now." I looked at Thanasset and Milda. "I'm sorry." Then I turned to Zaddorn. "I remember what happened that night—"

I told them the bare facts of what I had relived in the few short seconds it had taken for the memories to march by. And while I talked, all sorts of pieces, scattered and out of sequence, fitted together.

I had been with Illia at the time of the robbery. But I couldn't remember that, and no one had thought to ask her. If they had asked her, without telling her why, she would probably have fudged the time and circumstances so that, if her folks found out, they wouldn't be too angry.

The men in Thanasset's back yard had said: "The Chief says he's got it on him." I had thought that meant Zaddorn suspected me of carrying the Ra'ira. But no—one of Worfit's informants must have told him I was back in town.

What I "had on me" was enough money to pay my debt to him.

And one more piece of information was pertinent.

"There's something I haven't told you," I said. "When I woke up out in the desert, there was a dead man nearby. I've been concerned, ever since we found out that Gharlas took the Ra'ira, that it was his body, and that his vlek was wandering around loose somewhere, carrying the stone. But I know now, definitely, that it wasn't Gharlas."

"Who was it?" Zaddorn asked.

"One of the other men on the caravan," I said. "I never knew his name."

"What happened to Gharlas?" Ferrathyn asked me.

"I wish I knew. It's a blank between the last of Markasset and the beginning of Rikardon."

"How did the man die?" Thanasset asked softly.

"I can't be sure—but I think Keeshah killed him."

Thanasset nodded. "I'd have thought so. That man must have been my son's murderer. Why don't you ask Keeshah where Gharlas is."

I did, rousing him from a deep sleep. He didn't quite understand until I stopped using the name and tried to picture the man and his vlek, walking away.

He left, Keeshah said.

You didn't want to kill him, too?

Why? I kill the one who hurt Markasset. Then you came.

"He doesn't know," I told the others. "He revenged Markasset, then grieved for him until I surprised him by standing up."

"Well, we know where he's heading," Zaddorn said. "I'll alert every peace officer between here and Eddarta. We'll get the Ra'ira back."

"I certainly hope so," said Thanasset fervently, then he smiled at me. "Meanwhile, I have the pleasant task ahead of me of getting reacquainted with my son." His face clouded.

175

"Are you uncomfortable being called Markasset?"

"A little," I admitted. "I am not Markasset. His memories are accessible to me now—not yet assimilated in the sense that they are truly a part of my personality, but available on demand." *And I'm no longer Ricardo,* I admitted to myself. *I am too completely a part of Gandalara now. I'm someone new.*

"It is an ancient custom to give a boy a new name when he first carries a sword," Thanasset was saying. "I don't think anyone will be too surprised if I invoke the old custom on the occasion of awarding Serkajon's steel sword to my son. It will take a little while for word to get around everywhere, but it will eventually. Will that suit you, Rikardon?"

"Yes. Thank you."

Thanasset looked around at the others. "Of course, I don't need to say that no one here will reveal your secret. Now," he said, grimacing at me, "I think it's high time you had a bath. You, too, Zaddorn."

That night I lay in my own bed for the first time since I had awakened in Gandalara. In spite of being dead tired, my mind kept buzzing. I'd long since given up recriminating over not having asked Illia or Keeshah a long time ago to help fill in the gaps of my memory. They hadn't had all the answers in any case, and, until I touched that sword, I couldn't have asked the right questions to draw out the few they had.

The sword lay beside me, unsheathed. I reached out and touched the cool metal of the blade. The sword of Serkajon. I wouldn't even make a guess as to why it was the catalyst that unified Ricardo and Markasset. But the sword had felt just right in my hand. It seemed in its proper place, lying beside my sleeping pallet.

Gandalara—a strange world only a few weeks ago. Now it was my home, and I wanted no other. I belonged here. I thought of the people, now dispersed, who had been in this house today. My family: Thanasset, with his straight back and tiny scar and his infinite understanding even through his own pain; Milda, dear and kind and fragile, and stronger sometimes than the steel beside me. And my friends: Illia, special and exciting, trusting and loyal; Zaddorn, stubborn and proud and devoted to his job; and Ferrathyn, full of quiet, supportive strength. What I knew of them would change as they got to know me; we would forge new relationships, and I hoped I could heal some of the wounds Markasset had caused.

I thought, too, of Worfit. Thanasset had insisted that I use the stolen gold pieces to repay Markasset's debt. I would meet Worfit at last tomorrow because, as Markasset—that half of me which had been Markasset—had understood, that kind of debt must be paid in person.

Ricardo owed Worfit something, too. In fear and ignorance and error, Ricardo had killed one of Worfit's men. By law the death was self-defense, and unpunishable. But Worfit deserved an explanation, an apology.

Rikardon would honor both debts to Worfit, then end the association.

Last—deliberately so—I thought of Keeshah.

In the moment I had taken Serkajon's sword into my hand, one of the flashing memories had been particularly strong. I had been a young Markasset, just turned twelve, already tall and strong for my age, eager for the test of crossing the Khumber Pass into the Valley of the Sah'um. Eager at first, then weary, and finally moving along in an odd past echo of my desert awakening.

I dragged my trembling limbs a few feet at a time through the thin air at the top of the pass. My chest was on fire, my body felt almost useless, my eyes couldn't focus, my head was reeling. Purpose forgotten, I kept going out of sheer stubborn inertia.

I discovered gradually that I could breathe again, and the burning pain in my chest was abating. I had made it past the crest. There was no path on the other side of the mountain, only the hard-baked rock and a few scrubby bushes, and an occasional treacherous patch of loose shale. My coordination was gone. I had lost my pack of food and was shamefully weak. I stumbled and rolled down the steep hillside, finally crashing into a bed of vines tangled around a fallen tree. The sweet, cloying smell of the disturbed earth was my last memory for a long while.

I woke to a sharp pain in my left foot. It took a moment to remember where I was, then the pain increased as the foot was pulled against the weight of my body, dragging it a few inches through the vines. I yelled, thrashed my arms, sat up.

A sha'um, a yearling cub the size of a grown tiger, jumped away, crouched down and considered me. His ears lay back against his head; his mouth was ready to snarl.

He thought I was dead, Markasset was thinking. He thought I was food. He still thinks so.

As if to prove it, the cub chose that moment to spring for-

ward, knocking me backward again, reaching for my throat with his jaws. I slammed my forearm against his head, diverting the deadly teeth and calling forth a high-pitched roar. He swung his head back toward my neck and I grabbed handfuls of fur and skin behind his cheeks and strained to keep his teeth away from my skin. We weren't badly matched for strength, and I began to feel some hope of winning. He was furious now, roaring and lunging down, then back, trying to break my hold. When he began to press down steadily again, his jaws snapping, I shifted my position and let his own weight and strength push him off to my side. I let go my stranglehold on the sides of his neck, sat up and straddled his back, pressing him to the ground with my weight. I caught the hold again, this time from behind him. He couldn't move now, and I felt a glow of triumph, even though I knew I could not keep the hold for long. Already my arms were trembling from the strain and my hands were cramping.

Hurt me.

The message came from the cat beneath me, and it brought a flash of joy. So that's what it's like! My hands loosened, and I felt the muscles in the cat's sides ripple in anticipation. I grabbed again, more tightly, and tried to speak to the cat.

I am Markasset, I told it. *I want to stay in the Valley with you for a season. I will not hurt you again, and you will not let the other cats hurt me. Agreed?*

There was no message; I tightened my fingers in the fur, and the cat made a whimpering sound that made me want to let go. But I held on until I felt the cat's mind struggling to speak to me again.

Yes.

I let go then, and stood up. The cat leaped up and out of reach, then turned to look at me. I walked toward him and put out my hand. His ears went back and his head jerked away, but he held his ground and I stayed still, waiting. Then I moved my hand again, slowly bringing it closer to his head. He eyed it with a sidelong glance, growling nervously, but he didn't move away this time. I touched the place on his neck where I had pinched him so badly. I rubbed it lightly, then brought my hand forward to stroke the soft fur under his chin. His eyes closed and his ears twitched.

I'm sorry I had to hurt you, I said, savoring the special kind of speech.

Fair, he said, and reached down to lick the blood from my foot.

The memory had cleared up one more puzzle for me. The forest in which Markasset had wrestled with the sha'um cub had been full of straight, tall trees. It was the only place, I had learned, where such trees grew, and they were effectively guarded from potential lumber barons by the presence of the sha'um.

Now I understood, too, Keeshah's puzzlement from time to time since Ricardo's arrival in his world. There were subtle differences between his relationships with Markasset and Ricardo. His meeting with Markasset had set the tone for their relationship; although there was an unbreakable bond of affection between them, Markasset was always the master, demanding of Keeshah everything he was willing to give.

So the small things I had done out of simple consideration—sharing the last of my water, letting him rest simply for his own comfort and not because he could go no further—these things had been new to him. And we had communicated in a different way.

That had been Ricardo. Would Keeshah need to adjust again to the new combined form? I knew, this time, that he would accept the change—even as he had accepted a confused wretch in the middle of a salty desert.

Suddenly I needed Keeshah. He had slept through the afternoon and was still sleeping lightly. I reached out for him, and his mind roused to my touch.

Thank you for helping me, Keeshah. Before anybody else, you knew I was changed, but you trusted me. I appreciate it—more than I can say. . . .

As it had happened before in times of stress, it happened now in the name of friendship. Keeshah and I merged. I could feel the comforting solidity of the stone ledge, smell the fresh grass. And this time the understanding flowed both ways. With conflicting pride and humility, I felt Keeshah's commitment to me, whole-hearted and without reservations. He was not surprised by the change in me, only mildly curious. Though he didn't care about other people, he sensed that I was unique among the people of this world, and there was pride—no, not pride; *smugness*—that he was associated with me.

We couldn't hold the meld for long, and as it faded, I sensed Keeshah falling back into sleep.

Good night, Keeshah, I said softly, not expecting him to hear me. But he roused again and answered me sleepily.

Good night . . . Rikardon.

179

END PROCEEDINGS:

INPUT SESSION ONE

—Enough, you are tiring. We will withdraw together from the All-Mind. . . .

The Recording is complete for now. I will detach my mind from yours. . . .

How do you feel?

—I am exhausted.

—As it should be for the work you have done.

—There is more.

—When you have rested, we will Record again. For now, sleep. . . .

ABOUT THE AUTHORS

RANDALL GARRETT, a veteran science fiction and fantasy writer, and VICKI ANN HEYDRON, a newcomer to the field, met in 1975 in the California home of their mutual agent, Tracy E. Blackstone. Within a year, they had decided to begin working together and, in December 1978, they were married.

Currently, they are living in Austin, Texas where they are working on the Gandalara novels, of which *The Steel of Raithskar* is the first.

OUT OF THIS WORLD!

That's the only way to describe Bantam's great series of science fiction classics. These space-age thrillers are filled with terror, fancy and adventure and written by America's most renowned writers of science fiction. Welcome to outer space and have a good trip!

☐	23512	THE COMPASS ROSE by Ursula LeGuin	$2.95
☐	23541	WIND'S 12 QUARTERS by Ursula LeGuin	$2.95
☐	22855	CINNABAR by Edward Bryant	$2.50
☐	20499	LENSMEN FROM RIGEL by D. Kyle	$2.50
☐	22588	THE SUICIDE PLAGUE by E. Naha	$2.75
☐	01355	THE DINOSAURS by B. Preiss & Wm. Stout (A Large Format Book)	$12.95
☐	13031	THE ROBOT WHO LOOKED LIKE ME by Robert Sheckley	$2.50
☐	20310	THE EINSTEIN INTERSECTION by S. Delaney	$2.50
☐	22938	THE WINDHOVER TAPES: FLEXING THE WARP by Warren Norwood	$2.75
☐	23351	THE WINDHOVER TAPES: FIZE OF THE GABRIEL RATCHETS by Warren Norwood	$2.95 $2.95
☐	23394	THE WINDHOVER TAPES: AN IMAGE OF VOICES by W. Norwood	$2.75
☐	20752	HONEYMOON IN HELL by F. Brown	$2.25
☐	22968	THE MARTIAN CHRONICLES by Ray Bradbury	$2.75
☐	14144	MOCKINGBIRD by Walter Tevis	$2.95
☐	14274	THE MAN WHO FELL TO EARTH by Walter Tevis	$2.25
☐	23785	STAR TREK: THE NEW VOYAGES 2 by Culbreath & Marshak	$2.95
☐	20990	A CANTICLE FOR LEIBOWITZ by Walter Miller, Jr.	$2.95
☐	20761	SUNDIVER by David Brin	$2.50
☐	23828	THE FARTHEST SHORE by Ursula LeGuin	$2.95
☐	22563	A WIZARD OF EARTHSEA by Ursula LeGuin	$2.95

Buy them at your local bookstore or use this handy coupon for ordering:

Bantam Books, Inc., Dept. SF, 414 East Golf Road, Des Plaines, Ill. 60016

Please send me the books I have checked above. I am enclosing $_____ (please add $1.25 to cover postage and handling). Send check or money order —no cash or C.O.D.'s please.

Mr/Mrs/Miss_____

Address_____

City_____State/Zip_____

SF—7/83

Please allow four to six weeks for delivery. This offer expires 1/84.

FANTASY AND SCIENCE FICTION FAVORITES

Bantam brings you the recognized classics as well as the current favorites in fantasy and science fiction. Here you will find the most recent titles by the most respected authors in the genre.